**This book is to be returned on or before
the last date stamped below.**

**AYLESBURY COLLEGE
LIBRARY**

This book may be renewed by personal application, post or
telephone, quoting date, author and title.

LIBREX

# JOHN CHAMBERS'
## Wild Flower Garden

Introduction by
DAVID BELLAMY

ELM TREE BOOKS · LONDON

First published in Great Britain 1987
by Elm Tree Books/Hamish Hamilton Ltd
27 Wrights Lane, London W8 5TZ

Designed and produced by
Shuckburgh Reynolds Ltd
289 Westbourne Grove
London W11 2QA

Designed by Carol McCleeve
Text prepared by David Joyce
in collaboration with John Chambers

British Library Cataloguing in Publication Data
Chambers, John
   The wild flower garden
   1. Wild flower gardening.
   I. Title
   635.9'676     SB439

ISBN 0-241-12056-X

Typeset by SX Composing Ltd, Rayleigh, Essex
Colour separation by Aragorn Reproduction Co Ltd
Printed in West Germany by Mohndruck GmbH, Gütersloh

# CONTENTS

# FOREWORD
# BY DAVID BELLAMY

One of the most pleasant memories of my childhood was being able to go into the old brickfields opposite my home on the outskirts of London to pick a bunch of wild flowers to give to my mother.

It was in this way that I soon learned that the petals fall off Buttercups, how Dog Daisies got their first name and why my granny would never allow May Blossom in the house. Those flower-fringed experiences overflowed into the bomb sites where Rosebay Willowherb raised its ephemeral crop of blooms, hiding the destruction and sending squadrons of silken seeds parachuting on the summer breezes. The bomb craters on the North Downs exploded with colour, Crosswort, Squinancy Wort, Fragrant and even Pyramidal Orchids. In the post-war years it was possible to cycle from London to Brighton and it was flowers all the way, roadside verges, small fields with cows grazing contentedly on floriforous salads and in autumn the hedgerows groaning with Hips, Haws, Filberts, Sloes, Geans and Crabs, a surfeit of fruits to feed the birds and small mammals alike.

Each year our scout camp site was paid for by working in the farmer's coppice woodland, real hard graft, but rewarded by a patchwork of wild flowers, Anemone, Bluebell, Cowslip, Dwale, Earthnut, Foxglove, Geranium, Honeysuckle, Ivy, Jack-by-the-hedge, Kingcup, Lady's Mantle, Mint, Nettle, Primrose, Roses, Sanicle, Townhall clock, Ulmus, Violets, Willowherb, Yellow Archangel, Zerna. I almost made it, an alphabet of beauty, a nectar bar for all seasons to which butterflies, moths and all the other sugar-sipping insect addicts came again and again.

The countryside of my youth was indeed a place of great variety, dazzling beauty and, we then thought, everlasting interest. Now sadly much of that has gone, swept away by a thing called progress. Since the last world war the British countryside has lost so much, 95% of its lowland and 80% of its upland unimproved species-rich grassland, 80% of its chalk downland, 50% of its broadleaved and coppice woodland, and more of its hedgerows than I care to think about.

It is no use blaming the farmers, the developers and the politicians, we have all been at it together, demanding more of everything in an uncontrolled race to the top. The top of high rise buildings, grain and butter mountains, enormous import bills all set in a despoiled desolate landscape. It is no use, and never has been any use, just blaming other people, the time has come to change our ways, to do our bit for conservation. That means you, and this book shows you how to get cracking right in your own backyard.

More than one million acres of Britain lie neatly boxed by hedges, walls, fences and houses and are under the care of ordinary householders like you and me. That is more than six times the area of all our National Nature Reserves put together, and not much less than the area of all our SSSIs, Sites of Special Scientific Interest. So if everyone bought this book and used it to plan their gardens the John Chambers way, Britain would soon begin to bloom with its own wild flowers once more.

From the detailed lists of species, you can plan your own nature reserve. Blooming the year round to provide nectar for butterflies, scents to attract both day and night flying moths, and seeds in plenty for the birds and for the ants. What is more it could well save you the expenditure of energy, both petrol for the mower and rotovator and muscle power. It could also ward off those problems which come with using too many chemicals. Even the biggest chemical companies are now busy developing and producing whole ranges of safer, biodegradable herbicides and pesticides that kill the baddies like Couch and Twitch and leave the goodies like the aphid-eating ladybirds, the earwigs and woodlice that do much more good than harm.

Please don't run away with the idea that you can leave it all to itself. A wildlife section in your garden needs a lot of planning and preparation and this book provides all the necessary instructions to provide an ecocosm of natural features. Mini-meadows, sweet in spring, summer or autumn, short, medium or tall, dry bits, damp bits, wet bits, boggy bits, even subaqua bits with perennial plants for your own Dragon and Damsel flies to emerge on. When it is all at last complete, though requiring less intensive care than your more formal plots, it will never let you rest for it will provide a year round source of pleasure, interest and research. To help you on your way the description of each plant is garlanded with fascinating facts. A little bit of local history hidden in a local name. A little bit of mystery concerning the curative properties contained in these once so common flowers, culled from Culpeper, an amementarium of balms, cerecloaths, decoctions, electuaries, infusions, oyls, postums, salves and tinctures.

Please have a care, for even alternative medicine can be lethal in the hands of the untutored. Likewise, please never be tempted to take seeds, whether supplied by John Chambers or one of the other suppliers listed in the book, and plant them in the wild. Just as much damage can be done to a natural or semi-natural community by adding alien genetic stock as can be perpetrated by removing the local stock for planting in your garden. Immeasurable damage has been and is being done, often by people who say they are botanists or plantsmen, who steal from the wild both at home and abroad to add to their own collections. The laws which govern the import of plants into this country are there to protect our farms and gardens from alien stock and from disease. Anyone who flaunts them is a vandal of the worst sort. The fact that this country now needs laws to protect our wild plants – it is an offence for any unauthorised person to uproot *any* wild plant – shows the bad state our countryside is in. However, the Conservation of Plants and Animals Act is now firmly in force and convictions are a feature of many court rooms.

Fortunately JOHN CHAMBERS' WILD FLOWER GARDEN is now a REALITY, showing us all the way ahead – *it's blooming marvellous*.

DAVID BELLAMY
Bedburn, 1987

# WHY GROW WILD FLOWERS?

Even twenty years ago those who advocated gardening with wild flowers stood a good chance of being consigned to the crank fringe of the horticultural world. Traditionalists still occupied the centre ground and their rather narrow view of what was suitable for cultivation largely prevailed. Setting aside the fruit and vegetable sections of the garden, that view encompassed a lawn – ideally free of daisies and dandelions – and beds devoted to exotic ornamentals. But for a few exceptions, the wild flowers of Europe hardly featured at all.

In the last twenty years the change of emphasis has been quite dramatic. As someone who takes every opportunity to advocate the use of wild flowers in gardens – and, in particular, who recommends growing them from seed – I am pleased to discover that few people professionally engaged in gardening would now think of me and my fellow advocates as mere gardening cranks. Nonetheless, it is clear to me that we have a long way to go before European wild flowers are given their due as plants that are beautiful in their own right, particularly suited to the growing conditions that we can offer and more appropriate than many exotics can ever be if we are setting out to make our gardens mini-wildlife sanctuaries.

## The appeal of wild flowers

It was for their culinary and medicinal values that wild plants were first brought into the garden, Tansy, for example, as a bitter flavouring, White Horehound for the preparation of cough remedies and Yarrow as a wound herb. Although their use in cooking and in herbal remedies is one of the most fascinating aspects of the long exploitation of plants by man, for most gardeners this alone could never be an adequate reason for bringing these plants into the modern garden.

A very good reason for growing a number of wild flowers is simply that they are lovely garden plants. Part of the appeal of such favourites as Bluebells, Cowslips, Foxgloves and Primroses is that they have a simplicity that many cultivated plants have lost. These four are among the most popular wild flowers, so popular that no case needs to be made for them. There are, however, other plants as beautiful in their own way, as easy to grow and just as responsive to garden conditions and yet, in comparison with the favourites, more or less neglected. To those who know their merits it is difficult to see why Corn Marigold, Musk Mallow, Narrow-leaved Everlasting-pea and Red Campion, to take four outstanding examples, should be so rarely grown even by those with an interest in wild flowers. I very much hope that the readers of this book will be persuaded to try not only the plants with well established reputations but also some at least of those with which they are less familiar.

What will surprise many gardeners is that a large number of the wild flowers, if given good growing conditions with a reasonably fertile soil and freedom from competition, will make well-shaped vigorous plants, often flowering better and for a longer period than they do in the wild. It will soon become obvious that wild flowers are not a race apart and that they respond to good treatment in much the same way as other plants do.

### Environmental concern

Visitors to our stands at horticultural shows often comment how wild flowers have become a dwindling feature of the countryside. This sometimes vague sense of the physical world being less colourful and less varied than once it was corresponds to real and alarming changes in our landscape and gives us another very powerful incentive to grow wild flowers in the garden.

The way land has been used for agriculture, building and industry has had a tremendous effect in modifying our natural vegetation. By the end of the seventeenth century little was left of the vast forest that following the retreat of the great ice sheets, had covered Britain. The loss of the forest canopy, however, gave many herbaceous plants their chance, just as the planting of hedgerows in the eighteenth and nineteenth centuries favoured other species. Tremendously significant though changes often were in the long term, for the most part they occurred slowly, plants and other wildlife adapting to the gradual transformation of habitats.

This century, and particularly since World War II, the pace of change has quickened dramatically. Small fields surrounded by hedges do not allow the most efficient use of modern farm machinery. Out came the hedges (between 1946 and 1970 at an estimated rate of 4,500 miles per year). Fields of grain do not give maximum yields when there is competition from weeds. In went selective herbicides. Potentially rich wetlands can only produce crops if the water is taken away. Down went the drains. Since 1949, 40% of Britain's ancient wood-

land has been lost, 90% of hay meadows have been destroyed and 50% of wetland has been drained. Ten of Britain's native wild flower species have disappeared during the last fifty years and there is a serious threat to 300 of the remaining 1500. Have we become aware too late of the consequences of massive changes in land use and agricultural methods? It is not simply that some species of wild flowers are becoming less common but that whole habitats are being lost and that a range of species – birds, animals and insects as well as plants – are under threat.

It is disheartening that many large development projects still go ahead despite the well-argued cases put forward by conservationists. It is, however, encouraging to see what broad support there very often is for conservation measures and that the issues raised are no longer viewed as matters of local interest only.

Very few of us have it in our power to preserve a whole habitat, although through membership of local conservation groups we may be able to influence decisions on particular cases. Nor are we likely to have the heavy responsibility of saving some of our rarest plants. But the private gardens of Britain add up to a formidable area, hundreds of thousands of acres, and it can be no bad thing if an increasing number of our wild flowers find more and more space given over to them in a part of the landscape that is still neglected as a wildlife sanctuary. The explosion of interest in wild flower and wildlife gardening is a clear indication that more and more people think it is a constructive way of doing something to conserve native plants.

It is important to remember that the complex chemistry and biology of old grassland, woodland and wetland habitats cannot be reproduced simply by planting wild flowers in an appropriate setting. But that is a start and one that gives not only plants but also other wildlife the best chance of making something of the little niche we are offering them. By selective planting we can do a little bit more to attract certain categories of wildlife. By growing good nectar plants, for example, it is possible to entice an interesting range of moths and butterflies into the garden. If you grow the food plants of their caterpillars, you may find your garden becoming a small but valuable breeding site.

Weediness is very often the reason passionate gardeners give for not growing wild flowers. There is often a curious contradiction here, the person delighting in a plant when it is growing in a hedgerow and abhorring it when it strays into the garden. Wild flowers are not tidy respecters of man-made boundaries; it is our perception of a plant as something growing in the wrong place that makes a weed of it.

## My personal involvement

It is enormously encouraging to me and to many other people, including conservationists and naturalists, nurserymen and seedsmen, who have a professional interest in wild flowers, to find a re-newed public interest in our native plants. Twelve years ago I was working for Mommersteeg International, a large Northamptonshire-based company specialising in the mixing, packing and distribution of both amenity and agricultural grass seed mixtures. We began to respond to approaches from conservation-minded public authorities, landscapers and landowners who wanted wild flower seed to be added to some of the grass seed mixtures they were intending to sow in order to create flowering grassland.

Our first mixtures were mainly made up of suitable, commercially available, mineral-rich herbs and legumes being used for agricultural and some amenity purposes, such as Salad Burnet, Ribwort, Plantain, Yarrow, Sheep's Sorrel, Bird's-foot-trefoil, Kidney Vetch, Sainfoin, Suckling Clover (Lesser Trefoil), Trefoil (Black Medick) and Greater bird's-foot-trefoil. To these basic ingredients, we added an ever-increasing number of major grassland wild flowers, including Cowslip, Oxeye Daisy, Wild Carrot, Wild Parsnip, Lady's Bedstraw, Meadow Buttercup, Hoary Plantain and Selfheal.

At first the stocks used were obtained from Dutch horticultural seedsmen. However, these were quickly replaced by hand-collected seeds produced mainly from nursery rows by a small number of British enterprises, commercial growers and seed companies who were beginning to specialise in wild flower seed production. A range of mixtures for a variety of soil types and situations began to be formulated and marketed.

From this time, we originated and added an illustrated packet range of twenty-two of Britain's best known wild flowers to a small range of products being offered to shops, garden centres and by mail order. This was quite an innovation and they were extremely well received; it was the first time that gardeners had been offered a shop collection of wild flowers in illustrated packets containing full cultural information. This small but significant collection proved to be the starting point for the development of a range of seeds which I eventually took over from Mommersteeg in 1979.

In 1980, I produced my first mail order seed catalogue, which included 150 wild flowers. Over the years, this number has increased to over 500 packets accompanied by 50 wild flower, grass and wild flower and wildlife mixtures; wild flower plants and bulbs; associated books and posters; herbs and edible plants; everlasting flowers; cultivated nectar plants; sprouting seeds; green manure crops; crops; wild, ornamental and cultivated grasses and grass seed mixtures. The illustrated packet range of wild flowers currently stands at 70 separately packed species plus 20 wild flower mixtures and two grass and wild flower mixtures. This range, plus illustrated herb, everlasting flower and ornamental grass seed packets is also supplied to shops and garden centres. Many of the mail order species and mixtures, plus other mixes more suitable for amenity and agricultural purposes, are offered in larger quantities to local authorities, landscapers and landowners.

## A growing interest

Since the time that the original packet collection was introduced to retail and mail order customers, major seed packet and grass seed companies have been adding wild flowers to their ranges. In response to the rapidly increasing demand for wild flower seed from the public, local authorities, landowners, landscapers and seed merchants, a number of commercial nurseries and seed companies now specialise in wild flower seed production.

An increasing number of references and articles dealing with the use of wild flowers in the garden have appeared in recent years in the national and regional press and in all types of publications, especially gardening and women's magazines. Apart from the publications produced by conservation organisations, there are a number of magazines dealing entirely with wildlife. The BBC Wildlife magazine is Britain's only newsstand magazine devoted to natural history and conservation. In addition, radio and television wildlife programmes with a significant wild flower content occur much more regularly and wildlife writers and personalities such as David Attenborough, David Bellamy, Miriam Rothschild, Richard Mabey and Chris Baines promote public awareness of the beauty of our native wildlife and the threats to the conservation of flora and fauna.

Much information about cultivating and propagating many wild flowers under garden conditions has been generally available for many years. Influential gardening writers including Robinson, Jekyll, Ingwersen, Genders, Stuart-Thomas and Lloyd have encouraged their cultivation and most encyclopedias of gardening include some wild species and many cultivated forms of wild flowers or their closely related species. In the last few years they have been joined by many new books specialising in the cultivation of wild flowers or in wildlife gardening. Details of these and other useful publications can be found on page 139.

Many conservation organisations also promote greater public consciousness and understanding of the advantages of British wildlife and what can be done to preserve it for future generations. All encourage their members to make their gardens more attractive to wildlife, especially the Royal Society for the Protection of Birds, the British Butterfly Conservation Society, the Urban Wildlife Group (Birmingham), the British Trust for Conservation Volunteers and the Royal Society for Nature Conservation. The RSNC is one of the largest voluntary conservation organisations and is the umbrella body of 47 local nature conservation trusts throughout the United Kingdom. Together with 30 urban wildlife groups it has over 165,000 members and manages 1,684 reserves covering 53,342 hectares. WATCH, the junior wing of the RSNC, has a personal membership of around 23,000 with a further 700 affiliated schools. Just over a year ago it launched the British Wildlife Appeal to raise £10 million over five years. Last May, as part of this appeal, National Wild Flower Week was launched to focus public attention on Britain's priceless heritage of wild flowers.

One of the most effective ways I have found for engaging the interest of garden owners in the possibilities of growing wild flowers in their gardens is to put on displays alongside cultivated flowers in flower tents at gardening shows around the country. At Chelsea, the Royal Show and flower shows such as those at Shrewsbury and Southport, I have been able to prove how attractive, colourful and suitable wild flowers are for use in gardens. Our permanent wild flower garden at the Royal Showground shows that it is perfectly possible to make an attractive garden using only wild flowers. Our greatest undertaking so far has been a six-month wild flower garden mounted in conjunction with Woman's Weekly at last year's National Garden Festival at Stoke-on-Trent. It demonstrated how effectively plants from different habitats can be woven into garden settings and I was delighted when it was awarded a gold medal.

### Gardeners' question time

I long ago discovered that as well as giving me an opportunity to share my enthusiasm with a wide public these displays also give me a chance to discover what people want to know about wild flowers and how to grow them. This book cannot answer all the hundreds of questions that have been put to me by correspondents, customers and the many people I have met at shows who are keen to learn about wild flowers and the way that they can be best used in the garden. My scheme has been a modest one: to make a selection of interesting plants suitable for growing in a range of conditions and to provide adequate information on their cultivation and on more general aspects of wild flower gardening.

In the A-Z section I have dealt with 80 plants which are personal favourites in some detail but I have tried to incorporate within these entries and elsewhere in the text information about other interesting species. The supporting information will, I hope, enable more people to grow and enjoy wild flowers, whether in the significant but limited space of town or country gardens or on a grand scale with woodland and meadowland.

# WILD FLOWER GUIDE

M aking a selection of eighty wild flowers has been no easy task. About the inclusion of some plants – Cowslips, Primroses and Sweet Violets among them – there can be no dispute. However, crowding behind these plants of the first rank are many others, many more than could be given full treatment here, that are interesting and attractive. Wherever space has allowed I have unashamedly made reference in the eighty entries to other species, sometimes close relatives of the featured plants, sometimes plants from similar natural habitats, and sometimes plants of more distant connection but linked in some way.

In reviewing plants suitable for inclusion I have often gone back to the early writers on our wild flowers and in particular to three: John Gerard, John Parkinson and Nicholas Culpeper. These authorities, writing in the late sixteenth and seventeenth centuries, did not conform to modern standards of scientific accuracy and originality of observation. Their works, nonetheless, contain a great body of accumulated wisdom and belief, often expressed with pithy vigour. I have often quoted from them not only for the intrinsic interest of what they say but also because they seem to speak from an age in which our wild flowers were appreciated for their beauty and their usefulness to man.

# BETONY
## *Stachys officinalis*

**Flowering season**
June to September.

**Suitable growing conditions**
Well-drained ground in borders or in wild parts of the garden; reasonably fertile soil ranging from slightly acid to alkaline; a position in partial shade or full sun.

**Growing guide**
Sow thinly in early spring or early autumn in carefully prepared permanent position; lightly cover seed; thin out up to 30cm (1ft) apart. Preferably, sow in seed bed; transplant into growing bed; move to final positions in autumn. Plants can be propagated by division of the roots from October to April.

Betony is a curious case of a medicinal herb that has almost totally fallen from favour, although it was once the sovereign remedy for all manner of illnesses. According to Culpeper it was 'a very precious Herb'. Another common name, Woundwort, reflects its old prestige. All the old authorities list numerous conditions for which it was effective: it could ease toothache, cure the bites of mad dogs, heal old sores, draw out splinters, revive the weary and preserve men from what Gerard calls 'the danger of epidemical diseases'. Even wild animals, it was believed, recognized the plant's healing properties and, wounded or afflicted, would seek it out, eat it and be cured.

Its efficacy in the treatment of medical conditions was only part of a much broader potency, for it was a herb of powerful magical qualities and was supposed to protect from evil those who took it or wore it about them.

This European native, which was once so commonly grown in physic gardens, is a common plant on the Continent and the British Isles, although not extending into northern Scandinavia and only rarely found in Scotland and Ireland. It is a plant of copses and woodland clearings but is also sometimes found in more open grassland and scrub.

Betony is a perennial, growing from a woody root-stock sending up square stems to a height of about 60cm (2ft). The stems carry relatively few leaves, which are rough to the touch and have a jagged edge. Most of the leaves grow from the base and these are heart-shaped. The flowers, which appear in the second half of summer, are carried in a short, densely-packed spike, and in colour are a strong reddish purple.

In the garden Betony has made the transition from a herbal plant to an ornamental but it is generally a cultivated form with large flowers that is grown and not the plant as found in the wild. This itself is attractive and is useful for planting in clumps in lightly shaded parts of the garden. It is quite at home in borders mixed with other wild flowers or with cultivated varieties, or else forming stands in wilder parts of the garden.

Even after the decline of its reputation as a valuable medicinal herb, Betony has figured as a constituent of herbal tobaccos, particularly combined with Colt's-foot *(Tussilago farfara)* and Eyebright *(Euphrasia officinalis)*. It has also been used in snuff mixtures. It is said that an infusion prepared with the dried leaves is a fair substitute for conventional tea.

# BIRD'S-FOOT-TREFOIL

*Lotus corniculatus*

**Flowering season**
May to September.

**Suitable growing conditions**
Well-drained ground mixed with grasses and other wild flowers; acid or alkaline soil of low fertility; a position in full sun.

**Growing guide**
Scarify seed before sowing (see page 106). Sow thinly in early spring or early autumn in carefully prepared permanent position; lightly cover seed; thin out as required; spread can be over 60cm (2ft). Preferably, sow in seed bed; transplant to growing bed. Move to final positions in autumn. Plants are easily propagated by division from October to March.

Although such a modest creeping plant, Bird's-foot-trefoil is burdened with an exceptionally large number of local names. Some, such as Buttered Eggs, are a clear reference to the bright yellow splashed with orange of the flowers while others, including Boots-and-shoes, refer to their form. Many allude to the shape of the black pods, which when seen in groups of three or so with their little withered claws it is not too fanciful to find resembling a bird's foot or a cat's claw. In others, among them Hop-o'-my-thumb, we can recognize resonances of a magic fairy world that was once charged with a deeper, perhaps more sinister, significance than we can now easily appreciate.

Its many local names are a sign of the wide distribution of Bird's-foot-trefoil, which throughout Europe, and extending as far as North Africa and Asia Minor, is a common weed of grassland. It is often found growing very thickly on poor chalky soils and in pasture on sandy ground near the coast. As well as occurring wild it is commonly included as a constituent of seed mixtures for pasture, being particularly suitable for free-draining soils as its long tap-root allows it to draw on deep supplies of water. There are divided opinions about its value as a fodder plant for at certain times of the year some animals appear to avoid it. It has a reputation for being poisonous but in natural populations of the plant only some plants are toxic and the level of toxicity among these fluctuates seasonally. Despite its reputation, in parts of France it is grown as a crop.

This clover-like plant forms dense mats, the stems creeping along the ground for 30cm (12in) or so, sometimes becoming more upright near the tip. The pea-like flowers, which are about 12mm (½in) across, are carried in heads of two to six and the seed pods that follow grow as they mature until they are about 25mm (1in) long.

In the garden Bird's-foot-trefoil is often thought of as a weed of lawns, for it is one of those successful grassland plants that survives even when turf is cut quite short. The wild flower gardener will recognize it for what it is, a pretty native that is an integral part of grassland habitats, an important source of nectar for a wide range of insects and a major food plant for the caterpillars of several moths and butterflies, including those of the Common Blue. The best way to use it is as part of a grass and wild flower mixture that is left uncut in the summer, but because it does tolerate mowing it is a good plant to include in a rough lawn.

# BITING STONECROP
## *Sedum acre*

**Flowering season**
June to July.

**Suitable growing conditions**
Very well-drained stony ground and the tops of walls; acid or alkaline soil of low fertility; a position in full sun.

**Growing guide**
Sow thinly in early spring or early autumn in carefully prepared permanent position; barely cover seed; thin out as required; spread can be over 30cm (1ft). Preferably, sow in pots; prick out into tray; move to final positions in autumn. Plants are easily propagated from rooted stems.

The Stonecrops, mainly species of *Sedum*, include a number of plants that are well suited because of their fleshy leaves and stems to withstand periods of drought. Of the native species the most common is the Biting Stonecrop or Wallpepper, both names referring to the pungency of the leaves, as does the specific name *acre*.

It is a species that is widely distributed, occurring even in the far north on the coast of Scandinavia. Stony, sandy and chalky soils suit it well. It finds many man-made structures very much to its liking so that it is a familiar plant on old walls.

This is a perennial species with a very fibrous root system and numerous trailing stems forming mats 5 to 20cm (2 to 8in) tall. The thick leaves are cylindrical and arranged tightly along the stems. The flowering season starts in mid-summer and, although short, is vivid. The flowers are starry, bright yellow and borne in profusion.

The Biting Stonecrop is a genial little plant that is easy to fit even into a small garden if it has not already found its way there. Its good nature has been recognized in an oddly long-winded local name, Welcome-home-husband-though-never-so-drunk. It will quickly soften the edges of old masonry and rubble, it will happily scratch a living in the cracks of paving, it can make an attractive addition to a rock garden provided that it is not put among the choicest plants, and planted in quantity it can make good ground cover.

Some apothecaries considered preparations of Biting Stonecrop a valuable treatment for intestinal parasites but even among the old authorities there were those recommending caution in the use of this herb. The irritant substances that it contains are so powerful that it can cause blistering when applied externally.

The White Stonecrop (*S. album*) and the English Stonecrop (*S. anglicum*) are two other species that will thrive in harsh conditions.

A quite unrelated species, Ground Ivy (*Glechoma hederacea*), is an evergreen perennial of creeping habit that is another useful and attractive ground-covering plant. In contrast to the Biting Stonecrop, it prefers moist and fertile soils, in the wild generally occurring in damp grassland and open woods. The leaves are long-stalked and kidney-shaped and when growing in full sun are often purplish at the edges. This is a member of the Mint family; the connection can be smelt in the crushed leaves (though the smell is much less pleasant than that of the culinary herb) and seen in the lipped flowers. These begin to appear in early spring and continue for several months.

# BLUEBELL
### *Hyacinthoides non-scriptus*

**Flowering season**
April to June.

**Suitable growing conditions**
Well-drained ground; acid or alkaline soil that is reasonably fertile; sunny or shady positions.

**Growing guide**
Plants raised from seed take 4-6 years to reach flowering size. Sow thinly in shallow drills in a lightly shaded growing bed in autumn; cover seed; in spring, thin out as required. Artificial stratification is necessary if sowing in spring (see page 106). After two or three years, move to final positions 10cm (4in) apart. Plant bulbs 10-15cm (4-6in) deep in clumps in early autumn.

Woods hazy blue with the flowers of the Bluebell, or Wild Hyacinth, are such a feature of Britain in May – and so relatively uncommon in other parts of Europe – that it is astonishing how infrequently the plant is mentioned by early botanical writers. Modern taxonomists have rather cruelly made up for this neglect by moving the plant about from one genus to another. The specific name, *non-scripta*, means not written on and was intended to distinguish this plant from the Hyacinth of the Mediterranean region. According to legend Apollo, overwhelmed by grief at the death of the handsome Spartan youth Hyacinthus, raised from his blood the Hyacinth flower, on which were marked the letters *ai, ai*, as a lament to echo through the ages.

In its wild state the Bluebell often grows very densely, creating great sheets of blue in woodland. It flowers particularly freely in an open position where the shade is not too dense and therefore benefits from coppicing.

The strap-shaped leaves are deep green and slightly shorter than the flax flower spikes, which are usually from 15 to 40cm (12 to 16in) tall but bend over at the tip. Each stem carries about ten to fifteen bell-shaped flowers in a rather one-sided arrangement. The flowers are generally violet blue in colour and slightly fragrant.

The Bluebell is one of the loveliest plants for the wild or semi-wild garden, particularly for planting in dappled shade under trees. It is a robust grower, able to look after itself and build up large colonies but too vigorous to allow to compete with gentler plants in the rock garden. Wild stands suffer more from trampling than picking but as a cut flower it has a short life and is therefore better enjoyed as a growing plant.

It is a shame to mix the English Bluebell with the Spanish Bluebell *(Hyacinthoides hispanica)* which is widely grown as a garden plant, and has stouter stems and heavier flowers than the native. The two will hybridize, producing intermediates that are not true to either parent.

Bluebells are an important source of nectar and pollen for Bumble-bees but the flower-tubes are too long for Honey Bees.

The Bluebell does not feature prominently in traditional herbal medicine but the thick juice that is found in the bulbs, in fact in every part of the plant, has been used as a starch and glue.

# BROOM
### *Cytisus scoparius* subsp. *scoparius*

**Flowering season**
May to June.

**Suitable growing conditions**
Well-drained ground at the back of borders or as an informal hedging; acid or neutral soil of medium or low fertility; a position in full sun.

**Growing guide**
Soak seeds before sowing (see page 106). Sow thinly in early autumn in carefully prepared permanent position; cover seed; in spring, thin out as required; spread can be 3m (9ft). Preferably, sow in pots; prick out singly into pots; move to final positions.

There are not many plants that have such a precise auditory association as Broom; the snap of the bursting pods is a characteristic sound of heathland on hot days in summer. Although it was used for the humble purpose of making a rough implement for sweeping, to which it has given its name, Broom has distinguished connections. The *planta genista*, to give it its ancient Latin name, was adopted as the emblem of Henry II and from it is derived the family name Plantagenet.

This native European shrub is widely found throughout its range on the fringes of woodland, on roadsides and often is a dominant species of heath and scrubland. However, it is rarely found on chalk and limestone, preferring sandy and clay soils. It is deciduous, growing to 1.8m (6ft), and the spineless angular stems are rather thinly clothed with small three-lobed leaves. The bright yellow flowers, which are borne in great profusion in early summer, are butterfly-shaped, with a large standard petal, two wing petals and a keel. The pods, which are about 4cm (1½in) long, are green at first but turn blackish brown before exploding.

From a distance the plant might be confused with its close relative Gorse *(Ulex europaeus)* but the spiny character of this plant distinguishes it. Although Gorse has become a serious weed in some countries, in Britain it is much less hardy than Broom.

Many of the Brooms commonly grown as ornamentals are forms or hybrids of the wild European species, which is no less versatile in the garden. It makes an excellent background plant to other wild flowers and, planted as a low hedge, is useful for marking a transition from the more cultivated parts of the garden to wilder areas. It is a particularly useful plant for gardens with sandy dry soils.

Broom is a good source of pollen for bees and a food plant for the caterpillars of several moths and butterflies, including those of the Silver-studded Blue. In the garden it also makes a good refuge for small birds.

In the past, the flower buds have been pickled and eaten as a delicacy – they are said to have been served at the coronation feast of James II – and before the introduction of hops the tops were used to give a bitter tang to beer. Its principal medical use has been in diuretic preparations; we have it on Gerard's authority that Henry VIII 'was woont to drinke the distilled water of Broome flowers against surfets, and diseases thereof arising'.

# BUGLE
## *Ajuga reptans*

**Flowering season**
May to June.

**Suitable growing conditions**
Moist or well-drained ground in wild parts of the garden; reasonably fertile soils ranging from slightly acid to markedly alkaline; shady or open positions.

**Growing guide**
Sow thinly in early spring or early autumn in carefully prepared permanent position; lightly cover seed; thin out up to 45cm (18in) apart. Preferably, sow in a pot; prick out into a tray; move to final positions in autumn. Plants are easily propagated by root division and separation of the runners.

There is mystery surrounding the origins of the common name of this perennial, but the name Carpenter's Herb, by which it is sometimes known, is a straightforward allusion to its former use as a herb to staunch bleeding.

Bugle is a widely distributed European native, being found from North Africa to northern Britain and eastwards to the Caucasus, and it occurs as an introduced species in many other parts of the world. In Britain and continental Europe it is a common plant in woodland and grassy places, the blue spikes sometimes forming great patches.

The root-stock produces a rosette of smooth shiny leaves and also throws out numerous leafy runners, sometimes more than 60cm (2ft) long. Rootlets form at every pair of leaves and eventually, after the runner itself has died, a large colony of new plants comes away in the spring. Spring is also the flowering season. A stem, which is square in section and hairy on two sides, develops from the leafy rosette, growing to a height of about 25cm (10in) and bearing a head of six to twelve small dull-blue flowers. It seems that very often the seed does not set, and the plant must then rely on its runners to propagate itself.

Gardeners have tended to treat Bugle with some caution, fearing that such a ready colonizer will be too hearty among choice plants. However, a number of forms with distinctive foliage colour – deepest plum, wine red and variegated – have become popular ground-covering ornamentals to mix with other robust plants.

The wild plant is very effective as ground cover and in sunny or shady parts of the garden will spread in a way that is not difficult to control, excluding many less desirable plants in the process. It is in the wild garden that Bugle shows at its best, its masses of spiky blueness a sure sign that spring has really come. These early flowers are an important source of nectar to many insects.

John Ray, writing in the seventeenth century, reiterates centuries of confidence in Bugle for the treatment of wounds and sores: 'Those that have Bugle and Sanicle need no surgeon'. Culpeper also recommended Bugle as 'very effectual for any inward wounds, thrusts, or stabs in the body or bowels' and suggested the syrup of the herb for 'such as give themselves much to drinking'. Despite the regard the old apothecaries had for it, Bugle is today rarely used for medicinal purposes.

# COLUMBINE

*Aquilegia vulgaris*

**Flowering season**
May to June.

**Suitable growing conditions**
Well-drained ground in the border or with other woodland plants; neutral to alkaline soil that is reasonably fertile; a sunny or partially shaded position.

**Growing guide**
Sow thinly in early autumn or early spring in carefully prepared permanent position; lightly cover seed; thin out to 30cm (1ft) apart. Artificial stratification is beneficial if sowing in spring (see page 106). Preferably, sow in pots; prick out into a tray; move to final positions in autumn. Plants can be propagated by division between October and March.

The common name Columbine (and an even earlier one, Culverwort) refers to a supposed resemblance between the shape of the flower and a cluster of doves. The allusion is no more fanciful than that in the generic name *Aquilegia*, which sees a resemblance between the spurs of the flowers and the talons of the eagle.

Although the Columbine is a truly wild plant, rarely seen in the British Isles in its native state but ranging from northern Europe to North Africa, it is best known, under the name Granny's-Bonnet, as a favourite subject in the cottage garden. Most of the cultivated corms are, however, hybrids, several species contributing to the wide colour range which is now available. Amongst the most popular strains a conspicuous feature is the exceptional length of the spurs.

The Columbine is a relatively short-lived perennial which in early spring produces a tuft of pretty blue-green leaves. The slender but wiry flower stem grows to a height of 60cm (2ft), although flowering plants can be much shorter growing. The hanging flowers, up to 5cm (2in) across, are generally purplish blue, although there are variations in shade and white forms sometimes occur. All five petals are spurred.

The refinement of the wild Columbine, distinctive in flower and elegant in leaf, makes it an easy plant to accommodate in the border. It can, however, cope perfectly well in a wilder setting, self-seeding freely when planted among other plants that enjoy dappled shade and is a useful stand-by for a north-facing corner.

Vita Sackville-West, who at Sissinghurst gave cottage gardening a truly patrician stamp, recommends 'gaily blowing' Columbines for growing in enclosed spaces and against walls, either in sun or shade. She also mentions the old country saying, that their 'morals leave much to be desired', a reference to the fact that Columbines will hybridise freely amongst themselves. Seeds gathered from plants grown near cultivated Columbines or other Aquilegias will often not come true to type.

Like other members of the Buttercup family it is poisonous, so the Columbine is not a plant to meddle with in the making of herbal remedies. A preparation is still sometimes made from the roots for the external treatment of ulcers.

As a picked flower the Columbine is not long lived but it makes a graceful addition to a bunch of woodland flowers.

# COMMON COMFREY
## *Symphytum officinale*

**Flowering season**
May to September.

**Suitable growing conditions**
Moist ground in borders or the wild garden; a reasonably fertile soil that is not excessively acid or alkaline; a position in sun or part shade.

**Growing guide**
Sow thinly in spring or autumn in permanent position; cover seed; thin out up to 45cm (18in) apart. Preferably, sow in pots; prick out into a tray; move to final positions in autumn.

Comfrey's reputation as a healing herb is preserved in its common name, derived from a Latin word meaning 'to join together' and in such names as Knitbone, Bruisewort and Boneset by which it has also been known. It may not be the same plant that Dioscorides called *symphiton* but it has enjoyed the same regard as a herb that makes things whole.

Common Comfrey is native to Europe and Asia and is an introduced plant in other parts of the world. Gerard says that 'Comfrey groweth in watrie ditches, in fat and fruitful meadowes', a description of its natural habitat that still holds true.

This handsome perennial, which can grow to a height of 120cm (50in), has strong coarse stalks and large rough hairy leaves. The drooping bell-shaped flowers are carried in one-sided clusters and can range in colour from dirty white to pink or blue. They begin to open in early summer and sometimes continue until early autumn.

Comfrey was once widely grown in cottage gardens because of its supposed medicinal value. Even allowing for its coarseness, a clump can make a bold effect. In the more cultivated parts of the garden it should be treated with some caution for it spreads freely and the smallest fragment of root will grow, making it extremely difficult to eradicate it should you want to. In shady damp parts of the wild garden it makes a really attractive plant; there, its luxuriant growth and long flowering season can be appreciated without anxiety.

All the old authorities stress Comfrey's bone knitting and healing properties. 'Great Comfrey . . . hath the same property that Bugle hath', writes Richard Surflet in *The Countrie Farme* of 1600, 'that is to say, to soulder wounde'. The copious mucilage produced by the plant almost certainly served as a proof of its efficacy. In addition, herb teas prepared with Comfrey are believed to give relief to those suffering from colds and bronchitis.

It is exceptional among plants in being a source of Vitamin $B_{12}$ and rich in protein. On these counts alone it is of value to vegans but some research has suggested that the plant contains small quantities of toxic substances that may be harmful if consumed regularly over a long period. However, it can be eaten as a cooked vegetable (prepared like spinach) and in a traditional German dish the leaves are cooked in fritters.

# COMMON EVENING-PRIMROSE
*Oenothera biennis*

**Flowering season**
June to September.

**Suitable growing conditions**
Very free-draining ground in borders or in wild parts of the garden; slightly acid to alkaline soils of low or medium fertility; a position in full sun.

**Growing guide**
Sow thinly in early June in carefully prepared permanent position; lightly cover seed; keep well watered; thin out up to 40cm (15in) apart. Preferably, sow in seed bed; transplant to growing bed in July; move to final position in mid autumn.

The Common Evening-primrose is an introduction from North America. It began its European career in the first quarter of the seventeenth century at the Padua Botanic Garden in Italy; since then it has become a common plant in much of Europe, enjoying a double status, first as a showy garden plant and second as an attractive weed.

The Evening-primroses are misleadingly named: they do not belong to the Primrose family (not all even have flowers in the yellow range) and, although some do have flowers that open in the late afternoon or evening, this is not true of the whole genus. Their botanical name comes from two Greek words that apparently signify that the plant was used to whet the appetite for wine.

As a garden escaper the Common Evening-primrose thrives in poor stony soils, so it is most familiar as a weed of roadsides and railway embankments. This biennial species, which in favourable conditions can germinate and flower in the same season, produces a thick, deeply probing root from which grows a rosette up to 60cm (2ft) across of narrow strap-shaped leaves. The rough stems, which grow to a height of 90cm (3ft), carry a succession of yellow flowers over a long season. Generally there are two or three flowers open on a stem at any one time, each opening in the late afternoon by a series of jerky spasms to form a fragrant, rather papery bowl about 5cm (2in) across. By the middle of the following day the flowers have withered.

Any coarseness in the foliage of this plant is more than made up for by the lovely yellow of its large sweetly-scented blooms and the length of its flowering season. It self-seeds so freely that it is sensible to take off some of the heads before the seeds mature. In a garden of any size there is almost certainly room for it in less organized corners, where it can be left to itself. Wherever it grows it will attract night-flying moths and, in the early morning, bees.

The Common Evening-primrose does not have the weighty medical, culinary and herbal associations of native European plants. However, it may yet prove more valuable than previously supposed, for it has been found to contain a compound with anti-coagulant properties that might be used to reduce the risk of heart attack.

Several close relatives of the Common Evening-primrose are also naturalized in Europe. Of these the most common is the Fragrant Evening-primrose *(Oenothera stricta)*, which in southern England is generally found on sand dunes.

# COMMON RESTHARROW
*Ononis repens*

**Flowering season**
June to September.

**Suitable growing conditions**
Free-draining grassland or
bare ground; neutral to
alkaline soils of low fertility;
a position in full sun.

**Growing guide**
Scarify seeds before sowing
(see page 106). Sow thinly in
early spring or early autumn
in carefully prepared
permanent position; lightly
cover seed; thin out as
required; spread can be over
60cm (2ft). Preferably, sow in
pots; prick out into pots;
move to final position in
autumn taking care not to
disturb the long tap-root.
Plants can be propagated by
shoot cuttings.

The prettiness of
this small member of the Pea family was little
consolation to the ploughman, who found its long,
tough and matted roots catching the plough and
difficult to cut through. An earlier name than
Restharrow (really a translation into English of a
medieval Latin name), was Cammock. Cammocky
milk and butter was tainted, the cause being cows
browsing on this common weed. Donkeys are said
to be particularly partial to Restharrow and the
Greek word for an ass is the source of the generic
name *Ononis*.

The typical natural habitat of this native European perennial is dry grassland. In the British Isles
it is most common on chalky soils and near the
seashore. It is found much more frequently in the
south and east than in the north and west.

This hairy plant has stems up to 60cm (2ft) long,
generally trailing and often rooting near the base.
The small pink flowers, which appear throughout
the summer, are followed by rather stubby pods.
Spiny Restharrow *(Ononis spinosa)*, a closely related species and often found growing with Common Restharrow on chalky soils, has spiny stems
that are more erect and the seed pods are longer. It
seems that in the wild the two species hybridize,
producing a range of intermediate plants.

In the garden Common Restharrow makes
a lovely addition to a short mini-meadow
where, as it is one of the food plants of the Common Blue, it will have the added attraction of
enticing these butterflies. In more open ground it
will spread very freely but could be combined with
other low-growing plants such as Horseshoe Vetch
*(Hippocrepis comosa)* and Sainfoin *(Onobrychis
viciifolia)* to make a bright carpet.

Restharrow has never been a major medical
herb although, perhaps as a desperate measure, it
has been used in the past to calm the delirious.
Parkinson says that a decoction of Restharrow
'made with some vinegar and gargled in the mouth
easeth the pains of the toothache, especially when
it cometh of rheum'.

The juice in the roots is sweet enough to have
tempted children to dig them up and chew them.
In some parts it is known as Wild Liquorice or
Spanish Root.

Restharrow fell out of favour as a vegetable long
ago. However, 'in former times', according to Parkinson, 'the young shoots and tender stalks were
pickled up to be eaten as a meate or sause, wonderfully commended against a foul breath, and to
take away the smell of wine in them that had
drunke too much'.

# COMMON ST JOHN'S WORT
## *Hypericum perforatum*

**Flowering season**
June to September.

**Suitable growing conditions**
Well-drained ground in borders or wild parts of the garden; acid or alkaline soils of medium or poor fertility; a position in full sun or dappled shade.

**Growing guide**
Sow thinly in early spring or early autumn in carefully prepared permanent position; lightly cover seed; thin out as required; spread can be over 60cm (2ft). Preferably, sow in seed bed; transplant into growing bed; move to final positions in autumn. Plants can be propagated by division of the roots.

Of several plants associated with St John the Common St John's Wort has the most distinguished reputation. The Saint's day falls on 24 June, three days after the summer solstice, and throughout Europe, even until recent times, summer fires were lit on the evening of the 23rd according to traditions that were heavy with magic significance. The herbs of St John were picked early in the morning and in the evening subjected to the purifying smoke of the ceremonial fires, a process which fortified the medical and magical properties of plants that were already ranked as herbs of great potency. The generic name *Hypericum*, derived from the Greek name *hypericon* is said to indicate that the plant's smell was so obnoxious to evil spirits that it would put them to flight.

St John's Wort is a native of temperate Europe and western Asia and occurs also as a naturalized plant in the Americas and Australasia. Throughout its range it is common in hedgerows, roadsides, open woodland and meadows; as an introduced plant it has sometimes become a serious weed.

This perennial, which spreads from underground rhizomes, makes a bush about 60cm (2ft) high, with erect stems, rather woody at the base, bearing pointed leaves that are marked with numerous translucent dots (the feature alluded to in the specific name *perforatum*). The yellow five-petalled flowers, borne in clusters during late summer and early autumn, are about 3cm (1in) across and have a prominent boss of yellow stamens at the centre. When crushed the flowers turn red, a fact contributing to the superstitious regard in which the plant has been held.

Common St John's Wort can make an attractive border plant, its yellow flowers being very welcome in early autumn. However, it can prove a vigorous spreader and for this reason it may be better to start with it in the rough edges of the garden where its expansion will not be at the expense of choice plants.

This herb's reputation as a healing agent had much to do with the red – and therefore blood-like – juice it yielded and the bruise-like marks of the leaves. As a homeopathic wound herb it is still highly regarded.

In countries with more and brighter sunlight than Britain farm animals that have grazed on Common St John's Wort sometimes suffer from a form of poisoning in which unpigmented areas of skin become photosensitive.

# COMMON TOADFLAX
## *Linaria vulgaris*

**Flowering season**
June to September.

**Suitable growing conditions**
Well-drained ground anywhere in the garden but preferably in the wilder parts; neutral to alkaline soils of reasonable fertility; a position in full sun.

**Growing guide**
Sow thinly in early spring or early autumn in carefully prepared permanent position; lightly cover seed; thin out up to 30cm (1ft) apart. Preferably, sow in seed bed; transplant into growing bed; move to final positions in autumn. Plants can be propagated by division in autumn or spring.

The most widely cultivated of the Toadflax is an introduced hardy annual, *Linaria maroccana*, but Common Toadflax, which is found throughout Europe, is a true, although generally short-lived, perennial. It shares with its annual relatives a capacity for prolific seeding. Linnaeus gave the plant its botanical name because of its similarity before flowering to the true flax *(Linum)*, in crops of which it was a frequent and troublesome weed. The common name makes the same connection, the prefix perhaps drawing a slightly fanciful comparison between the shape of the flower and that of a toad's head. A number of local names, such as Eggs and Bacon, allude to the flower's two colours.

As a wild plant Common Toadflax is found not only as a weed of cultivated fields, but among grass on roadsides and wasteland, even in open woodland. From the creeping root-stock grow slender stems up to 60cm (2ft) high, well clothed with long narrow leaves that stand at right angles to the stem. The long-spurred flowers, somewhat similar to those of the garden Snapdragon, are borne in a dense spike. The lower lip is orange, in contrast to the creamy yellow of the rest of the flower. The large bees that pollinate this species have to force

their way in to get nectar as the flowers never open.

Common Toadflax is one of the best wild flowers for making a bold splash of colour in the garden but as a border plant it is not easy to control unless it is closely hemmed in by other vigorous growers. Once established it is difficult to eliminate. It is at its best in wilder parts of the garden as part of a grass and wild flower mixture or better still as a clump, for instance on a sunny bank, where the flowers growing densely together can assert their pretty yellow. Wherever it is planted, it will propagate itself freely.

In the garden, as in the wild, Common Toadflax is a valuable nectar plant, Honey Bees and Bumblebees benefitting when the plant is growing in stands. It is also a food plant of the lovely Spotted Fritillary's caterpillars.

Toadflax contains poisonous substances and, if eaten in sufficient quantities, it might be harmful to animals. Among the herbalists its main reputation has been as a diuretic but it has featured in many other treatments, even sometimes as a rejuvenating lotion for, as Gerard says, 'a decoction of Toadflax taketh away the yellownesse and deformitie of the skinne'.

# CORN CHAMOMILE
*Anthemis arvensis*

**Flowering season**
June to July.

**Suitable growing
conditions**
Well-drained ground in
borders; soils of
medium or low fertility
that are not excessively
acid or alkaline; a
position in full sun.

**Growing guide**
Sow thinly in early
autumn or early spring
in carefully prepared
permanent position;
barely cover seed; thin
out up to 30cm (12in)
apart. For large
flowering plants, sow in
seed bed in early
autumn; move to final
positions in early
spring.

Few herbs have enjoyed so high a reputation and for so long as the Chamomile *(Chamaemelum nobile)*, of which it has been said, 'No simple in the whole catalogue of herbal medicines is possessed of a quality more friendly and beneficial to the intestines'. Even in Ancient Egypt it was greatly esteemed. 'Nechessor saith the Egyptians dedicated it to the sun, because it cured agues,' reports Culpeper but he was not impressed by the logic of their herbalism, adding, 'and they were like enough to do it, for they were the arrantist apes in their religion I ever read of'.

Chamomile, a perennial, occurs as a wild plant in parts of Britain but Corn Chamomile, an annual but closely related plant, is much more common. Throughout its range, which extends to North Africa and Asia Minor, it is a common field weed and is also found on verges and waste places, particularly where the soil is chalky. It forms a sometimes straggly bush up to 40cm (15in) tall with very finely divided leaves. The daisy-like flowers, which are white with yellow discs, are borne from early to mid-summer.

It is not always easy to distinguish between the Mayweeds and the Chamomiles, which all have similar flowers and feathery foliage. Corn Chamomile is most frequently confused with Wild Chamomile or Scented Mayweed *(Matricaria recutita)*, but on this plant the petals reflex once the flowers are mature, whereas with Corn Chamomile the petals either stand out at right angles to the stem or incline upwards.

The best way of using Corn Chamomile in the garden is to combine it with other wild flowers such as Corn Marigold *(Chrysanthemum segetum)* and Field Poppy *(Papaver rhoeas)*. Even when contrived, a combination of these annuals in the garden can recreate some of the freshness and gaiety that were a feature of cultivated fields before selective herbicides reduced wild populations of these plants to a fraction of what they were. However, rather than mixing seed in a random way you may prefer the bolder effect that is achieved by planting separate clumps of each species. The flowers of this species, like those of many other members of this family, are a source of nectar that attracts many insects.

Many wild flowers do not last well when picked for indoor decoration. The cut stems of Corn Chamomile are, however, exceptionally long lasting.

# CORNCOCKLE
## *Agrostemma githago*

**Flowering season**
June to August.

**Suitable growing conditions**
Well-drained ground in borders or in wilder parts of the garden; a neutral or slightly acid soil of reasonable fertility; a position in full sun.

**Growing guide**
Sow thinly in early autumn or early spring in carefully prepared permanent position; cover seed; thin out up to 20-40cm (8-16in) apart. In order to produce large flowering plants, sow in seed bed in early autumn; move to final positions in early spring.

As a wild plant Corncockle has had its moment. This native of southern Europe entered the north as a weed of arable land, flourishing in grain crops and contaminating the harvest, so that now the means to control it are available it has been reduced to a mere token presence. In the nineteenth century it was still a common field weed; now you might with great difficulty find it on poorly managed farmland.

Throughout its range in Europe and western Asia this annual member of the Pink family is associated with agriculture, germinating quickly where land has been turned and then flowering and seeding within the summer months. It rapidly develops into an erect and sparingly branched plant up to 90cm (3ft) tall that is given a greyish appearance by a covering of white hairs. The paired leaves, which are narrow and pointed, clasp the stem, which terminates in a solitary showy flower that is purplish pink in colour. The hairy calyx behind the flower and the five teeth growing from it, which are longer than the petals, are characteristic features of the plant.

This is one of the prettiest wild annuals and can stand comparison with many cultivated plants that give a quick and vivid display of colour; its bright effect is not achieved at the expense of grace. It is best used, grown fairly close together so that plants give one another support, as a patch in a border, or in wilder parts of the garden.

The seed-heads are very attractive and are worth gathering and drying for winter decoration. It can be embarrassingly prolific if allowed to self-seed so it is sensible to remove some seed-heads before they mature. Farmers rightly still see Corncockle as an undesirable weed so this is a plant that should never be let loose in the countryside.

There are reports from Poland of farm animals suffering Corncockle poisoning in the post-war period and in parts of southern Europe there may still be a problem of contaminated flour as a result of seed being harvested with rye and wheat. A diet with a sustained intake of contaminated flour, which is grey and has an unpleasant taste and smell, can lead to chronic poisoning, with the victims becoming gradually weaker. Cooking, for instance when the flour is used in bread, in no way reduces the toxicity of the contaminant.

Enjoy Corncockle as a wild plant of rare beauty that is quite at home in the garden, but be thankful that it is no longer a weed in our own grain crops.

# CORN MARIGOLD
## *Chrysanthemum segetum*

**Flowering season**
June to August.

**Suitable growing conditions**
Well-drained bare ground; neutral to acid soil that is reasonably fertile; an open sunny position.

**Growing guide**
Sow thinly in early autumn or early spring in permanent position; lightly cover seed; thin out up to 30cm (1ft) apart. For large flowering plants, sow in seed bed in early autumn; move to final positions in early spring. Add to grass and wild flower mixtures to give first year colour.

Beauty has been no protection for the colourful annual weeds of arable land. Corncockle, Cornflower and Corn Marigold, three of the loveliest, are now rarely seen mixed with crops, although the Corn Marigold at least survives fairly commonly on the verges of worked ground.

In the case of Corn Marigold there are records dating from the fourteenth century ordering tenant farmers to remove what was a particularly common weed in crops of barley. Uprooting was not really an effective method of control; it is only as a result of more efficient cleaning of grain seed and the ever increasing use of herbicides that Corn Marigold has become a less common and therefore less troublesome plant.

Gold, Boodle or Yellow Oxeye Daisy – Corn Marigold has many local names – is almost certainly a very early introduction from the Mediterranean region and it was probably a weed of some of the first crops grown in Britain and northern Europe. The 'gold' in some early place-names, for instance Goldhanger in Essex, is very likely a reference to this weed with clear yellow flowers.

The plant, which germinates in autumn or spring, grows to a height of 30cm (12in), the tooth-ed or lobed leaves being, as Culpeper says, 'somewhat clammy in handling'. Their waxy texture may give them some protection from herbicides. The upper leaves clasp stems bearing solitary daisy-like flowers up to 5cm (2in) across, which are slightly fragrant and which are borne throughout the summer months.

As the normal habitat of Corn Marigolds is disturbed ground, they are best used in the garden planted in bare ground, grown as colourful, free-flowering annuals on their own or mixed with other bright annuals such as Field Poppy, Corn Chamomile, Corncockle and Cornflower. The flowers are a source of nectar for insects and the cut flowers are exceptionally long-lasting. It is important to recognize that to farmers these annuals are still weeds, so on no account should the seed be scattered in the open countryside.

Corn Marigolds do not feature prominently in the old herbals although they were used in the treatment of fevers. In the nineteenth century it was reported that in China the lightly boiled petals served with vinegar were considered a delicacy.

# COWSLIP
## *Primula veris*

**Flowering season**
April to May.

**Suitable growing conditions**
Well-drained bare ground or a mini-meadow; acid or alkaline soil that is not too rich; an open or partially shaded position.

**Growing guide**
Sow thinly in carefully prepared permanent position in autumn; lightly cover seed; in spring, thin out to 20cm (8in) apart. Artificial stratification is necessary if sowing in spring (see page 106). Preferably, sow in seed bed; transplant into growing bed; move to final positions in autumn. Plants are easily propagated by division after flowering.

According to John Parkinson, Apothecary to King James I, 'In some countries they call them Paigles, or Palsieworts, or Petty Mulleins, which are called Cowslips in others'. The most common name, a polite version of 'cowslop', is only one of many, some of which refer to a resemblance between the flowerhead and a bunch of keys. The wealth of local names hints at the affection felt for this spring-flowering perennial, once very common on meadowland and in open woodland throughout Europe. It is still widely distributed and often numerous locally, particularly on dry limey soils, but its numbers have declined, partly as a result of changes in farming.

A rosette of pale green crinkled leaves up to 20cm (8in) long grows from a short rhizome with long thin roots. The fragrant deep-yellow flowers, each about 12mm (½in) across, are borne in one-sided nodding clusters of ten to thirty on a stem about 25cm (10in) high. The notched petals, marked orange near the eye, form a tubular corol-la that is rather small in relation to the inflated greenish-yellow calyx behind it.

A bare description cannot convey the charm of a plant that ranks as one of the most desirable wild flowers for the garden. When grown in clumps in the border Cowslips make a good spring show, in rock gardens or raised beds they combine well with other spring flowers, and they give a really authentic stamp to a wild spring mini-meadow. They also provide nectar for insects and food for the caterpillar of the Duke of Burgundy Fritillary.

In herbal remedies Cowslips have been held effective in the treatment of numerous ailments, particularly paralysis and nervous complaints. Unfortunately the making of Cowslip wine, a traditional country beverage valued for its sedative and calming properties, cannot now be encouraged, as it calls for very large quantities of flowers. Cowslip balls or 'tosties', produced by stringing together flowerheads, also make an unacceptable demand on plant populations, fifty or sixty heads being needed to make a ball.

# DAISY
## *Bellis perennis*

**Flowering season**
May to October.

**Suitable growing conditions**
Well-drained ground mixed with grasses and other wild flowers; soils of reasonable or poor fertility ranging from mildly acid to strongly alkaline; a sunny position.

**Growing guide**
Sow thinly in early spring or early autumn in carefully prepared permanent position; barely cover seed; thin out up to 10cm (4in) apart. Preferably, sow in seed bed; transplant into growing bed; move to final positions in autumn. Plants can be propagated by division.

When you can put your foot on seven daisies, an old proverb says, summer is come. This beguiling little flower, which for all its charm pricks the nightmares of lawn perfectionists, is at its peak in late spring and early summer but begins flowering very early and continues well into autumn. Its common name is simply derived from 'day's eye', a reference to its shining prettiness in full sun. At night and in cold dull weather the flowers close. The northern name Bairnwort is a delightful reminder of a time when the flowers of a lawn or meadow were literally within the reach of a hand.

This perennial member of the Daisy family is common throughout Europe, including the British Isles, and western Asia and as an introduced species in many other countries. Lawns suit it very well for in this environment man is keeping its competition under control. It is common, too, in short meadow grass and on verges. It is in praise of a meadow flower that Chaucer writes so fervently of 'Swiche as men callen daysies in our toun'.

Daisies grow from a sturdy root and form a basal rosette of slightly hairy spoon-shaped leaves, rounded at the end but with faintly jagged edges. Plants produce numerous solitary flowers on stems generally not more than 6cm (2½in) high.

The bright yellow disc is surrounded by numerous white, sometimes pink-tinged, florets, in all making a flower about 2.5cm (1in) across.

The Daisy was early developed as a garden flower, double kinds being particularly favoured. In *The Country Housewife's Garden* of 1615 William Lawson says that Daisies 'be good to keep up and strengthen the edges of your borders, as Pinks, be they red, white, mixt'. The cultivated forms are still widely grown as they are among the most reliable winter-flowering plants for bedding, edging or growing in containers. They are usually treated as biennials. The simple wild plant is a very modest thing set beside the monster varieties but its unforced beauty warrants giving it encouragement in any areas of short grass, particularly in rough lawns and grassed paths. Provided you can dispel the notion of its weediness, it will be a pleasure to the eye as well as being a useful source of nectar to many insects.

Some claim that the young leaves are edible but they are sufficiently acrid to deter cattle from browsing on them. In herbal medicine the Daisy was formerly much used in the treatment of wounds and, as the old name Bruisewort suggests, to relieve aches and pains.

# DOG ROSE

*Rosa canina*

**Flowering season**
June to July; hips, August to November

**Suitable growing conditions**
Well-drained ground in wilder parts of the garden and in hedgerows; acid and alkaline soils, even those of low fertility; a position in full sun or part shade.

**Growing guide**
Plants raised from seed usually take two or three years to reach flowering size. Sow in pots (or seed bed) in autumn; cover seed; over-winter outdoors; in spring, transplant into growing bed. Artificial stratification is necessary if sowing in spring (see page 106). After two years, move to final positions.

'The Plant of Roses, though it be a Shrub full of prickles, yet it had been more fit and convenient to have placed it with the most glorious flowres of the world, than to insert the same among base and thornie shrubs; for the Rose doth deserve the chiefest and most principall place among all flowers whatsoever; being not only esteemed for his beautie, vertues, and his fragrant and odoriferous smell, but also because it is the honour and ornament of our English Sceptre.'

The opinion of John Gerard, writing in *the Herball* of 1597, is shared by all the classical, medieval and Renaissance authorities but almost certainly they had in mind early cultivated forms. In the surprisingly complex genetic background, however, of such long established roses as the Old Cabbage Rose (*Rosa centifolia*) and the White Rose of York (*Rosa alba*) the simple Dog Rose or Brier has played a part. This rose's apparently perjorative common name most probably refers to a belief that has come down to us from Pliny that the root was a cure for the bite of a mad dog.

The species covers a rather variable complex of plants distributed throughout Europe and western Asia. In continental Europe and Britain it is a familiar plant of hedgerows, thickets, scrub and wasteland, and in Britain it is by far the most common of the wild roses. This deciduous shrub, which can grow to a height of 3m (10ft) produces a tangle of arching and much-branched woody stems, fiercely armed with tough curved prickles. The simple five-petalled highly fragrant flowers, which are pink or white and generally borne in small clusters, appear in mid-summer and are followed in autumn by bright scarlet hips.

The hardiness and resistance to disease of the Dog Rose has long been recognized by gardeners. Its summer flowers and autumn fruits make the Dog Rose an attractive plant in the wild garden and in rough hedges where it can provide a refuge for small mammals and birds. Bees collect the pollen with great industry.

The hips of the Dog Rose were once commonly used in sweet dishes; as Gerard writes, they 'maketh the most pleasants meats, and banqueting dishes, and tartes, and such-like'. Their high Vitamin C content was recognized between the wars and during World War II there was a national programme to gather hips for the preparation of rose-hip syrup.

# FEVERFEW
*Tanacetum parthenium*

**Flowering season**
July to August

**Suitable growing conditions**
Well-drained ground in borders or in wilder parts of the garden; reasonably fertile soil that is not excessively acid or alkaline; a position in full sun.

**Growing guide**
Sow thinly in early spring or early autumn in carefully prepared permanent position; lightly cover seed; thin out up to 45cm (18in). Preferably, sow in seed bed; transplant into growing bed; move to final positions in autumn. Plants are easily propagated by dividing established clumps in March or April.

Feverfew may well not be a native in Britain but this leafy aromatic perennial is widely distributed here and in other parts of Europe, perhaps because it was so much valued in physic gardens. The common name is derived from the Latin *febrifugia*, applied to substances that could drive out fevers. Although it appears subsequently to have lost favour in folk medicine, among medieval and Renaissance authorities it enjoyed high standing, its mere presence in the vicinity of a house helping, it was believed, to keep the air wholesome and giving the occupants protection from pestilential diseases.

The plant is found in hedgerows, on roadsides and in waste ground, often surviving and spreading near abandoned cottage gardens.

The light green leaves, which have a pungent smell when crushed, are delicately cut and have probably given rise to the corruption of Feverfew in another common name, Featherfew. It makes a bushy plant, up to 60cm (2ft) high, carrying numerous heads of small white flowers, each about 2cm (¾in) across, throughout the summer. The white ray florets characteristically curl back from the yellow disc. The daisy-like flowers produce copious quantities of seed. This may not be a long-lived perennial but the leaves do not die down in winter.

A number of selected forms are widely grown in gardens, flowers of the double forms being longer lasting than those of the wild plant. Feverfew is often used as an edging plant, and is grown in containers as well as in borders. The wild plant can be used in much the same way and is a partiularly good subject where you want to make a transition from areas of the garden that are highly cultivated to areas of wilder planting. In the wild garden proper it can be mixed with other plants or form a stand on its own.

Although some insects visit the flowers, the plant's pungency appears to repel bees. A tincture prepared from Feverfew exploits these insect repellent properties and is said to give relief where bites have already been inflicted. Dried leaves in muslin bags placed among clothes and linen are said to deter moths.

As a tonic Feverfew is usually taken as an infusion but decoctions prepared with sugar and honey are said to be effective in the treatment of coughs and chest complaints. Fresh interest has recently been taken in this herb for it has been discovered that it can give relief from migraine headaches, rheumatism and arthritis.

# FIELD FORGET-ME-NOT
## *Myosotis arvensis*

**Flowering season**
April to September

**Suitable growing conditions**
Free-draining ground in borders; acid or alkaline soil of reasonable fertility; a position in full sun or light shade.

**Growing guide**
Sow thinly in early autumn or early spring in carefully prepared permanent position; lightly cover seed; thin out up to 20-30cm (8-12in) apart. For large flower plants, sow in seed bed in early autumn; move to final positions in early spring. Add to grass and wild flower mixtures to give first year colour.

The Forget-me-nots all show a strong family likeness and are easily recognized as related to the popular garden flower. Until the nineteenth century they were known in this country as Scorpion Grass. This was a book name that linked them, because of the more-or-less coiled flower stems, to plants that the first century Greek authority Dioscorides likened to the scorpion's tail. Coleridge used the name Forget-me-not in *The Keepsake*, a poem first published in 1802, adding in a note that throughout the Austrian Empire the Water Forget-me-not (*Myosotis scorpioides*) was known by the name *Vergiss-mein nicht*, of which Forget-me-not was a translation. The German name and the French *Ne m'oubliez pas* are said to refer to the story of a knight who, walking with his lady by the side of a river, in stretching to pick flowers to give her slipped and fell in. The weight of his armour was so great that he could not extricate himself, but before drowning he had the presence of mind to throw her the flowers, calling out the pathetic words that have since been attached to them.

The Field Forget-me-not is an annual or biennial species that is widespread as a native in Europe. In the British Isles it is common on dry rather than damp open ground and is often found on cultivated land, on dunes and even in woodland. It is a hairy slender plant, rarely growing taller than 30m (12in). When the flowers are in bud the stems are coiled but they unfold as the flowers open.

This is a free-flowering annual that will do well in an open position or in light shade, as a clump or as an edging. Once a colony has been established it will self-seed. Staggered sowing, starting in autumn for flowering in early spring and continuing through till early summer for flowering later in the same season, will give you a long and satisfying display.

Wood Forget-me-not (*M. sylvatica*) is a perennial species but best grown as a biennial. In the wild it is found in damp woods but it is more common as a garden plant, tolerating light shade but flowering best if given an open position. It is larger in all its parts than the Field Forget-me-not and the flowers have an orange ring in the centre.

Anywhere that is damp or boggy will be suitable for the Water Forget-me-not. For maximum effect plant it at the water's margin, even with its feet covered by 75mm (3in) of water. It will flower the summer through, whether in sun or part shade.

# FIELD POPPY
## *Papaver rhoeas*

**Flowering season**
May to August

**Suitable growing conditions**
Well-drained ground in the border; most types of soil that are reasonably fertile; a sunny position.

**Growing guide**
Sow thinly in early autumn or early spring in carefully prepared permanent position; barely cover seed; thin out up to 30cm (1ft) apart. Can be added to grass and wild flower mixtures to give first year colour.

Although the Field or Common Poppy is still a common annual of disturbed land, on waste ground, on roadside verges and beside railway lines, the use of herbicides and efficient seed cleaning mean that it is very rare to see fields of corn stained red with its bright flowers. In this context it had a privileged status in the past, being inseparably associated with the earth renewing itself in its annual cycle of fecundity. There is a hint of pagan symbolism in the Flanders Poppy, whose crop seemed nurtured by the blood of slain warriors.

The Field Poppy is very widely distributed in the British Isles, Europe and eastwards, as well as North Africa. The seed can remain viable for many years, germinating in favourable conditions when ground is disturbed. It grows quickly into a slender, erect plant, up to 60cm (2ft) high, with branched hairy stems and pale green, deeply lobed or toothed leaves. The solitary buds hang down but the brilliant scarlet, four-petalled flowers face up. They are up to 75mm (3in) across and are blotched black at the base. The seed capsules are smooth, globular and flat-capped.

The Shirley Poppies, so popular as garden annuals, have been derived from this wild plant and generally revert to type in a few generations of self-breeding. The true species has its own distinct charm and makes an excellent subject in the border, when planted in a large patch giving the impression of dense redness once seen in cornfields and rarely conveyed by the scattered plants found growing on roadsides. Part of its beauty in the garden results from the simultaneous presence of buds, open flowers and seed-heads.

Provided they are treated appropriately, Poppies are excellent flowers for cutting. Pick only those that are ready to open or are partly unfolded. Dip the ends of the stems immediately in boiling water for about a minute and then leave the flowers overnight plunged to their necks in deep, warm water, preferably in a cool, dark room. The dried seed-heads are useful for winter decorations.

The Opium Poppy *(Papaver somniferum)* is a major source of useful but extremely harmful drugs. The Field Poppy, however, is not a herbal or culinary plant of great significance. All parts of the plant are said to be poisonous in some degree.

# FIELD SCABIOUS
## *Knautia arvensis*

**Flowering season**
June to September

**Suitable growing conditions**
Well-drained mini-grassland
or bare ground in a border;
reasonably fertile soil
ranging from slightly acid to
markedly alkaline; a position
in full sun.

**Growing guide**
Sow thinly in early spring or
early autumn in carefully
prepared permanent
position; cover seed; thin out
up to 60cm (2ft) apart.
Preferably, sow in seed bed;
transplant into growing bed;
move to final positions in
autumn. Plants can be
propagated by dividing
established clumps in March.

The Field Scabious is the most conspicuous of a group of plants belonging to the Teasel family that in the wild are attractive members of grassland communities. Their common name and the botanical name *Scabiosa* they once all shared refer to their former use in the treatment of scabies and other skin conditions that were common ailments when personal hygiene was little understood or appreciated. The modern botanical name acknowledges a seventeenth-century botanist, Dr Knaut.

The Field Scabious is found throughout Europe and is common in Britain, more so in the south than the north. It is typically found on dry grassland, particularly on chalky downland, but it is also found on roadsides and in hedgerows.

It is a tenacious wiry plant with a perennial rootstock from which grow two or three stems to a height of between 60 and 90cm (2 to 3ft). These stems are rather bare and only slightly branched. The dull green leaves at the base, which persist throughout the winter, are not much divided but those further up the stem are more slender and cut almost to the mid-rib. The flowerheads, which are carried on long stalks, consist of flat cushions, up to 40mm (2in) across, packed with many small bluish or lilac flowers. The outer flowers are larger than those in the centre and differences in the size of the petals are more exaggerated. A number of local names refer to the way the flower-heads resemble pin-cushions, the pins being the mature stamens. These pass their peak before the stigmas mature so that there is little chance of self-pollination.

In the garden Field Scabious is a first-rate ingredient of a grass and wild-flower mixture. If you are dividing your garden into different mowing regimes, this is one to include in the late-summer flowering mini-meadow. Although it does not attain the size of the Caucasian Scabious, which is such a popular flower for cutting, it can make an attractive border plant, growing more compactly than it does in grass.

Another closely related species worth including in a grass and wild flower mixture is the Small Scabious *(Scabiosa columbaria)*, a perennial most commonly found on chalky soils. It is smaller in all its parts than the Field Scabious, although if grown as a border plant it can reach 90cm (3ft). Both plants are excellent sources of nectar and are attractive to butterflies as well as to bees.

# FLAG IRIS
## *Iris pseudacorus*

**Flowering season**
May to July.

**Suitable growing conditions**
Water margins or moist ground in borders; fertile soil that can range from slightly acid to alkaline; a position in full sun or light shade.

**Growing guide**
Sow in early autumn or early spring in carefully prepared permanent position; cover seed; thin out to 30cm (1ft) apart. Artificial stratification is beneficial if sowing in spring (see page 106). Preferably, sow in pots; prick out singly into pots; plant in final positions in September.

This stately plant of the water's edge is said to be the origin of the Fleur de Lys, the heraldic emblem of the kings of France. It is strongly argued that Lys is a corruption of Louis after Louis VII, who adopted the emblem, which had already featured on the banner of the Frankish King Clovis, when he embarked as a Crusader for the Holy Land. Although the name Flag Iris seems an obvious reference to the fluttering segments of the flower, 'flag' in this case seems to be a word of obscure origin. We can be certain that another allusion in such local names as Sword Flower is to the blade-like shape of the leaves. The Flag Iris might be confused with the Sweet Sedge (*Acorus calamus*) when it is not in flower and for this reason the botanical specific name describes the Yellow or Flag Iris as the 'false acorus'.

This is a widely distributed plant, found almost everywhere throughout Europe growing by still and running water, even in ditches and low-lying moist ground. It is a perennial with sword-like bluish-green leaves growing from stout rhizomes to a height of 90cm (3ft). Stiff stems, which sometimes grow taller than the leaves, carry two or three bright yellow flowers with brown mottling on the falls. The flowers, which can be up to 10cm (4in) across, are followed by large green seed capsules. These split to release the yellowish-brown seeds.

The Yellow Iris is an almost indispensable component in any waterside planting. As a marginal it breaks the line between land and water and its severely erect habit makes a nice contrast to plants of rounded shape and a looser way of growing. It is seen to such good effect in and near water that it is often not appreciated how well it will do in the border. 'Although it be a watery plant of nature,' said Gerard, 'yet being planted in gardens it prospereth well.' A number of named forms, selected for flower colour or variegated foliage, are sometimes available from nurserymen but these have no more grace and elegance than the wild plant.

At one time Flag Iris was much used as a medicine – for coughs, toothache, weak eyes, as a cathartic and as a treatment for serpents' bites, to mention only some of its applications – and as a cosmetic. It is not likely to be eaten by man but even in the eighteenth century Linnaeus recognized that the plant was poisonous and potentially dangerous to cattle.

# FOXGLOVE
## *Digitalis purpurea*

**Flowering season**
June to September.

**Suitable growing conditions**
Reasonably moist or damp ground in the border or in wilder parts of the garden; acid soil that is moderately fertile or rich; in full sun or part shade.

**Growing guide**
Sow thinly in May/June in carefully prepared permanent position; barely cover seed; keep well watered; thin out up to 60cm (2ft) apart. Preferably sow in pots; transplant to growing bed as soon as possible; move to final position in mid autumn.

The most stately of woodland flowers, the Foxglove conveys in its Anglo-Saxon name something of its magical potency: the fairies are said to have given the fox the hanging bells to wear as magic slippers, ensuring a silent approach to victims in the poultry yard. Many local names allude to the thimble-like form of the flowers but the more sinister Dead-Men's-Fingers is apparently a reference to the poisonous nature of the plant.

Foxgloves are characteristic plants of glades and woodland fringes, particularly on acid soils. The plant is found throughout the British Isles and the western edge of continental Europe. Large stands are often found in areas that have recently been cleared or burnt off. This is a biennial plant which first forms a rosette of downy grey-green leaves and sends up in its second year a spike up to 150cm (5ft) tall bearing a one-sided tier of ten to forty hanging flowers. These are usually pink but sometimes white marked with purple spots in the tube and can be up to 5cm (2in) in length.

A number of cultivated forms have long been popular garden plants but the simple wild plant conveys better than almost any other native the essence of untamed natural beauty. It is an excellent plant for the back of the border, for growing along hedges or in dappled shade under trees. Although it will self-seed freely, it is not a difficult plant to control. The long stems make handsome cut flowers but in smaller arrangements it is possible to show the beauty of the individual bells.

The leaves, roots and seeds of Foxglove are poisonous and the plant has occasionally been responsible for the death of farm animals. It has even been suggested that Digitalis poisoning, resulting from the consumption of medical preparations, may have affected the artistic vision of Vincent van Gogh. Digitalin, one of the active principles, is cumulative in the body.

The value of Foxglove in the treatment of heart conditions has been known since the eighteenth century and preparations of the plant were sometimes prescribed for chest conditions. Before World War I it was widely grown on a commercial scale, particularly in Britain and Germany.

Foxgloves are important nectar plants for Bumble-bees, which work their way up the flower spikes from thimble to thimble, crawling right into each flower.

# GERMANDER SPEEDWELL
## *Veronica chamaedrys*

**Flowering season**
March to July.

**Suitable growing conditions**
Well-drained ground in wild parts of the garden; lightly acid to alkaline soils of moderate fertility; a position in part shade or full sun.

**Growing guide**
Sow thinly in early spring or early autumn in carefully prepared permanent position; lightly cover seed; thin out as required; spread can be over 60cm (2ft). Preferably, sow in seed bed; transplant into growing bed; move to final positon in autumn. Plants are easily propagated by division in March or April.

The Speedwells, which are members of the Foxglove family, form a large group that includes as well as a number of rather insignificant plants, several well-known weeds and numerous garden-worthy plants. The botanical name *Veronica*, which at one time also included the shrubby plants now classified under the name *Hebe*, is of uncertain origin, although some have been tempted to connect it to the saint whose handkerchief was found to bear the image of Christ's face after she had used it to wipe his brow on his way to the Cross.

The common name Speedwell may simply refer to the way the flowers of the Germander Speedwell are so lightly attached that almost any interference causes them to fall. On the other hand many of the Speedwells are plants of waysides; perhaps the name is a kind of parting salute. 'Germander' is a corruption of the Greek word preserved now in the specific name, which signifies that the plant resembles a small oak. It has to be admitted that the comparison is a forced one for the leaves are rather nettle-like.

Germander Speedwell, the prettiest of the native species, is a common plant in the British Isles and the rest of Europe, generally found growing among grass in woodland and copses as well as in more open positions. This creeping perennial has rather lax stems, along which run, on opposite sides, two lines of long white hairs. The flowering stems stand up to 40cm (16in) high and carry the white-eyed bright-blue flowers in great profusion. It was almost certainly of this plant that Tennyson was thinking when he wrote of 'the little Speedwell's darling blue'. At night and in bad weather the flowers close and the colour cannot be seen.

Germander Speedwell is too vigorous a plant to leave unchecked in borders but it is a lovely addition to the wild garden, where the brightness of its flowers lasts for several months. As it tolerates partial shade it is a good plant to grow in grass under trees and at the bottom of hedges. It can even grow with sufficient density to form a ground cover that will exclude most other plants.

Of the other Speedwells probably the most common is the annual Field Speedwell *(V. persica)*. This plant, an introducton of the early nineteenth century, is particularly common as a lawn weed. If you can tolerate intruders in your lawn you will have the pleasure of its white and blue flowers very early in spring, for it and the Daisy are two of the first flowers to bloom.

# GLOBEFLOWER
## *Trollius europaeus*

**Flowering season**
June to August.

**Suitable growing conditions**
Moist ground by water, in the wild parts of the garden or in borders; neutral to acid fertile soil; a sunny or lightly shaded position.

**Growing guide**
Sow thinly in early spring or early autumn in carefully prepared permanent positions; lightly cover seed; thin out up to 45cm (18in). Preferably, sow in seed bed; transplant into growing bed; move to final positions in autumn. Plants can be propagated by division of the fibrous roots in September or April.

The incurved sepals of the Globeflower have given it its common name and very likely its botanical name, too. It has been suggested that *Trollius* is a latinized form of a Swiss-German vernacular name that referred to the rolled up form of the flowers. In Scotland and the Borders it has been known by several variants of Locker Gowlan, meaning a closed-in yellow flower.

Although not often seen as a wild plant in the west of Europe it is quite common in the north and east. In the British Isles its centre of distribution is Scotland and northern England. It is a plant of the uplands, most frequently found in damp pastures of mountainous areas. Reginald Farrer, an influential writer on alpine plants in the early twentieth century, wrote of having seen alpine meadows in which 'whole acres [were] shining with the bland and moony citron of its unbroken mass of bloom' in alpine meadows. This is a sight difficult to imagine when all one has seen are isolated or scattered clumps of the plant.

The Globeflower is a vigorous perennial that makes a fine clump of deeply divided and toothed leaves. The lemon-yellow globular flowers, usually one to a stem, are carried well above the leaves on a stalk about 50cm (20in) high. The true petals are concealed by the sepals that curve in tightly, leaving only a small hole by which insects can enter to collect nectar and pollinate the flowers. Flowering is in summer, at higher altitudes generally later than in the lowlands.

The Globeflower has long been valued as a garden plant. This species is not now so often grown but many hybrids of which it and *Trollius asiaticus* are parents are widely available. These show variations in colour from pale lemon to deep orange and the flowers are large globes. The beauty of the simple wild plant matches theirs. It is one of the best natives to grow as a waterside plant but it will do well in a wild garden where the soil does not dry out or in borders with rich moist soil, doing as well in light shade as it does in the open.

The Globeflower was little commented on by the early botanical writers and herbalists so that there appear to be few uses to which it has been put other than as a garden ornamental. It must, in any event, be treated with some caution as it contains poisonous principles similar to those found in other members of the Buttercup family.

# GOAT'S-BEARD
## *Tragopogon pratensis*

**Flowering season**
June to July.

**Suitable growing conditions**
Well-drained mini-grassland; any reasonably fertile soil that is not excessively acid or alkaline; a position in full sun.

**Growing guide**
Sow thinly in May/June in carefully prepared permanent position; cover seed; thin out up to 21cm (9in) apart. Preferably, sow in a pot; prick out into pots as soon as possible in July; move to final position in mid-autumn.

The Composite family includes many yellow-flowered species that are common in grassland and of them the Goat's-beard is outstanding for the beauty of its relatively large flowerheads, which can be more than 5cm (2in) across. Both the common name and the generic name *Tragopogon* refer to the silky hairs of the seeds. It has sometimes been known as Jacob's Flower, for the husband of the Virgin Mary is normally depicted as bearded. This is one of the plants included in Linnaeus's floral clock, for, as Gerard writes, 'it shutteth itself at twelve of the clocke, and sheweth not his face open untill the next dayes Sun doth make it flower anew'. The prompt closing of the flowers has earned the plant another name, Jack-go-to-bed-at-noon.

Goat's-beard is a widely distributed European native that normally grows as a biennial but individual plants will sometimes persist for more than one flowering season. In the British Isles it is a common plant of meadows, roadsides and dunes in the south and east but less frequently seen in the north and west.

The bluish-green grass-like leaves that sheath the stems are a distinctive feature of this sturdy upright plant, which can grow to a height of 60cm (2ft). The flowering season starts in early summer. There is one yellow flower to a stem and each flower is surrounded by a ring of about eight greenish bracts which extend beyond the florets and almost completely enclose the flower when it folds. The feathery down of the clock or 'blowball', as Gerard calls it, is dispersed by the wind when the seeds are ripe, the interlaced filaments providing a parachute for the seed.

This is a really worthwhile species to include in a flowering mini-meadow, where it will be perfectly at home with such characteristic plants as Red Clover, Hoary Plantain, Rough Hawkbit, Oxeye Daisy and Yellow Rattle. Like many of the closely related composites it is a nectar plant that is attractive to bees and butterflies.

Goat's-beard has long lost favour as a medical herb, although Culpeper considered it a valuable restorative. It has had some reputation as a vegetable, the tap-root being prepared in the same manner as parsnips and the leaves used in salads. As a root vegetable it has been eclipsed by the closely related species Salsify *(T. porrifolius)*, sometimes called the Vegetable Oyster.

# GREATER KNAPWEED
## *Centaurea scabiosa*

**Flowering season**
June to September.

**Suitable growing conditions**
Well-drained mini-grassland or bare ground in borders; neutral to alkaline soil of reasonable fertility; a position in full sun.

**Growing guide**
Sow thinly in early spring or early autumn in carefully prepared permanent position; cover seed; thin out up to 45cm (18in) apart. Preferably, sow in seed bed; transplant into growing bed; move to final positions in autumn. Plants can be propagated by division between October and March.

The Knapweeds are among the most conspicuous herbaceous members of the composite family found in pasture land. They owe their common name to their knobby flowers but their generic name *Centaurea* alludes to a fable in which the Centaur Chiron healed a foot wound with a plant of this kind. It may be that Greater Knapweed was once used to treat skin conditions such as scabies, hence the specific name *scabiosa*.

Greater Knapweed is widely distributed as a native in Europe, most often found on dry grassland, roadsides and steep rough country, especially where the soil is chalky. In the British Isles it is common but much more so in the south and east than in the north and west.

This is a very tough hairy but spineless perennial growing from a stout and sometimes woody root-stock to a height of 90cm (3ft). The lower leaves are very large, sometimes more than 30cm (1ft) in length and all are deeply divided. The main stem is generally unbranched until above the middle. In mid-summer the tight knobs at the end of the stems open as purplish-red flowers up to 5cm (2in) across bearing a close resemblance to those of the Cornflower *(C. cyanus)*, a closely related

plant. The outer florets are larger and less tightly arranged than those in the centre. When the seed-heads mature they have a dense tuft of white hair at the top.

Greater Knapweed and Common Knapweed or Hardheads *(C. nigra)* are frequently and understandably confused. The latter is also an erect plant, although rarely taller than 60cm (2ft) and its leaves are less divided and notched than those of the Greater Knapweed. It is found on a broader range of soils.

Both of these Knapweeds should feature in a summer meadow and are striking plants to add to a border, where, free of competition, they make well-balanced sturdy growth and give a long flowering season. The unopened buds and flower are good material for cutting and the attractive seed-heads, when empty of seeds are worth drying and using for winter decoration.

Both species are a valuable source of nectar for bees and butterflies and on that account are worth including in any garden where wildlife is being encouraged. Dead-heading before the seeds disperse will prevent a build-up of unwanted plants but you will then miss out on the sight of seed-eating birds such as the Goldfinch plundering the heads.

# GREATER STITCHWORT
*Stellaria holostea*

**Flowering season**
April to June.

**Suitable growing conditions**
Reasonably moist ground in the border or wild parts of the garden; neutral or slightly acid soil that is reasonably fertile; a position in full sun or part shade.

**Growing guide**
Sow thinly in early spring or early autumn in carefully prepared permanent position; lightly cover seed; thin out as required; spread can be over 60cm (2ft) Preferably, sow in seed bed; transplant into growing bed; move to final positions in autumn.

The Stitchworts and their close relative chickweed *(S. media)* have been given their generic name *Stellaria* on account of the star-like shape of their flowers, the effect being heightened by the way the petals are deeply divided. Greater Stitchwort is a flopping species with stems that snap very readily. This was interpreted as a sign that the plant was effective in the treatment of fractures and it was mistakenly identified with a plant that in ancient medicine had the name *holosteon*, meaning 'whole bone'; hence the specific name. Local names such as Brandy Snap and Jack Snaps refer to the ready way the stems break but the name Stitchwort indicates that it was used, as Gerard says, 'against the paine in the side, stitches, and such-like'.

Greater Stitchwort is a perennial with a wide distribution in Europe. In the British Isles it is a common plant of hedgerows, woodland fringes and copses, generally showing a preference for heavy soils. The long, narrow and pointed leaves grow in opposite pairs from the brittle straggling stems that are square in section. Using other plants for support these gain a height of up to 60cm (2ft). The flowering season starts in mid-spring and the white flowers are pricked with ten prominent stamens.

The Lesser Stitchwort *(S. graminea)* is a very similar plant with narrower leaves and smaller flowers but, despite its name, it can grow rather taller, even reaching 90cm (3ft). It is generally found in more open positions and on lighter soils than the Greater Stitchwort.

Both of these plants are suitable for growing as clumps in the border or naturalizing in rough parts of the garden, Greater Stitchwort being particularly useful at the foot of hedges and in damp shaded ground under trees. Its profusion of white flowers in a sombre corner of the garden early in the season is very welcome. Lesser Stitchwort is a good plant to establish on grassy banks.

Whether you choose to have it in your garden or not Chickweed is almost certainly going to be there so perhaps you should aim to make the best of it. This must count as one of the most widely distributed plants in the world, seeding prolifically and flowering at any time of the year, even in the dead of winter. Birds love it and no doubt the fondness all fowl show for it is the origin of its common name. In the past it has been much used as a vegetable either uncooked as an addition to salads or simmered lightly in butter.

# GREAT MULLEIN
## *Verbascum thapsus*

**Flowering season**
June to August.

**Suitable growing conditions**
Well-drained ground in the border or wild parts of the garden; ordinary soil, even of low fertility, that is not excessively acidic or alkaline; an open sunny position.

**Growing guide**
Sow thinly in May/June in carefully prepared permanent position; barely cover seed; keep well watered; thin out up to 60cm (2ft) apart. Preferably sow in seed bed; transplant to growing bed in July; move to final positon in mid autumn.

M any of the local names by which this statuesque plant is known allude to the felted softness of the foliage and stem. Even the botanical name *Verbascum* may be derived from the Latin *barba* (a beard), a reference to the plant's hairiness. Less obvious is the name Candlewick Plant. It is said that the dry down of the foliage and stems was used for lamp wicks and that the stalks, dipped in tallow, served as candles. Wherever it is seen, the taller tapering spikes of the Great Mullein or Aaron's Rod, as it is also known, resemble nothing so much as impressive church candles.

This biennial is a very widely distributed plant, common in continental Europe and the British Isles, except for the north west. It is a plant of sunny dry habitats, often flourishing in inhospitable rough places.

In the first year it builds up a rosette of large thick silvery leaves with hairs on both surfaces. From this rosette, in the second year, grows a sturdy solitary stem that can be up to 2m (7ft) tall. The flower spike proper is about 30cm (12in) long and is densely packed with buds that appear to open in a random way and not in progression from the bottom buds up. The flowers are yellow and up to 3cm (1in) across and appear over a long season in summer. Each of the hard seed capsules contains numerous seeds.

Mulleins were early adopted as cottage garden flowers, their tall spires if anything more stately than those of the Hollyhock. The species and forms most widely cultivated now are perennial but the biennial Great Mullein is in no sense an inferior plant standing at the back of a sunny border or allowed to self-seed in a wilder part of the garden. Because it is a true biennial, in order to get an annual display from self-seeding plants it is necessary to plant two years in succession.

The flowers of the Great Mullein attract many insects, including the Bumble-bee and the Honey Bee. The Mullein Moth caterpillar, which feeds on the foliage, is particularly handsome but has a gross appetite.

The leaves and flowers of the Great Mullein have been used in various herbal and medical preparations particularly in the treatment of chest complaints and haemorrhoids. The dried leaves were used to make herbal tobacco which when smoked, it is claimed, gave relief from asthma and even the dry cough of consumption.

# HAREBELL
*Campanula rotundifolia*

**Flowering season**
July to September.

**Suitable growing conditions**
Well-drained mini-grassland or bare ground in borders; acid or alkaline soil of low fertility; a position in full sun or light shade.

**Growing guide**
Sow thinly in early autumn or early spring in carefully prepared permanent position; barely cover seed. Artificial stratification is beneficial if sowing in spring (see page 106). Thin out as required; spread can be over 45cm (18in). Preferably sow in pots, prick out into a tray; move to final positons in autumn. Plants can be propagated by division in October or by basal shoot cuttings.

S hakespeare's 'azur'd harebell' is almost certainly not *Campanula rotundifolia* but the Bluebell or Wild Hyacinth *(Hyacinthoides non-scriptus)*. In Scotland and northern England the 'round-leaved bellflower', to translate this delightful Campanula's name, is known as the Bluebell.

Botanical names present their own problems. The stem leaves of Harebell in flower are spindly. When Linnaeus, who had observed the plant growing in the grounds of the University of Uppsala, gave it its name he was thinking of the rounded basal leaves that are carried through the winter.

Given that the Harebell is a sinister fairy plant – local names include Witch Bell and Witches' Thimble, and the hare is an animal associated with witches – we should not be surprised that there is a certain contrariness in its naming.

Throughout the temperate regions of the northern hemisphere the Harebell is a fairly common plant of dry grassy places, often appearing to flourish best on poor soils. It is a perennial species of Bellflower, producing the flowering stems from the basal rosette of rounded leaves in the second half of summer. The stems range from 20 to 40cm (8 to 16in) in height and carry one or several hanging flowers. These are of an exquisitely refined shape, about 20mm (¾in) long and pale blue in colour, although darker forms are sometimes found in the wild.

As well as being a very beautiful plant, the Harebell can be successfully grown in a variety of ways. The graceful nodding flowers are a fine embellishment to a flowering meadow. It is an easy plant to establish in a wall, making a pretty association with Herb Robert *(Geranium robertianum)* and Ivy-leaved Toadflax *(Cymbalaria muralis)*. In borders, where it has less competition, it has a slightly different habit, growing in a rather tight clump and often forming a loose pyramid.

The Campanulas include a number of plants of outstanding garden merit. Another European native which is an attractive perennial for the border or for wilder parts of the garden is the Clustered Bellflower *(C. glomerata)* a plant that is also reasonably common on chalky grassland. It is rather variable in habit, sometimes growing to 45cm (18in) but generally less. The purplish-blue flowers are bell-shaped but erect and carried in distinct clusters. The wild plant is invasive and therefore is best reserved for rougher parts of the garden.

# HEART'S-EASE
## *Viola tricolor*

**Flowering season**
April to September.

**Suitable growing conditions**
Well-drained bare ground or in thin grass; neutral to acid soil that is reasonably fertile; an open sunny position or partial shade.

**Growing guide**
Sow thinly in early autumn or early spring in carefully prepared permanent position; lightly cover seed; thin out up to 15-30cm (6-12in) apart. In order to produce large flowering plants, sow in seed bed in early autumn; move to final positions in early spring. Can be added to grass and wild flower mixtures to give first year colour.

In less than two hundred years of selective breeding the elegant little Heart's-ease has been transformed into the bold round-faced modern garden Pansy. When seen beside this the Wild Pansy may seem an inconspicuous plant but it is still one of the best-loved wild flowers.

Its Anglo-Saxon name was Bonewort, but by the early sixteenth century the two common names by which it is best known were current. Pansy, from the French *pensée* (a thought) and Heart's-ease, a name originally shared with the Wallflower, are mildly fanciful in comparison with local names such as Kiss-at-the-garden-gate, Love-in-idleness, Meet-her-in-the-entry-kiss-her-in-the-buttery and Three-faces-under-a-hood. Many of these names suggest playful rustic gallantry; in a more solemn tone, Herb Trinity presents the three-coloured flower as emblematic of Christian doctrine.

The Wild Pansy is still a common plant in Britain (particularly northern Britain) and Europe and its range extends eastwards to the Himalayas. It is most frequently seen as a weed of cultivated ground, in fields and gardens, but it is also to be found on waste ground and grassy banks. In the right conditions it will grow as a short-lived perennial but it seeds with the prodigality of an annual.

The plant has deep green narrow leaves, lobed and deeply cut at the base, and is a somewhat straggly and angular grower, rarely reaching a height of more than 25cm (10in). The flowers, which start to appear in mid-spring and continue well into autumn, are about 25mm (1in) across and the colouring is a combination of white and shades of purple and yellow. The bottom petal forms a spur behind.

When grown in the garden the Wild Pansy is happiest if allowed to establish self-seeding colonies in borders, rockeries or in thin grass. Regular picking prevents seed-heads from developing and therefore prolongs the flowering season.

According to the old herbals, Heart's-ease was used in the treatment of skin conditions and also for diseases of the heart; perhaps its name owes more to a belief in its effectiveness for such physical conditions than to any supposed value as a love potion. Nonetheless it has been given a certain notoriety by the spell Oberon cast on Titania in Shakespeare's *A Midsummer Night's Dream*. Oberon calls for flowers of Love-in-idleness:

'The juice of it, on sleeping eyelids laid,
Will make or man or woman madly dote
Upon the next live creature that it sees.'

# HEATHER

## *Calluna vulgaris*

**Flowering season**
July to September.

**Suitable growing conditions**
Free-draining ground in rock gardens and raised beds or rougher open ground; neutral to acid soil of low fertility; a position in full sun.

**Growing guide**
In spring, sow the very small seed on the surface of a sandy peat seed compost in a tray; do not cover seed; firm gently; cover tray with glass and keep shaded until germination occurs. Prick out into small pots as soon as possible; grow on in shade until they become established; pinch out the growing points to induce bushy growth; re-pot in the following spring or plant out in permanent position 30cm (1ft) apart.

The English name Ling seems to be losing out in competition with Heather, the Scottish name of a plant that is common on poor soils throughout Europe, including the British Isles, and as an introduced species in America. Perhaps association with the word 'heath' has reinforced the Scottish name, although a real connection between the two words does not appear to exist. The botanical name *Calluna* goes back to a Greek word meaning 'to cleanse', a reference to the way the plant has been used to make brooms.

This small perennial sub-shrub is found throughout its range on sandy acid soils, frequently covering very large tracts as the dominant species, although Gorse, Pine and Birch, as well as some of the other Heathers (species of *Erica*), are often found growing with it. Heather is a sociable plant, thriving in colonies.

The much branched woody stems of this evergreen, which can vary in height and spread from 75mm to 90cm (3in to 3ft) are closely covered with scale-like leaves. The purple bell-shaped flowers, which are borne over a long season in the second half of summer, form one-sided spikes at the end of stems. It is not uncommon to find clumps with white flowers growing among purple-flowered colonies in the wild.

Although there is only one hardy species of *Calluna*, this has given rise to several hundred varieties that are popular garden plants. The varieties show considerable differences in flower and foliage colour so that a selection combined with species and varies of *Erica* will gradually knit together to form an interestingly patterned ground cover that effectively excludes weeds. For a rough piece of poor ground, even such a difficult area to plant as a windswept plot near the sea, the wild Heathers are unequalled. A judicious planting of Heather can also be effective in rock gardens and raised beds.

The poor, living on poor land, have had cause to be grateful for Heather. It has been used as fodder for sheep, as thatching, as fuel, as bedding material, for weaving rough baskets, to make an orange dye, and instead of hops in beer. Heather is a major source of nectar and the honey produced from it is distinctive and of good quality. On moorland it is an important source of food for Red Grouse. In the garden it can give good cover to small mammals and serve as a food plant for the caterpillars of several butterflies and moths, including those of the Silver-studded Blue and the Mottled Beauty.

# HEDGE WOUNDWORT
## *Stachys sylvatica*

**Flowering season**
May to August.

**Suitable growing conditions**
Reasonably moist ground in
the border or in wild parts of
the garden; fertile ground that
is not excessively acid or
alkaline; a position in full sun
or part shade.

**Growing guide**
Sow thinly in early spring or
early autumn in carefully
prepared permanent position;
lightly cover seed; thin out as
required; spread can be over
60cm (2ft). Preferably, sow in
seed bed; transplant into
growing bed; move to final
positions in autumn. Plants are
easily propagated by division
of the roots between October
and April.

The Mint family, a very numerous group of plants, is well represented in Europe by a number of attractive herbs that are found in hedgerows and woodland. Hedge Woundwort, like Betony *(Stachys officinalis)*, belongs to this group and must count as one of the most striking European members. To an earlier age Betony was the equivalent of a wonder drug; extravagant claims were made for the way it could cure all manner of diseases and conditions. Hedge Woundwort, its close relative, was also considered a valuable medicinal herb, particularly effective in staunching the flow of blood and in aiding rapid healing. Its common name is therefore easily understood.

In most parts of Europe this is a very common plant and almost everywhere in the British Isles it is a familiar species in woodland and hedgerows, particularly where these lie on fertile soil. Although it is often found at the sunlit edge of copses and hedgerows, it will tolerate dappled and even fairly dense shade.

Hedge Woundwort is a perennial with an erect habit, the hairy stems, which are square in section, sometimes attaining a height of 100cm (40in). The heart-shaped leaves, which are arranged in opposite pairs, are long stalked and coarsely toothed.

The dull red flowers, brightened by white markings, are carried on an elongated spike in an arrangement that is rather gappy at the bottom but much denser towards the tip. The flowering season lasts throughout the second half of summer.

For areas of semi-shade, either in a border or in wilder parts of the garden, Hedge Woundwort is a very useful species. For the best effect it should be planted in a dense clump and there its consistent flowering, with all plants beginning and ending very close together, will give a nice massed effect. A disadvantage not shared by some of its close relatives is that when bruised it gives off a rather unpleasant smell. Perhaps this lies behind the old belief that toads liked to shelter under it.

Marsh Woundwort *(S. palustris)* is another perennial worth finding a place for in the garden. This is another reasonably common species, although in the British Isles more frequently found in the south and west than in the north and east. It is a plant of ditches and marshy ground and is often found on soils that are markedly acid. In most respects it is very similar to Hedge Woundwort but the leaves are longer and narrower with short stalks and the flowers are pale mauve.

# HONEYSUCKLE
### *Lonicera periclymenum*

**Flowering season**
June to September.

**Suitable growing conditions**
Free-draining ground near an adequate support; almost any soil unless it is excessively acid; a position in full sun.

**Growing guide**
Sow in autumn in pots outdoors or, preferably, in a cold frame; cover seed; prick out into pots, three seedlings to a pot; transfer to larger pots; plunge in growing area; plant out in permanent position in autumn, incorporating well-rotted compost. Plants raised from seed take a few years to reach flowering size. Plants can also be propagated by hardwood cuttings, stem sections or layering.

There are many cultivated species of *Lonicera* but few can match the native Honeysuckle for sweetness of perfume. In the evening and after rain its scent is as powerful as that of almost any exotic. The specific name *periclymenum* and the other common English name, Woodbine, refer to the plant's twining habit. A sixteenth-century German naturalist, Adam Lonicer, is honoured by the generic name.

Honeysuckle has been introduced in many parts of the temperate world but it is a native of Europe, western Asia and North Africa. In the British Isles it is very common in hedgerows and woodland, generally scrambling up into trees and bushes but sometimes trailing nearer the ground.

The stems of this climbing deciduous shrub are reddish when young but they gradually become woody. The oval leaves are arranged in pairs and are dark green above and pale, almost bluish, on the underside. In mid-summer numerous fragrant pale yellow flowers, often flushed with purplish-red, are carried in terminal clusters. Each flower is about 5cm (2in) long in the shape of a lipped trumpet from which the stamens protrude. The flowers are followed by bright red berries, which have a reputation for being poisonous. However, there are few if any reported cases of human poisoning.

Honeysuckle is very attractive to a wide range of insects. Night-flying moths, in particular, come to feed on the nectar. The tongue of the Honey Bee is not long enough to reach to the bottom of the flower tube, but Bumblebees sometimes resort to piercing the base of the tube in order to plunder the honey. The caterpillars of one or two moths and butterflies, including those of the lovely White Admiral, will feed on the plant's leaves.

The garden merits of the Honeysuckle have long been recognized. In Elizabethan England, Honeysuckle was frequently used to enclose bowers. Given something to hold on to it can clamber up an ugly wall or fence and, with a trellis or similar support, it can be used to screen one part of the garden from another. In the wild garden Honeysuckle is best left to grow freely, supported either by a hedge or by a shrub. The Woodbine's clasp can be very close so that it will sometimes smother or distort the shape of its host. Therefore choose carefully where you plant.

# HORSESHOE VETCH
## *Hippocrepis comosa*

**Flowering season**
May to July.

**Suitable growing conditions**
Very free-draining mini-grassland; a strongly alkaline soil of low fertility; sunny position.

**Growing guide**
Scarify seeds before sowing. Sow thinly in early spring or early autumn in carefully prepared permanent position; lightly cover seed; thin out as required; spread can be over 60cm (2ft). Preferably, sow in seed bed; transplant into growing bed; move to final positions in autumn. Plants are easily propagated by division.

The small grassland members of the Pea family include a curious mixture of valuable and villainous plants. Both the Hairy Tare *(Vicia hirsuta)* and the Smooth Tare *(V. tetrasperma)* have in the past been serious weeds of agriculture, smothering corn and other crops. On the other hand, Common Vetch *(V. sativa)*, which probably comes from western Asia but is now thoroughly naturalized in the British Isles and other parts of northern Europe, is an early forage plant that farmers have long cultivated for their cattle.

The name 'vetch' comes from the Latin word *vicia* by which these plants were known to the Romans. The 'tare' was originally the seed of the offending weed but was later applied to the plant. The botanical and common names of the Horseshoe Vetch, which is closely related to species of *Vicia*, refer either to the shape of the seed-pod or to the arrangement of the flowerhead.

This perennial species is rather patchily distributed in Europe and in the British Isles is only common in southern England, where it favours dry grassland on chalk.

The trailing stems grow from a woody rootstock and carry leaves composed of about six paired leaflets with a single terminal leaflet. In the flowering season, which begins in mid-spring, the stems turn up to carry the flower-heads, which consist of five to eight yellow pea flowers arranged in a half circle. The flowers secrete nectar that attracts Bumble-bees and Honey Bees. A pumping mechanism, which is triggered by the weight of an alighting insect, ejects threads of pollen on to it. The pods consist of a string of seeds, each section roughly horseshoe shaped.

In its natural habitat the Horseshoe Vetch flowers with great profusion. That lovely blaze of gold can easily be part of a flowering mini-meadow or untamed lawn in a garden, where the plant is not difficult to establish and maintain provided that the competition is not too vigorous. Many of the Vetches have attractive flowers and leaves and as well as being a source of nectar some are food plants for the caterpillars of moths and butterflies. Those of the lovely Adonis Blue and those of the Dingy Skipper are found on Horseshoe Vetch.

Kidney Vetch *(Anthyllis vulneraria)*, another small pea flower of dry grassland, is much more widely distributed than Horseshoe Vetch.

# JACOB'S-LADDER
### *Polemonium caeruleum*

**Flowering season**
May to July.

**Suitable growing conditions**
Moist ground in borders or wild parts of the garden; fertile soil that is neutral or alkaline; a position in full sun or light shade.

**Growing guide**
Sow thinly in early spring

or early autumn in carefully prepared permanent position; lightly cover seed; thin out up to 45cm (18in) apart. Preferably, sow in seed bed; transplant into growing bed; move to final positions in autumn. Plants can be propagated by division between autumn and March.

All the evidence suggests that in the British Isles Jacob's-ladder has never been more than a rare and localized species. Even elsewhere in Europe its distribution is very uneven and perhaps has more to do with escapes from cultivation than the remnants of wild populations. The regular paired arrangement of the leaves have earned it its common name. The plant was once more commonly known as Greek Valerian but its only connection with true Valerian *(Valeriana officinalis)* is that the leaves of both plants have a similar shape.

In the wild it is a plant of fertile alkaline soils, most often found in open or lightly shaded ground near streams. The flowering stem grows from a basal clump of finely divided leaves to a height of about 60cm (2ft). The pale blue flowers, which are white in bud and carried in dense clusters at the end of stems, are bell shaped and as much as 25mm (1in) across. The anthers are a conspicuous feature, being bright yellow.

Jacob's-ladder has been a popular garden plant for several centuries; we know, for instance, from Culpeper that it was widely cultivated in the first half of the seventeenth century. Some say that its history as a garden plant goes back to Roman times. It has not lost its appeal. As great a gardener as Margery Fish, who packed into the gardens of East Lambrook Manor a connoisseur's collection of cultivated plants, admitted that she would not want to be without this species. 'Its blue spires are seconded to the wilderness, with Pulmonarias, Bugles and some of the more rampant Geraniums'. Such a mixture would be worth repeating if you were to confine the use of Jacob's-ladder to the rougher parts of the garden. However, very few gardeners have Margery Fish's wealth of plants competing for limited space and most would be happy to enjoy it as a showy border plant. For a good display it should be grown on rich soil.

The Pulmonarias mentioned by Margery Fish could include the most common, Lungwort or Jerusalem Cowslip *(Pulmonaria officinalis)*. This is almost certainly an introduced species in Britain, having escaped from gardens, where it was grown principally as a medial herb, being valued in the treatment of all lung complaints. It has large spotted leaves and pink flowers that appear very early in the year when the handsome Stinking Hellebore *(Helleborus foetidus)*, a wild plant of alkaline soils, shows its strange green and maroon cups.

# LADY'S BEDSTRAW

*Galium verum*

**Flowering season**
June to August.

**Suitable growing conditions**
Well-drained mini-grassland or bare ground in borders; acid or alkaline soil, even of low fertility; a position in full sun.

**Growing guide**
Sow thinly in early spring or early autumn in carefully prepared permanent position; lightly cover seed; thin out as required; spread can be over 60cm (2ft). Preferably, sow in seed bed; transplant into growing bed; move to final positons in autumn. Plants are easily propagated by division between October and March.

According to a legend that was widespread in medieval Europe, Lady's Bedstraw, sometimes referred to more explicitly as Our Lady's Bedstraw, and Bracken formed the rough bedding in the stable where the Virgin Mary bore the infant Jesus. Because of its yielding softness and fragrance it has certainly been much used since to stuff mattresses or simply as an elastic layer under a sheet.

The botanical name *Galium* (derived from a Greek word meaning milk) and such English local names as Cheese Rennet refer to the herb's properties as a curdling agent. 'The people in Cheshire,' wrote Gerard, 'especially about Namptwich where the best cheese is made, do use it in their rennet, esteeming greatly of that cheese above other made without it.' The greenish-yellow of the flowers helped to give cheese its colour.

This native perennial of Europe and western Asia, which is also a common introduced weed in eastern states of America, is found throughout the British Isles, favouring dry grassland, particularly on chalk or sand dunes. It sometimes occurs as a weed in lawns. A creeping root-stock sends up a number of slender stems that are square in section; they tend to sprawl but can be erect to a height of 100cm (40in). The spindly dark green leaves are arranged in whorls of eight or twelve. The dense flower clusters are bright yellow, giving off a fragrance of honeyed sweetness when fresh but smelling of hay when dry.

Lady's Bedstraw is probably not a major source of nectar but it is a food plant of the caterpillars of several Hawkmoths. The Bedstraw Hawkmoth is only a visitor to Britain but its caterpillars have occasionally been found in this country.

Provided that lawns are not cut closer than 50 to 75mm (2 to 3in), Lady's Bedstraw can be encouraged as one of the constituents. However, it may be easier to manage it as part of a flowering mini-meadow that is not cut in the second half of summer. As a border plant it gives a long flowering season with taller, denser heads than it produces when grown in grass. It is a good plant for cutting, the flowers being long-lasting in water, and the dried seed-heads make an attractive addition to winter arrangements.

The old authorities mention a decoction of Lady's Bedstraw as an effective foot bath. As a medicine this herb has been used to treat gout and epilepsy and also as a styptic: 'the herb or flower bruised and put into the nostrils, stayeth their bleeding', says Culpeper.

# LADY'S-SMOCK
## *Cardamine pratensis*

**Flowering season**
April to July.

**Suitable growing conditions**
Damp wild parts of the garden or in moisture-retentive borders; fertile soil that is neutral or slightly alkaline; a position in full sun.

**Growing guide**
Sow thinly in early spring or early autumn in carefully prepared permanent position; lightly cover seed; thin out up to 30cm (1ft) apart. Preferably sow in a pot; prick out into a tray and keep moist; move to final positons in autumn. Plants are easily propagated by division in October and by leaf cuttings.

Cuckooflower is an equally common name for this pretty plant of damp meadows. Cuckoo time is spring time and that is when Lady's-smock starts to bloom, although not usually 'silver-white' as the spring song in *Love's Labour's Lost* would lead us to expect.

The botanical name *Cardamine* suggests that it was once considered beneficial to the heart but the herbalists seem to have neglected this plant, perhaps because it was thought unlucky to pick it. According to a reputation widespread in Europe, it is associated with thunder and lightning.

Lady's-smock, a member of the Crucifer family (which includes Cabbage and Mustard), is a perennial that is widely distributed in temperate areas of the northern hemisphere. In the British Isles it is common in moist pasture and as a marginal plant of still and running water.

Erect slender stems grow from a basal rosette to a height of from 30 to 60cm (1 to 2ft). The leaves are divided but those at the base are much broader than those growing from the stems. The lilac flowers, which are about 12mm (½in) across, are carried in loose heads. Seed sets freely, the pod opening explosively and ejecting the seed, and the plants also increase vegetatively by the formation of plantlets between the basal leaves.

If you have water in the garden, you will find this plant very easy to establish on the margins. There it will combine well with other moisture lovers, such as the Marsh-marigold *(Caltha palustris)*. It will also flourish in a damp mini-meadow of the kind that suits the Snake's-head *(Fritillaria meleagris)* and, more surprisingly, does well as a border plant in moisture-retentive soil. To get the full benefit of it in a border it needs to be planted in a good-sized clump.

Such an early, free-flowering plant is very attractive to a wide range of insects, including butterflies and bees. The Orange Tip is one butterfly that is particularly associated with it, the adults taking nectar and the caterpillars feeding on the leaves.

The leaves are also suitable for human consumption; they are bitter but a few young shoots in soup or a salad will add a distinctive flavour. The name Bittercress, by which it is sometimes known, refers to its use as a salad vegetable. Watercress *(Nasturtium officinale)* another Crucifer of damp places, is better known as an edible plant. The cultivated plant is the same as the plant found in the wild.

# LESSER BULRUSH
## *Typha angustifolia*

**Flowering season**
June to July.

**Suitable growing conditions**
Wet ground; the roots can be covered by up to 22cm (9in) of water; moderately acid to alkaline soils of reasonable fertility; a position in full sun.

**Growing guide**
Sow the minute seed in early spring or autumn in pots; barely cover seed; prick out into pots; keep moist; plunge in moist area of growing bed for one or two growing seasons before planting out in permanent position 15-30cm (6-12in) apart. Plants can easily be propagated by dividing the rhizomes in April or May.

The plants of the water's margin are a particularly interesting and attractive group, tolerating, or enjoying, wet feet but often able to get along quite happily provided that the soil remains moist. Several are grouped here with the Lesser Bulrush.

The Bulrushes are often known as Reedmaces. The best known of these hardy herbaceous perennials is the Bulrush or Great Reedmace *(T. latifolia)* which is widely distributed in Europe and common in the British Isles except in the far north. It is found at the edges of still and slow-moving water, sometimes in water as much as 120cm (4ft) deep. This is a majestic plant that can grow to a height of 240cm (8ft) but unless you have a very large pond or lake it is almost certainly not suitable for your garden. It is a very vigorous spreading plant that will quickly take over a small stretch of water; once established it is difficult to eliminate.

Its close relative, the Lesser Bulrush or Lesser Reedmace, is not such a common plant, in Britain more frequently seen in the south and east than in the north and west. It is generally less than 180cm

(6ft) tall and it is not quite as aggressive as its relative.

Both of these species have magnificent flowering heads that are beautiful on the plant and attractive as indoor decorations; for this purpose cut them when they are young.

The Flowering-rush *(Butomus umbellatus)* is a plant of the water margin that is easier to manage at the edge of a garden pond. This is another species with a scattered distribution in the wild and more common in the south of the British Isles than the north and west. Despite its grass-like leaves and fondness for water, this perennial is not a true rush. In mid-summer the flowering stems, which can sometimes grow to a height of 150cm (5ft), carry numerous pink flowers, which have their parts arranged in threes.

The Bog Asphodel or Lancashire Asphodel *(Narthecium ossifragum)*, in the wild a plant of marshy places on moorland and mountains where the soil is acid, is common in the British Isles in the north and west. In mid-summer, stems about 30cm (1ft) high carry heads of yellow flowers, which have curiously furred stamens.

# LESSER CELANDINE
*Ranunculus ficaria*

**Flowering season**
March to May.

**Suitable growing conditions**
Moist but not waterlogged ground under trees, in hedgerows and in banks by water; reasonably fertile soil that is not excessively acid or alkaline; a position in partial or full shade.

**Growing guide**
Sow thinly in early spring or early autumn in permanent position; lightly cover seed; thin out up to 15cm (6in) apart. Preferably sow in a pot; prick out into a tray and keep semi-shaded; move to final positions in autumn. Can be propagated by separation of the tuber clusters in the autumn.

Although its most widely used name suggests a family connection with the Greater Celandine *(Chelidonium majus)*, these two plants have little in common other than a similarity of flower colour. The Lesser Celandine's 'glittering countenance', to use Wordsworth's phrase, is one of the delights of spring, when a profusion of burnished yellow flowers spangles damp woodland.

Figwort, another common name of this perennial herb, like the specific name, *ficaria*, alludes to the shape of the underground tubers. Pilewort, yet another common name, is suggested by the similarity of the swollen roots to haemorrhoids, a fact seized on by the old herbalists.

The Lesser Celandine is widely distributed and common in Europe, including the British Isles, and western Asia. Throughout its range it is most frequently found in woods, where it can form dense carpets, even in fairly dense shade. It is, however, also found in more open positions, in hedgerows, damp meadows and by water.

The long-stalked leaves, dark green, heart-shaped and shining, appear in early spring followed within a matter of days by the flowers. These are borne on stems about 20cm (8in) long and consist of eight or more golden yellow petals with a centre of short yellow stamens. The flowers, which are up to 75mm (3in) across, only open fully in sunlight and when closed are greenish and therefore inconspicuous. As they age they become almost white.

Perhaps because in cold climates insect fertilization in early spring is unreliable, the Lesser Celandine can also reproduce by means of small bulblets that form at the junction of the leaves and main stem. When the leaves die down, as they do in early summer, these grain-like tubers fall to the ground and, in favourable conditions, develop into new plants.

The Lesser Celandine is a vigorous spreading plant so that some thought should be given to where it is planted in the garden. It is seen at its best forming large patches naturalized under trees, where its dazzling early flowering makes it so appealing. In such a setting it can be combined with other early woodland plants, such as the Violets and the Wood Anemone, to be followed later by Bluebells.

As with other members of the Buttercup family, the plant is poisonous and has occasionally been responsible for losses of sheep and cattle. The juices can cause blistering and allergic reactions.

# MARSH-MARIGOLD
## *Caltha palustris*

**Flowering season**
March to July.

**Suitable growing conditions**
Boggy ground at the water's edge or somewhat drier ground in shade; reasonably fertile soil that is not excessively acid or alkaline; a position in full sun or shade.

**Growing guide**
Sow thinly in early spring or early autumn in carefully prepared permanent position; lightly cover seed; thin out up to 30cm (1ft) apart. Preferably, sow in a pot; prick out into a tray and keep moist and shaded; move to final positions in autumn. Plants are easily propagated by division of the roots in May or early June immediately after flowering.

The most handsome of the native Buttercups is the Marsh-marigold, a plant with an exceptionally wide distribution in the northern hemisphere. This cheering plant, which is sometimes in flower as early as February, has many local names and a very familiar common name, Kingcup. The name Marigold is puzzling, because the plant is not related to any of the garden plants that go by that name. In the British Isles, as elsewhere in northern Europe, it is a common perennial in marshy ground, ditches and even in damp woodland, for it thrives in shady conditions.

The kidney-shaped leaves are in themselves an attractive feature. Gerard describes the 'great broad leaves' as 'somewhat round, smooth, of a gallant greene colour, slightly indented or purlde about the edges'. They set off to perfection the 'goodly yellow flowers, glittering like gold'. The plant is rather variable in size but is generally shorter than 60cm (2ft).

Gardeners have long been attracted to the Marsh-marigold, appreciating its uncomplicated beauty, very often growing the undeveloped form as it is found in the wild. Nurserymen also offer double and white varieties. It is a more versatile plant that it might at first appear. Planted at the water's edge so that its beauty is doubled by reflection it is superb. In open positions it should be in ground that will never dry out but, planted in shade, it will tolerate slightly drier conditions.

It is said that the flowerbuds of this plant have been pickled and used as a substitute for capers. However, like all members of the buttercup family, it contains poisonous principles and therefore should be treated with the greatest caution. Marsh-marigold has very little reputation as a medical herb but in the past people believed that it was powerful in warding off evil spirits.

Three other plants with yellow flowers could be added to a waterside planting. Yellow Loosestrife *(Lysimachia vulgaris)*, which does not belong to the same genus as another good waterside plant, Purple-loosestrife *(Lythrum salicaria)*, is a native perennial found beside still and running water. It is a downy plant with flowering stems growing to about 90cm (3ft), which carry a mass of yellow five-petalled flowers in mid-summer. A related species, Creeping-Jenny *(Lysimachia nummularia)*, is a plant that gets about at a lower level, although its stems can be up to 60cm (2ft) long. It is an evergreen perennial that flowers in the second half of summer. Gardeners have taken to this plant because it thrives not only in boggy conditions but also in much drier borders.

# MEADOW BUTTERCUP
*Ranunculus acris*

**Flowering season**
April to May.

**Suitable growing conditions**
Damp or reasonably moist mini-grassland; acid or alkaline soils that are reasonably fertile; a position in full sun.

**Growing guide**
Sow thinly in early spring or early autumn in carefully prepared permanent positon; lightly cover seed; thin out up to 45cm (18in) apart. Preferably, sow in seed bed; transplant into growing bed; move to final positions in autumn. Plants are easily propagated by division in October or March.

The rich yellow colour of their flowers has given the Buttercups their common name, but only over the last two centuries has it gained its present dominance. It appears to be a combination of the earlier names Butterflower and Gold-cups or King-cups. These plants are common, however, and the wealth of local names, many alluding to a resemblance between the leaves and the shape of a crow's foot, testifies to this. According to the eighteenth-century gardening authority Philip Miller, the name Buttercup may have gained the ascendancy 'under the notion that the yellow colour of butter is owing to these plants'.

Meadow Buttercup, a perennial, is a typical flower of damp meadows throughout most of Europe and eastward into Asia. In Britain it is common everywhere, though less so on acid soils.

The plant is rather hairy with erect and creeping stems, the latter not rooting as those of Creeping Buttercup *(R. repens)* do. The numerous basal leaves are deeply divided into as many as seven lobes, and each lobe is itself often deeply cut. This is the tallest of the Buttercups, producing stems that can reach to a height of 90cm (3ft), although in normal conditions they are more likely to be a little more than half this height. The burnished yellow flowers (occasionally paler or white) are carried in small clusters, each flower about 25mm (1in) across. The main flowering season is generally over by June but in some years Meadow Buttercups continue to flower well into autumn.

Many gardeners are hostile to the Buttercups, rigorously eliminating them from lawns. But if you want to create a flowering mini-meadow and your ground is reasonably moist, the Meadow Buttercup should be a major ingredient of your grass and wild flower mixture. It is one of the early-flowering constituents that makes a good companion for Oxeye Daisies *(Leucanthemum vulgare)*.

The Creeping Buttercup is an attractive plant of heavy moist soils but such a vigorous spreader that it may be wiser to admire it in the wild rather than to introduce it into the garden. Its runners take root very freely so that a single plant can quickly become a large patch.

All the Buttercups are poisonous. What is surprising is that, given how common these plants are, the instances of cattle poisoning are very few and far between.

# MEADOW CLARY
## *Salvia pratensis*

**Flowering season**
June to July.

**Suitable growing conditions**
Well-drained ground in a border; neutral to alkaline soil of reasonable fertility; a position in full sun.

**Growing guide**
Sow thinly in early spring or early autumn in carefully prepared permanent positon; lightly cover seed; thin out up to 45cm (18in) apart. Preferably, sow in a seed bed; transplant into a growing bed; move to final position in autumn. Plants can be propagated by division from October to March.

Rather than the origin of the common name, 'clear-eye' is a connection made by the old apothecaries. 'Wild Clary', as Gerard wrote, 'is called after the Latine name *Oculis Christi*, of his effect in helping the diseases of the eies'. The Wild Clary of which Gerard wrote *(S. verbenaca)* has seeds that swell and become mucilaginous when soaked in water. When introduced into the eye they would pick up motes and grit.

The true origin of the name is the Latin word *sclarea*, which is preserved in the specific name of the Garden Clary or Clary Sage *(S. sclarea)*, a biennial species that is a common native of southern Europe. It is sometimes known as the Muscatel Sage because its slightly aromatic leaves were once used to prepare an adulterant that, it is claimed, gave to wine a muscatel-like flavour.

Meadow Clary is a perennial and in Britain a very rare plant that is found in only a few locations in the south and east, always on chalky grassland.

This is a sturdy species, growing to a height of 80cm (30in). There is a good clump of leaves at the base of the plant but there are relatively few carried on the stems. The few there are have bluntly toothed margins, are wrinkled and somewhat coarse. When crushed they are slightly aromatic. In summer there is a striking display of large violet-blue flowers that are borne in long spikes. The flowers themselves are arranged in whorls of four and can be up to 25mm (1in) long. The upper lip, which is noticeable compressed, arches tensely and the stigma and anthers protrude.

Meadow Clary's reputation as a good hardy perennial for the garden is long standing and a number of cultivated forms are available. Most have deeper colouring than the wild form and some have white or pink flowers. For maximum effect plant this handsome species as a clump in a free-draining sunny border.

Another member of the Mint family that will do well in a similar position is White Horehound *(Marrubium vulgare)*, a hardy perennial growing to a height of 50cm (20in). The whole plant is downy, even the crowded clusters of whitish flowers having a woolly appearance, and the leaves have a distinctly musky smell.

Formerly it was grown in almost every cottage garden, for it has long been a standard remedy for colds and chest complaints. As Gerard says, 'Syrup made of the greene fresh leaves and sugar is a most singular remedie against the cough and wheezing of the lungs'.

# MEADOW CRANE'S-BILL
*Geranium pratense*

**Flowering season**
May to September.

**Suitable growing conditions**
Well-drained ground in borders or wilder areas of the garden; neutral to alkaline soil of reasonable or high fertility; a position in full sun.

**Growing guide**
Scarify seed before sowing (see page 106). Sow thinly in early spring or early autumn in carefully prepared permanent position; lightly cover seed; thin out up to 60cm (2ft) apart. Preferably, sow in a pot; prick out into a tray; move to final positions in autumn. Plants are easily propagated by division.

The Crane's-bills, which include a number of hardy perennials that are very popular with gardeners, owe their common name and their botanical generic name to a resemblance between the shape of their seed-heads and that of the head and beak of a crane. This slightly fanciful allusion does not apply to the colourful half-hardy bedding 'Geraniums' that make such useful plants for growing in containers; they are more accurately known as Pelargoniums.

The Meadow Crane's-bill is a plant of considerable distinction, as lovely for its foliage as it is for its flowers. As well as being a native of the British Isles it is found widely distributed in northern Europe and eastwards into Asia. In the wild it is most often seen growing in limestone areas, generally in an open position where the ground is reasonably dry.

The deeply divided leaves, with five to seven distinct lobes, are carried on long stalks, forming an attractive clump about 60cm (2ft) high and about the same across. In the autumn the foliage takes on lovely russet colouring so that even at the end of the flowering season this plant still earns its keep in the garden.

The violet-blue flowers, which have earned the plant the local name Blue Basins, appear over a long period in the summer. They are carried above the foliage in small clusters, each bloom about 40mm (1½in) across. It is only when looked at closely that their dark crimson veining is obvious.

Gardeners have generally preferred to grow selected forms of the Meadow Crane's-bill, partly because some have particularly subtle flower colour, partly because some of them are double and therefore do not seed with the sometimes overwhelming prodigality of the type.

The species as found in the wild needs no apology but its capacity to increase must be taken into account when a place is being found for it in the garden. Provided its expansionist tendencies do not present a problem, it makes a lovely plant in the border, benefitting from good soil to make a more compact bush that flowers more uniformly and profusely than is generally found in the wild.

It will also do well sown with grasses and other plants as part of a summer-flowering mixture. Where you want to exclude other plants it can be grown fairly successfully as ground cover.

The Meadow Crane's-bill has been curiously neglected by the herbalists but bee-keepers have long known that the flowers are an important source of nectar and pollen.

# MEADOWSWEET
## *Filipendula ulmaria*

**Flowering season**
June to August.

**Suitable growing conditions**
Moist ground in borders or in wild parts of the garden beside water; rich soil that is slightly acid to alkaline; a position in full sun or part shade.

**Growing guide**
Sow thinly in early spring or early autumn in permanent position; lightly cover seed; thin out up to 45cm (18in) apart. Preferably, sow in seed bed; transplant into growing bed and keep moist; move to final positions in autumn. Plants can be propagated by division.

A fragrant flower so characteristic of damp meadows must, one might reasonably expect, owe its common name to a neat combination that describes it and indicates its habitat. It is sometimes called Queen of the Meadow, but earlier names, such as Meadsweet and Meadwort, indicate its use as a flavouring of mead.

This European and Asian perennial, which is now naturalized in North America, is a common plant throughout its range, particularly on rich soils at the edge of still or flowing water.

Meadowsweet has a stout root-stock, which is itself slightly aromatic, from which grow reddish stems to a height of about 90cm (3ft). The dark green leaves, which are silvery on the underside, bear a slight resemblance to those of the Elm, hence the specific name *ulmaria*. Flowering starts about mid-summer, the small creamy five-petalled blossoms carried in feathery heads. There is a marked difference between the scent of the flowers before and after picking, a fact that explains the local name Courtship-and-matrimony.

Several closely related plants, including the Spiraeas, are valuable ornamental perennials. Selected forms of Meadowsweet are widely culti-vated, in particular the form 'Aurea', the young leaves of which are a glorious golden green, making it an outstanding foliage plant for damp soils. The common form is a lovely plant in its own right, either massed in the border or growing with a medley of other moisture-loving plants in a boggy wild garden or round the edge of a garden pond. In a really damp position it will grow much more luxuriantly than in the drier soil of a border.

When the rooms of medieval and Elizabethan houses were scented with leaves and flowers scattered on the floor, Meadowsweet ranked as one of the most pleasant strewing herbs. A few leaves were often also used in the past to flavour claret and punches.

One of the principal medical uses of Meadowsweet was in the treatment of malarial fevers. It was probably much more effective than many alternative medications for in the first half of the nineteenth century the flowerbuds were found to contain salicylic acid, which was later used in the manufacture of aspirin. The name of this important compound is derived from *Spiraea*; when the great botanist Linnaeus classified Meadowsweet he called it *Spiraea ulmaria*.

# MUSK MALLOW
### *Malva moschata*

**Flowering season**
June to August.

**Suitable growing conditions**
Well-drained ground in borders or in wild parts of the garden; reasonably fertile or even poor soil ranging from slightly acid to very alkaline; a position in full sun or light shade.

**Growing guide**
Sow thinly in early spring or early autumn in carefully prepared permanent position; lightly cover seed; thin out up to 45cm (18in) apart. Preferably, sow in seed bed; transplant into growing bed; move to final positions in autumn. Plants can be propagated by basal shoot cuttings take in April.

The Mallows have given their name to a large family that includes several plants of great economic importance (particularly species of *Gossypium*, which yield cotton) and many attractive ornamentals, among them the Hollyhock *(Althaea)* and Hibiscus. The common name Mallow is derived from the Latin *malva*, meaning soft, a reference to the texture of the leaves and to the emollient properties of plants in this genus. The musky scent is not an obvious feature of the plant until it is brought into a warm room.

The Mallows are among the most showy of wild flowers and of them the Musk Mallow is the loveliest. It is widely distributed in Europe and in the British Isles is reasonably common in grassy places and in hedgerows, although rarer in the north.

This perennial, which grows to a height of 75cm (30in), produces several upright stems that are slightly hairy and often marked with purple spots. The lower leaves are kidney-shaped but the stem leaves are deeply divided. The rose-pink flowers, up to 5cm (2in) across, and consisting of five deeply notched petals and a prominent bunch of stamens, are borne over a long period in summer. The nutlets that follow the flowers turn almost black when ripe.

Musk Mallow has long been recognized as a first-rate garden plant. The most sought-after form is a lovely white variety but the wild plant with pink flowers is hardly inferior. Musk Mallow responds well when given good growing conditions in a border, a clump planted in full sun or light shade giving a long and colourful display. It can be grown in grass but because of competition it will not make the same vigorous growth.

Although it shares in some degree the properties of other Mallows, Musk Mallow is less important as a culinary and medicinal herb than Common Mallow *(M. sylvestris)* and Marsh Mallow *(Althaea officinalis)*. The former, sometimes called Billy Buttons or Fairy Cheeses because of its round fruits, has been widely used as a vegetable but its flavour is said to be insipid and the texture glutinous.

Marsh Mallow, a rather uncommon plant found in salt marshes and along the margins of tidal streams and rivers, has given its name to a kind of confectionery. Preparations of this herb are also considered effective in the treatment of coughs, bronchitis and other chest complaints.

# MUSK THISTLE
## *Carduus nutans*

**Flowering season**
May to August.

**Suitable growing conditions**
Well-drained ground in a border; neutral to alkaline soil of reasonable fertility; a position in full sun.

**Growing guide**
Sow thinly in May/June in carefully prepared permanent positon; cover seed; keep well watered; thin out up to 30cm (1ft) apart. Preferably, sow four seeds in potting compost in a pot; grow on one seedling only; plant in final position in mid-autumn taking care not to disturb the tap-root.

Early botanical authorities in Britain failed to record even quite common Thistles, perhaps because they looked on them all as a tribe of pestilential weeds. Some have certainly warranted the despairing anger of farmers but there are among them others that are less troublesome to agriculture or horticulture and many that are interesting for their flowers and seeds and also for their statuesque form.

It was Gerard who gave the Musk Thistle the name it is best known by. He said it was 'of a most pleasant sweete smel, striving with the savour of the musk'. Gerard had a good nose for the smell is rather faint. It is also sometimes known as the Nodding Thistle because of the way the large flower hangs down.

This is a native European biennial that is common throughout its range. In the British Isles it is rare in Ireland and Scotland but otherwise it occurs frequently in fields, hedgerows and roadsides, particularly on chalky soils.

Musk Thistle is an erect plant, normally little branched except in the case of large specimens, which can reach a height of 1m (40in). The leaves, which have scattered hairs on both sides, are very deeply cut. In the second year flowering begins in late spring or early summer, the nodding heads being carried on spineless stalks. The bright purple flower is surrounded by a ring of spiny bracts and of these the outer ones are turned back. The down of the seed-head is beautifully soft.

This, the showiest of the native thistles, is handsome enough to grow in a border, where it will respond well to good growing conditions. It is a useful nectar plant and very attractive to a variety of butterflies.

Another species worth finding a place for in the garden is the Carline Thistle *(Carlina vulgaris)*. This is a reasonably common wild flower but it is rarely found other than on chalk. It, too, is biennial, in the second year producing a branched stem up to 60cm (2ft) high carrying flowerheads from mid-summer to autumn. The leaves are pale green, wavy at the edge and softly spiny. The flowerheads have conspicuous straw-yellow ray-like bracts. Even long after the seeds have dispersed the skeleton of the flowerhead remains, its durability making it an attractive plant for winter decorations.

Other thistles that could be featured in the wild garden or border are Dwarf Thistle *(Cirsium acaule)*, Meadow Thistle *(C. dissectum)*, Melancholy Thistle *(C. heterophyllum)* and Woolly Thistle *(C. eriophorum)*.

# NARROW-LEAVED EVERLASTING PEA

*Lathyrus sylvestris*

**Flowering season**
June to August.

**Suitable growing conditions**
Well-drained ground in borders or in wilder parts of the garden; neutral to alkaline soil of reasonable fertility; a position in full sun or light shade.

**Growing guide**
Scarify and soak seed before sowing to speed germination. Sow thinly in early spring or early autumn in carefully prepared permanent position; cover seed; thin out up to 45cm (18in) apart. Preferably, sow in a pot, prick out individually into pots or trays; move to final positons in autumn. Plants can be propagated by division of the rootstock.

The true Sweet-pea *(Lathyrus odoratus)* is a native annual of southern Italy and Sicily. Although it first came to Britain at the end of the seventeenth century, it was not until the nineteenth century that it was developed into the plants with which we are now so familiar. The species has a delicious scent (a quality not retained in all its progeny) and perhaps this was a major feature that encouraged breeders to transform the modest original into the prodigious range of varieties we know today.

The flower of the Everlasting-pea (everlasting in the sense that the plant is perennial) is not significantly more modest than that of the wild Sweet-pea. True, it has no scent but perhaps plant breeders will yet take it up and make of it something we hardly recognize. Agriculturalists have already looked at the plant but with a view to its use as fodder. The Wagner Pea, developed from a sub-species in Austria, is said to be more palatable to stock than the normal wild plant.

Although fairly common in Europe as a whole, the Narrow-leaved Everlasting-pea has a scattered distribution in the British Isles. It is a plant of rough hedgerows and the fringes of woodland. Like the Sweet-pea this is a scrambling climber, pulling itself up, sometimes to a height of 150cm (5ft), by wrapping tendrils round anything that will support it. The purplish-red flowers are borne in clusters of three to eight on stiff stems, the flowering season lasting throughout the summer.

At a first glance this species is difficult to distinguish from the Broad-leaved Everlasting-pea *(L. latifolius)*, an introduced European species that is often grown as an ornamental but which is naturalized in Britain, flourishing even on sand dunes. This species has broader leaflets and broader stipules at the base of the leaf than the native species.

The Narrow-leaved Everlasting-pea, and for that matter its close relative, can be accommodated in almost any garden. It looks best when it is allowed to grow quite freely scrambling up other plants, which it is not likely to smother, but can be directed by staking. Provided that it is given something else to cling to, it can be a useful plant to grow in hedges, clothe walls and soften the outline of man-made features. The removal of spent flowers will help extend the flowering season and the fresh flowers are excellent for cutting.

# CORNFLOWER
## Centaurea cyanus

**Flowering season**
June to August.

**Suitable growing conditions**
Well-drained ground in the border; neutral or acid soil that is reasonably fertile; an open sunny position.

**Growing guide**
Sow thinly in early autumn

or early spring in carefully prepared permanent position; cover seed; thin out up to 20-40cm (8-16in) apart. In order to produce large flowering plants, sow in seed bed in early autumn; move to final positions in early spring. Can be added to standard grass and wild flower mixtures to provide first year colour.

I n Britain fields of rye and other grain crops blued by the annual Cornflower are a thing of the past, although in some parts of Europe the plant is still reasonably common. The use of cleaner grain seed and the widespread application of herbicides have reduced to near rarity a plant that not only competed with crops for moisture and nutrients but which also had a reputation for blunting the reaper's sickle; it was sometimes known as Hurt Sickle.

The Cornflower is, however, a widely distributed plant, found throughout Europe, including the Mediterranean area, western Asia and in many other parts of the world where it has been introduced as a weed.

The Bluebottle, to give it another common local name, makes a rather slender wiry plant with narrow long leaves that are grey in appearance because of a downy covering. The solitary flowers have conspicuous ray florets that are generally bright blue, although the blue varies in intensity and white and pink forms sometimes occur.

Annual and perennial Cornflowers have long been popular in the cottage garden. The double cultivated forms are, however, heavier with less airy grace than the wild plant. In its own right it makes an excellent subject for a bold planting in a sunny border but it can also be combined with other annuals such as Field Poppies, Corn Marigolds and Chamomiles to make a bright display that in some measure recaptures the colourfulness of an old cornfield.

Bluebottles make attractive, long-lasting flowers for cutting. The interesting shape and texture of the unopened buds can be preserved by dipping the heads in clear varnish. Dead-heading prolongs the flowering season.

Bees, butterflies and other insects are attracted in great numbers to patches of Cornflower, as the flowers are a valuable source of nectar and pollen.

Culpeper rather grandly says that the powder of the Cornflower 'being taken in the water of Plantain, Horse-tail, or the Greater Comfrey . . . is a remedy against the poison of the scorpion' but it seems that a more commonly used preparation derived from the plant was an eyewash – and apparently one that was more effective in the treatment of blue than brown eyes.

# OXEYE DAISY
## *Leucanthemum vulgare*

**Flowering season**
May to August.

**Suitable growing
conditions**
Well-drained ground with
grass and other flowers or
in the border; neutral or
slightly acid soil of
reasonable fertility; a
position in full sun.

**Growing guide**
Sow thinly in early spring
or early autumn in
permanent position; lightly
cover seed; thin out up to
30cm (1ft) apart.
Preferably, sow in seed
bed; transplant into
growing bed; move to final
positions in autumn. Plants
are easily propagated by
division of established
clumps in March or April.

Despite the loss of extensive areas of traditional meadowland, the Oxeye Daisy remains a common plant and a prominent feature of all kinds of grassland, including fields, roadsides, railway embankments and churchyards. Although so familiar, it is still one of the delights of early summer, and is associated in many European countries with traditional flower-gathering on the eve of St John's Day, 24 June.

The name Oxeye Daisy was given to the plant because it was believed by the Renaissance writers on plants to be the same as a plant given this name by Dioscorides. It is also widely known as Dog Daisy and Moon Daisy and even as Marguerite.

This perennial is very widely distributed in temperate parts of the world, growing either as a native or as an introduced species. In Europe, including the British Isles, it shows a preference for better soils.

The plant, which grows from a woody creeping root, has dark green leaves, somewhat rounded near the base but small and coarsely toothed higher up, and tough stems up to 60cm (2ft) high, bearing the solitary flowers. Each flower, as much as 50mm (2in) across, has a central yellow disc surrounded by white ray-florets.

In the garden this is one of the most valuable ingredients in a 'flowering meadow' mixture, a small proportion of it combined with the less aggressive grasses and other wild flowers creating an easily maintained but beautiful expanse of grassland. The Oxeye Daisy can be included with early-flowering plants, including the spring bulbs, Cowslips and Oxlips. A mowing regime that begins in mid-summer, which many find most convenient with the early season plants, need only be delayed a week or two so as not to remove the dazzling white flowers at their peak. But the Oxeye can also figure as one of the first flowers of the summer and late-summer meadow, which will probably not be cut until the autumn.

Oxeye Daisies can be effectively planted as stands in grassland, although most certainly in subsequent years they will colonize quite widely. Judged simply on its ornamental value, it is worth including in the border, but because of its tendency to spread it should be used with some caution. A clump will attract many insects, as this is a good nectar plant.

# PRIMROSE
## *Primula vulgaris*

**Flowering season**
March to May.

**Suitable growing conditions**
Reasonably moist ground in borders or in wild parts of the gardens, and also in containers; soil of moderate fertility that is neither excessively acid or alkaline; a position in partial shade.

**Growing guide**
Sow thinly in permanent position in autumn; lightly cover seed; in spring, thin out up to 20cm (8in) apart. Preferably, sow in a pot; prick out into a tray; move to final positions in autumn. Plants are easily propagated by division after flowering.

In northern countries the Primrose has become the very emblem of spring and, as Parkinson described them in the *Paradisus* of 1629, 'the first ambassadors thereof'. Even on days of rough weather in March and April its flowers seem almost luminous but, sadly, the Primrose has paid a heavy price for its pale yellow beauty. Although still a common plant, it has been so heavily picked and so often uprooted that in the vicinity of large towns it is now rarely seen studding woodland as it does when left undisturbed. *Prima rosa*, from which its common name is derived, means simply the first rose or flower.

The Primrose is widely distributed in Europe but is more common on the western edge of the continent and in the south, extending into Turkey and North Africa. Throughout its range it is most frequently found on rich moist soils in woodland, hedgerows and on shady banks.

This perennial grows from a short, knotty rootstock, forming a rosette of crinkled leaves, up to 12cm (5in) long and slightly toothed towards the base. The flowers, which are borne on separate stalks up to 20cm (8in) high, have five notched creamy yellow petals marked orange yellow at the centre. The deep yellow eye gives the impression of a flower more strongly coloured than the Primrose really is; there is even a hint of green in its creamy pallor.

Although at first sight all the flowers seem alike they are of two kinds, which never grow mixed on the same plant. In 'pin-eyed' Primroses the style and stigma stand like a pin above the stamens; in 'thrum-eyed' plants the stigma lies below the stamens. This arrangement ensures cross-fertilization, pollination only being possible when the pollen of a 'pin-eyed' flower reaches the stigma of a 'thrum-eyed' flower, or vice versa.

The multi-coloured cultivated forms of Primrose and the robust Polyanthus hybrids that are widely grown as early-season bedding plants or winter pot plants are said to be derived from the wild Primrose. These are useful plants but they have lost the grace of the Primrose, which also makes an excellent plant in borders, containers and window boxes. Given good growing conditions and freed from competition with grass, it will form a larger plant and flower over a longer season than it does in the wild. Many will prefer to try to establish the Primrose at the foot of banks or hedges and under trees so that it grows in natural clumps. However you grow it, the Primrose will be a useful source of nectar to early insects.

# PURPLE-LOOSESTRIFE
## *Lythrum salicaria*

**Flowering season**
June to August.

**Suitable growing conditions**
The margins of ponds and streams or moist ground in borders; any fertile soil that is not excessively acid; a position in full sun or shade.

**Growing guide**
Sow thinly in early spring or early autumn in carefully prepared permanent position; lightly cover seed; thin out up to 45cm (18in). Preferably, sow in seed bed; transplant into growing bed and keep moist; move to final positions in autumn. Plants are easily propagated by division of the roots in October or April. They can also be propagated by basal cuttings in April.

Purple-loosestrife, one of the most showy of European wild flowers, owes its name to a mistaken connection with Yellow Loosestrife *(Lysimachia vulgaris)*. The Greek source of the generic name of this plant was taken to mean 'ending strife', and interpreted as indicating that it helped settle beasts that might otherwise be unruly at the plough. Purple-loosestrife's own botanical name refers somewhat imaginatively to its gory colouring and to the willow-like shape of the leaves.

This European native perennial is now a common plant in many temperate areas of the world. In the British Isles it occurs frequently in the south and west, growing abundantly in marshy places and on the margins of still water or slow-moving streams. It is a tall plant, in ideal conditions growing to 120cm (4ft) at least. The erect stems, which are square in section, grow from a creeping rhizome. The lower leaves are arranged in whorls of three, the upper ones in opposite pairs. The purplish flowers appear during the second half of summer, when many other plants are beginning to look decidedly tired, and are carried in closely packed spikes that are about 30cm (1ft) long. A curious feature of Purple-loosestrife is that, although on any one plant the arrangement in the flowers of the stamens and styles will be the same, three different arrangements are possible. The cross-fertilization that results helps to keep the species vigorous.

Purple-loosestrife prefers really damp ground at the edge of a pond or the like but will perform well in a reasonably moist border, even in shade, flowering for many weeks and then giving the bonus of good autumn colour. Nurserymen offer several named forms that show variations in flower colour, but the wild plant is lovely in its own right. It tends to seed very freely; prompt dead-heading will help to keep populations under control.

Another virtue of Purple-loosestrife is that it provides a source of nectar late in the year and is therefore attractive to butterflies and bees. The leaves are food for the caterpillars of the Emperor Moth and the Small Elephant Hawkmoth.

Another good plant for moist soils is Hemp-agrimony *(Eupatorium cannabinum)*. This is a handsome species with upright reddish stems and in late summer dense clusters of reddish-purple flowers that are attractive to butterflies.

# RAGGED-ROBIN

*Lychnis flos-cuculi*

**Flowering season**
May to June.

**Suitable growing conditions**
Damp mini-meadows or moist ground in borders; ordinary soil that is reasonably fertile; an open sunny position.

**Growing guide**
Sow thinly in early spring or early autumn in carefully prepared permanent position; lightly cover seed; thin out up to 45cm (18in). Preferably, sow in seed bed; transplant into growing bed; move to final positions in autumn. Plants can be propagated by division in April.

Despite the Ragged-Robin's specific botanical name, which means 'flower of the cuckoo', it generally flowers later than April, when cuckoos are commonly heard in much of northern Europe. In the sixteenth century, according to Gerard, it was known as Crowflower. Stems of Ragged-Robin are probably the 'Crowflowers' that feature with 'Nettles, Daisies, and Long Purples' in the fantastic garlands worn by the deranged Ophelia in Shakespeare's *Hamlet*. Other country names include Drunkards, Indian Pink and Shaggy Jacks.

In some parts it is still known as Batchelor's Buttons, a name it shares with a number of common wild flowers. It is said that unmarried girls wanting to know the young man they would marry used to pick and name buds after their admirers. The bud named after the man to be married would open first. Ragged-Robin, like the Field Poppy, was sometimes known as Thunder-flower. Perhaps, like the Field Poppy, the flowers were picked and hung in a building to protect it from lightning though, just as probably, picking might provoke a storm.

Throughout Britain and Europe Ragged-Robin is a common perennial of damp places, including meadows, marshes and woods. It makes a slender plant, sparsely furnished with rough hairy leaves, sending up an erect stem to 70cm (25in). It produces throughout early summer numerous five-petalled flowers up to 40mm (1½in) across. The flowers are not unlike those of the Red Campion, which like Ragged-Robin is a member of the Pink family (that includes garden plants such as Carnations, Pinks and Sweet Williams), but the petals are daintily frayed.

For the unique shape of the flower alone, the Ragged-Robin would be worth growing. It is a striking plant for almost any moist position in the garden, whether in a damp mini-meadow, on the fringe of pools or in the border. It is most effective when grown in clumps in the border, where its pretty flowers will attract butterflies and moths.

It is surprising, perhaps, that in the past herbalists have not invented qualities in such a pretty plant, even if they could not find real medicinal values in it. However, Gerard says that the flowers 'serve for garlands and crowns, and to decke up gardens' but that it is 'not used either in medicine or in nourishment'.

# RED CAMPION
### *Silene dioica*

**Flowering season**
May to November.

**Suitable growing conditions**
Well-drained soil in the border or wild parts of the garden; any reasonably fertile soil that is not excessively acidic or alkaline; a partially shaded or open position.

**Growing guide**
Sow thinly in early spring or early autumn in carefully prepared permanent position; lightly cover seed; thin out up to 45cm (18in). Preferably, sow in seed bed; transplant into growing bed; move to final positions in autumn. Plants are easily propagated by division and basal shoot cuttings.

According to some authorities the name Campion, first used of the garden flower Rose Campion *(Lychnis coronaria)*, is simply derived from 'champion', that is to say, 'champion of the garden'. Whatever the case, the group to which the name was applied were highly thought of as garden flowers in the sixteenth and seventeenth centuries.

In its wild state the Red Campion is found throughout Europe and extends south into North Africa and west into Asia. It is a common plant of hedgerows and woodland glades and verges, where its bright rose flowers are conspicuous in late spring, right through summer and even into autumn. The plant is rather slender, with pointed oval leaves that are hairy and sticky to the touch. The flowers, borne on stems up to 80cm (30in) high, have the characteristic five-petalled shape of the Pink family, to which this plant belongs.

When it forms a large clump Red Campion makes a good show in a lightly shaded border, coming into flower early and continuing over a long period. In wilder parts of the garden it combines well with Bluebells – in coppiced woodland it is often associated with this plant and with the Early Purple Orchid *(Orchis mascula)* – and will self-seed freely.

Red Campion is one of the prettiest of our native wild plants, which is also effective and long-lasting in flower arrangements.

Other wild members of the Pink family that are well worth growing include the Sea Campion and the White Campion. The Sea Campion *(Silene maritima)* is a smaller perennial of sprawling habit, growing to a height of 20cm (8in). It is found wild on rocky and shingly coasts and also in the mountains. It can look quite at home in a raised bed or rock garden, where it will flower profusely in late spring and the first half of summer.

The White Campion *(Silene alba)*, another perennial of fields and roadsides, is close in appearance to the Red Campion, with which it will sometimes hybridize. The flowers of the White Campion, which are scented in the evening, are of a pure whiteness not matched by any other wild flower.

# RED VALERIAN
*Centranthus ruber*

**Flowering season**
May to July.

**Suitable growing conditions**
Well-drained ground in the border and stony soil in wild parts of the garden; neutral to alkaline soil and particularly suitable for soil of low fertility; a sunny and in cold areas, a sheltered position.

**Growing guide**
Sow thinly in early spring or early autumn in carefully prepared permanent position; lightly cover seed; thin out up to 30cm (1ft) apart. Preferably, sow in seed bed; transplant into growing bed; move to final positions in autumn. Plants can be propagated by division in autumn or spring.

Linnaeus classified this plant as *Valeriana rubra* but later botanists have placed it in a separate genus and not simply because it lacks the medicinal properties of the Common Valerian *(Valeriana officinalis).* The generic name *Centranthus*, from the Greek words for 'spur' and 'flower', highlights one feature that distinguishes the plant from the true Valerian, namely a spur at the base of the tubular flower.

Red Valerian is almost certainly a plant introduced as an ornamental to northern Europe from the Mediterranean area. Gerard and Parkinson, the one writing at the end of the sixteenth century and the other toward the middle of the seventeenth, both refer to the plant as a garden flower. It is not uncommon in many parts of Europe and is widely naturalized in southern England, where it is most frequently seen flourishing in surprisingly inhospitable ground, including rocky cliffs, railway cuttings and, very commonly, ineradicably established in old walls.

It is not surprising that such a handsome, strong-growing perennial should have been so valued as a garden plant. The sturdy stems, woody at the base, are well-clothed in bluish green foliage that is covered with a distinct bloom. The small flowers, which are usually deep pink, although sometimes darker and occasionally white, are borne in dense heads at a height of about 90cm (3ft) and open over quite a long period from late spring to late summer. The seed, which is equipped with a feathery parachute, is distributed by wind.

Red Valerian has lost none of its appeal as a garden plant, although it is most effective when it is massed to create a bold effect. William Robinson, the nineteenth-century advocate of wild gardening, said that it 'is seen best only on banks, rubbish-heaps or old walls, in which positions it endures much longer than on the level ground'. He was right to point out that it succeeds best on poor soil, but he failed to say how useful it can be as a low hedge when it can separate more highly cultivated parts of the garden from areas that are less closely controlled.

It is said that in parts of continental Europe the very young leaves of Red Valerian are eaten either mixed with other salad vegetables or lightly cooked and served with butter. They have a rather bitter tang. However, it is much more important as a nectar plant for insects than it can ever be as a food plant for humans.

# ROCK-ROSE
*Helianthemum nummularium*

**Flowering season**
May to August.

**Suitable growing conditions**
Well-drained ground in the rock garden, border or a rough bank; neutral to alkaline soil of low fertility; a position in full sun.

**Growing guide**
Sow thinly in permanent position in autumn; lightly cover seed; in spring, thin as required; spread can be up to 60cm (2ft). Artificial stratification is necessary if sowing in spring (see page 106). Preferably sow in seed bed; transplant into growing bed; move to final positions in autumn. Plants can be propagated by lateral shoot cuttings taken from June to August.

The name Rock-rose is misleading; it is often found in rocky terrain but it is not a Rose. It belongs with the *Cistus* family, which includes many southern European species with flowers of short-lived but exquisite beauty, the petals having the quality of crushed tissue.

The Rock-rose is a sun-loving plant of open positions. Without sunlight the flowers remain closed, hence the generic name *Helianthemum*, meaning 'sunflower'. In the British Isles it has a very scattered distribution (in Ireland it is extremely uncommon) but in other parts of Europe, particularly towards the south, it occurs more evenly. It favours chalky soils and is most often found on dry grassland or scrubby country.

The Rock-rose is best described as a sprawling sub-shrub. The bases of the stems are woody but the plant is curiously lacking in backbone, flopping about at ground level, with stems often rooting and so extending the area covered by the plant, or else being propped up by other plants. The small narrow leaves, which are arranged in opposite pairs, are pale on the underside. The long flowering season lasts right through summer but individual flowers only hold their petals for a day or so. The very lax style of the plant extends to the way the buds hang but the open flowers are a lovely bright yellow and the petals have something of the texture that distinguishes species of *Cistus*. Occasional variations of flower colour occur; in some forms the petals are marked at the base with an orange dot.

The cultivated Rock-roses have become very popular garden plants, the breeders having produced from the native plant and closely related species some very free-flowering and unusually coloured hybrids. The hybrids bear, however, the unmistakable mark of the parent, which in its own right is a very attractive plant to grow in a sunny position. It can quite easily stand being added to a rock garden or raised bed which is planted with cultivated varieties. Grown in this way it could be underplanted with small spring bulbs.

To enjoy its wild character, however, it would be better to plant it in a less sophisticated setting, in a mini-meadow, on a dry sunny bank where it will not be overshadowed by taller plants or as part of a simple collection of prostrate native plants. Wild Thyme *(Thymus praecox* subsp. *arcticus)* would go well with it as would the lovely Mountain Avens *(Dryas octopetala)*.

# ROUGH HAWKBIT
*Leontodon hispidus*

**Flowering season**
May to September.

**Suitable growing conditions**
Reasonably well-drained mini-grassland; ordinary soil that is not excessively acid or alkaline; a position in full sun.

**Growing guide**
Sow thinly in early spring or early autumn in carefully prepared permanent position; lightly cover seed; thin out up to 22cm (9in) apart. Preferably, sow in seed bed; transplant to growing bed; move to final positons in mid-autumn. Plants can also be propagated by division in October or March.

The Hawkbits owe their common name to the belief that birds of prey ate the plant in order to sharpen their eyesight. The generic name, meaning 'lion's tooth', refers to the jagged edge of the leaves. It was to this genus that Linnaeus originally assigned the Dandelion *(Taraxacum officinale)*, whose common name is a corruption of the French for 'lion's tooth'. Rough Hawkbit is a common plant of grasslands, particularly those on chalk, and is found in most parts of the British Isles. It bears a strong resemblance to the Dandelion and is probably often mistaken for it.

Rough Hawkbit is a perennial, growing from a tough root-stock, with the jagged leaves arranged in rosettes. The lobes point backwards, as do those of the Dandelion, but its leaves are roughly hairy whereas those of the Dandelion are smooth. Slender stems, which are up to 30cm (1ft) high, carry solitary flowers, which droop when in bud. When open, the flowers are up to 35mm (1½in) across and are a lovely golden yellow with reddish streaks on the underside. They are rich in nectar and have a honeyed fragrance.

In the wild garden this plant belongs to the flowering mini-meadow, where some will be happier with it than with the more aggressive Dandelion.

However, the Dandelion is a plant that cannot lightly be dismissed. It flourishes in fields and roadsides and, to its cost, in lawns, where its large flat rosettes tolerate close mowing. The leaves are shiny dark green and the flower stalk, which is hollow and up to 40cm (16in) tall, contains a bitter white juice. As many as two hundred individual florets are contained in the golden flowers, which are rich in honey and very attractive to many insects. Honey Bees take the nectar and pollen very freely. Although they are so familiar, the plumed seeds of the clock are extraordinarily beautiful.

The young leaves can be used in salads and can also be cooked in the manner of Spinach. The roasted roots are used in the making of a coffee substitute.

# SCARLET PIMPERNEL
## *Anagallis arvensis*

**Flowering season**
May to August.

**Suitable growing conditions**
Well-drained bare ground in the border; moisture-retentive soil of reasonable fertility; a position in full sun.

**Growing guide**
Sow thinly in early autumn or early spring in carefully prepared permanent position; barely cover seed; thin out up to 15cm (6in) apart. In order to produce large flowering plants, sow in seed bed in early autumn; move to final positions in early spring.

Poor Man's Weatherglass and Shepherd's Glass are other common names of this annual herb that need little explanation; the flowers of the Scarlet Pimpernel react promptly to humidity and failing light. Once closed they are inconspicuous. Pimpernel is something of a puzzle. It was formerly the name of the Salad Burnet *(Sanguisorba minor* subsp. *minor)* and was probably derived from a word meaning 'two-winged', a reference to a paired arrangement of the leaves. It is believed that it was to this plant that Dioscorides gave the name *Anagallis*, from a word meaning 'to laugh', for the plant was used to dispel melancholy. Whether this is the plant described by Dioscorides as having scarlet and blue flowers, *Anagallis* is now its generic name.

The Scarlet Pimpernel is found almost everywhere in the temperate world, flourishing on cultivated land and roadsides. It remains common despite the use of herbicides.

This is a creeping plant with much-branched stems, square in section, that can grow up to 30cm (12in), occasionally sending up more erect stems.

The paired leaves are rich green in colour and spotted black on the underside. The flowers, which are borne throughout the summer, are carried on slender stalks growing from the junction of leaf and stem. Although not much more than 12mm (½in) across, they have a bright starry appearance and an intense orange-red colour. Sometimes the flowers are blue, pink or white. According to Renaissance authorities, such as William Turner, 'it that hath the blewe floure is called the female, but it that hath ye cremesine is called ye male'. The blue form, sometimes now treated as a subspecies, is said to be more common on the Continent than in Britain. Plants set copious seed and when the capsules are ripe the top of the fruit splits off and the seeds are dispersed.

Scarlet Pimpernel is such a prolific seeder that once you have grown it in the garden it will follow on from year to year. It can be used as a pretty, rapid-growing ground-covering herb that will respond well in a fertile soil without competition from grass and other plants.

The plant was recommended by Culpeper for treating the 'stinging and biting of venomous beasts or mad dogs'.

# SEA-HOLLY
## *Eryngium maritimum*

**Flowering season**
July to August.

**Suitable growing conditions**
Well-drained, even gravelly
ground in the border; neutral
to alkaline soil of low fertility; a
position in full sun.

**Growing guide**
Sow thinly in early spring or
early autumn in carefully
prepared permanent position;
cover seed; thin out up to
30cm (1ft) apart. Preferably,
sow seed in seed bed;
transplant to growing bed;
move to final positions in
autumn. Plants can be
propagated by careful division
of the roots and by root
cuttings.

There is no mystery in the common name of the Sea-holly, a curious and striking plant that is found, except under cultivation, only at the seashore. To refer to it now as Eryngo would seem affected but it was once a common name, derived from the Greek work meaning 'to belch' and referring to the supposed value of the plant in the treatment of flatulence. Sea-holly is fairly widely distributed on the European coastline but it is rare in the north of Britain. It survives, even flourishes, on shingle and sand where few other large perennials can find a living.

This spiny plant, which grows to a height of 50cm (20in), has grey stems and grey-green leathery leaves, spikily toothed and margined in a paler grey. The rounded heads of powdery-blue flowers are borne in summer. The superficial resemblance to the thistle is misleading for Sea-holly belongs to the umbellifers.

Discerning gardeners have very much taken to the Eryngiums, valuing them for their distinctive form, the beautiful colour of their foliage and their usefulness for winter drying. The native plant is often neglected in favour of exotic species and hybrids even though its unique charms are a match for theirs. In a sunny border where the ground is absolutely free-draining it makes a handsome subject planted singly or as a group. As it is a useful nectar plant it will attract many insects.

Eryngo root has, in the past, been considered a delicacy and one with aphrodisiac qualities. Gerard, who gives a recipe for candying or 'conditing' the roots, says 'they are exceeding good to be given to old and aged people that are consumed and withered with age, and who want natural moisture'. The candied roots were also used as a flavoursome ingredient in various dishes. It is said that the young flowering shoots were also considered of culinary merit, being cooked and eaten in the same way as asparagus.

Although not closely related to the Sea-holly, two other conspicuous plants of the seashore can be grown in similar conditions. The Yellow Horned-poppy *(Glaucium flavum)* and Sea-kale *(Crambe maritima)* are both plants of distinctive character. The Yellow Horned-poppy is a striking plant, found on shingly beaches, which needs very free-draining conditions and an open position. Sea-kale, known also as Sea Cabbage, has been highly regarded as a vegetable, the stems being blanched to moderate the plant's tanginess.

# SNAKE'S-HEAD
*Fritillaria meleagris*

**Flowering season**
April to May.

**Suitable growing conditions**
Reasonably moist ground in grassy mini-meadows, borders or rock gardens; fertile soil that is not excessively alkaline or acid; a sunny position.

**Growing guide**
Plants raised from seed take four to five years to reach

flowering size. Sow thinly in early spring or early autumn in seed bed; lightly cover seed; transplant to growing bed. After two or three years, move to final positions. Preferably, sow in pots; prick out into pots or a tray; grow for two or three years before moving to final position. Plant bulbs 7.5-10cm (3-4in) deep in early autumn. Stocks can be increased from offsets from the parent bulb.

Only one of the Fritillaries, an interesting group of bulbs that includes the stately Crown Imperial *(Fritillaria imperialis)*, has any claim to being a native of Britain and that is the Snake's-head. Even that is not certain for, although the plant is found wild in a few meadows, early authorities are curiously silent about it.

Whatever its true status in Britain this European species is one of the loveliest of spring flowers, its common name alluding to the elegant menace of the hanging bud. Both generic and specific names refer to the finely chequered pattern of its petals: *Fritillaria*, derived from the Latin for a dice-box, alludes, by extension, to the squared dicing board, while *meleagris* is derived from the name of the guineafowl, a bird with closely patterned plumage.

Throughout its range the Snake's-head, or Fritillary as it is commonly known, is found in damp meadows, where it sends up its grassy foliage in early spring. The slender stem, up to 45cm (18in) high, carries one or two bell-like flowers in mid-spring. The flowers are mainly purple with a darker tessellation, although white with green markings and intermediate forms are not uncommon. The weather is often cold and wet at the time when

the flowers are open, but the style, pollen and pollinating insects – generally the Bumble-bee queens – are fully sheltered in the hanging bells.

This is an outstanding plant for naturalizing in damp but not waterlogged meadow, where, once it is happily established, it will self-seed freely and build up sizeable colonies. It will even do quite well naturalized in open woodland, surviving the boisterous company of Bluebells but not tolerating dense shade. Wherever it is naturalized the mowing regime must allow it to die down after setting seed; effectively this means no cutting until mid-summer.

This unusually beautiful bulb can make a lovely show planted as a clump in a moist border if its rather subtle colouring is not overwhelmed by the brightest of the spring flowers. It may be even more effective planted in pockets in the rockery where the delicacy of the flowers can be appreciated at close range.

Despite the sinister ring of its common name and some of its more local names – in certain areas it has been known as Dead Men's Bells – this plant does not appear to be loaded with associations in folklore and there are few uses to which it has been put. The bulb is poisonous.

# SOAPWORT
## *Saponaria officinalis*

**Flowering season**
July to September.

**Suitable growing conditions**
Reasonably moist ground in the border; fertile soil that is not excessively acid or alkaline; a position in full sun.

**Growing guide**
Sow thinly in early autumn or early spring in carefully prepared permanent position; lightly cover seed; thin out up to 60cm (2ft) apart. Artificial stratification is beneficial if sowing in spring (see page 106). Preferably, sow in seed bed; transplant into growing bed; move to final positions in autumn. Plants are easily propagated by root division or remove underground roots between October and March.

Soapwort or Bouncing Bet is almost certainly an introduced plant in Britain. Its real home is central and southern Europe but it came as a washing plant, one that could make a serviceable lather, and as a washing plant it was taken to America. An early name was Fuller's Herb and very likely it was specifically for the woollen trade and the fulling process, in which wool is cleaned and thickened, that the plant first reached Britain. At one time it was grown and harvested in the vicinity of woollen mills – and it is probably from these plants that the wild populations in Britain are descended.

Soapwort is now widely distributed in Europe, western Asia and other parts of the world. In Europe it is a plant of waysides and hedgerows, and in Britain is more common in the south.

This perennial has a creeping root-stock from which grow a few upright stems to a hight of 90cm (3ft). These have few branches but are well clothed with opposite elliptical leaves that are smooth and narrow and have prominent longitudinal veins. The flowers, which are borne in late summer and autumn, are pink or white and, although not showy when looked at individually, form very attractive compact clusters.

This is a coarser plant than many members of the Pink family, to which it belongs, but it is one of our loveliest wild flowers and has been widely cultivated as an ornamental since the seventeenth century at least.

The common form makes a fine show in the border late in the season. It is seen to best effect growing as a clump but it will need checking as the roots are invasive. The flowers seem to be scentless but Hawkmoths and other insects are attracted to them for nectar.

To make a lather from the plant you must bruise the leaves and stems and then boil them in water for about half an hour. Then strain off the soapy liquid. The lather is not long lasting but is mildly astringent. It is sometimes recommended for cleaning old tapestries and similar fabrics and even for use as a mild shampoo.

A decoction of the plant has enjoyed a particularly high reputation as an effective remedy for what many writers coyly refer to as 'the itch'. On this point Culpeper does not mince words, recommending it as 'an absolute cure in the French-Pox'. It was also considered beneficial in the treatment of gout and rheumatism.

# SWEET VIOLET
## *Viola odorata*

**Flowering season**
February to April.

**Suitable growing conditions**
Well-drained ground in the border or in wilder parts of the garden; slightly acid to alkaline soils that are reasonably fertile; a sunny or partially shaded position.

**Growing guide**
Sow thinly in permanent position in autumn; lightly cover seed; in spring, thin as required. Artificial stratification is necessary if sowing in spring (see page 106). Preferably, sow in a pot; prick out into a pot; move to final positions in autumn. Plants are easily propagated by division of the roots.

Despite its fugitive sweet scent and refined flowers, *Viola odorata* is a plant that has been curiously neglected by modern gardeners. The Sweet Violet is a perennial found very widely in most parts of the British Isles except the far north and in parts of continental Europe, including the Mediterranean region. It is most often seen in hedgerows and on the edge of woods and is particularly common on chalky soils.

The plant grows from a creeping rhizome, which sends up stalks bearing dark green heart-shaped leaves. The flowers, borne on stems up to 15cm (6in) high, start to appear at the end of February. They are generally deep purple in colour, although paler variations and white forms are quite common. In autumn there is another crop of flowers, but these are minute and without petals. They are, however, self-fertilizing and produce seed. The Sweet Violet does not rely exclusively on seed to propagate itself. After flowering in spring plants send out runners which, when rooted, are independent of the parent plant.

In the garden the Sweet Violet is easy to establish in lightly shaded positions, for example along hedge bottoms, under trees and at the front of borders. If potted up and grown under glass plants can be brought into flower for Christmas.

Quite apart from its distinctive beauty, the Sweet Violet is worth growing in the garden as an early-season nectar plant and as an important source of food for the caterpillars of some butterflies; those of the High Brown Fritillary and the Pearl-bordered Fritillary will feed on it.

'Pliny saith', as Gerard reminds us, 'that Violets are as well used in Garlands as smelt unto; and are good against . . . heaviness of the head'. In *A Little Herball* of 1525 Anthony Ascham recommends that a person suffering from sleeplessness should prepare a decoction of the flowers.

Undoubtedly, syrup of Violets has been the most widely used preparation made from the flowers. Many early writers not only recognised it as a gentle laxative but held it effective in the treatment of ailments as diverse as epilepsy and jaundice. Violet plate, a crystallized paste prepared from the flowers mixed with sugar, was another of the apothecaries' standbys. Candied Violets are almost all that is left of this long tradition.

# TEASEL

*Dipsacus fullonum* subsp. *sylvestris*

**Flowering season**
July to August, dry heads
remaining throughout
autumn and winter.

**Suitable growing
conditions**
Well-drained bare ground
in the border or wild parts
of the garden; neutral to
alkaline soil even of low
fertility; a sunny position.

**Growing guide**
Sow thinly in May/June in
carefully prepared
permanent position; lightly
cover seed; keep well-
watered; thin out up to
60cm (2ft) apart. Preferably
sow in pots; prick out into
pots as soon as possible;
move to final position in
mid autumn, taking care
not to disturb the tap-root.

The Teasel is often most conspicuous in autumn and winter, when other foliage has died down, leaving its gaunt candelabra shapes as prominent clusters on verges and wasteland. It is a biennial with a wide distribution in Europe but in the British Isles it is most frequently found in the south and the Midlands.

In its first year the Teasel makes a spiny rosette of leaves from which, in the spring of the second year, grows a handsome flower stem that can reach a height of 180cm (6ft). A curious feature of the prickly stems are the cups formed by leafy bracts at the junction of side shoots. Small insects are often trapped and drowned in the little pools that collect here. Some have thought that the plant might be to some degree carnivorous, absorbing nutrients from the victims that have fallen into its watery traps. The botanical name *Dipsacus* suggests only that the plant is thirsty.

The bristles of the globular flowerhead are at first soft and green and the tiny flowers begin to open as a purple band almost halfway down the head. After a few days, as these are finishing, a pair of fresh bands opens either side, the flowering rings gradually moving further and further apart.

When flowering is over the whole plant turns brown and stiffens.

The Teasel makes a really striking garden plant, particularly when it is allowed to establish self-seeding colonies. However, because it is biennial, you will need to sow seed two springs in succession in order to ensure an annual display. It is a particularly good plant for attracting wildlife to the garden. When in flower it attracts many small butterflies, including the Common Blue and Small Copper, and large Bumble-bees. In autumn and winter the ripe seeds are a favourite food of Goldfinches, small parties of which work their way through stands of the plants.

The heads of Fuller's Teasel, a sub-species *(fullonum)* that has been widely cultivated, are still used in the wool trade, though not as widely as in the past, to raise the nap of material.

For the flower arranger the Teasel is a very useful plant for winter decorations. Stems should be picked as soon as flowering is over and hung to dry in a sunny place with good ventilation. Perhaps its use as a winter decoration developed from the old practice of hanging a stem in an airy part of the house as a weatherglass, the spines closing up with the prospect of rain.

# THRIFT

### *Armeria maritima* subsp. *maritima*

**Flowering season**
April to August.

**Suitable growing conditions**
Well-drained ground at the edges of borders, in rock gardens or raised beds and wilder plantings on banks; slightly acid, neutral or alkaline soils of reasonable or low fertility; a sunny open position.

**Growing guide**
Sow seed in autumn or spring, preferably in seed trays placed in a cold frame. Transfer seedlings to pots or a nursery bed and plant in permanent positions in autumn. The plant is easily propagated from cuttings, preferatly taken in mid- or late summer but at almost any time during the growing season.

Thrift, or Sea-pink, is a familiar plant of the seashore, often growing in association with Common Sea-lavender *(Limonium vulgare)*, a close relative. The ground-hugging hummocks of grassy leaves are well suited to exposed conditions at sea level and at higher altitudes. In fact the plant is found in mountainous areas as well as along the coast in much of the northern hemisphere.

It has never been widely used as a medicinal herb but since the sixteenth century at least it has been greatly valued as a garden plant, particularly, in Gerard's words, 'for the bordering up of beds and bankes'. Its neat habit made it particularly suitable as an edging for the formal beds that featured so prominently in Renaissance gardens.

Thrift is a perennial with a woody root-stock from which grow tufts of rather fleshy linear leaves about 75mm (3in) in length. The tight globular heads of flowers are generally rose pink but there are variations in intensity of colour. They appear in late spring and summer, borne on stems up to 20cm (8in) tall.

Through all the changes of fashion in gardening Thrift has never really lost its popularity, although what is now grown is rarely the simple wild plant but instead cultivated forms, selected for size of flower or brightness of colour, and closely related species. It is still, perhaps, most successfully used as an edging plant, effectively breaking the hard line where borders and paths meet. As it is a plant that thrives on a lean diet in free-draining soil it can be worked into gaps in paving, where it slowly builds up its tight cushion of leaves. Planted in this way it proves reasonably tolerant of light wear. A plant that is so demanding of good drainage is not surprisingly well suited in the rock garden or raised beds, even on the top of a sunny bank, and in these positions it combines well with other low-growing plants. For those whose gardens are blasted by wind, even spray-laden wind near the sea, it is a must, for these are the conditions it has adapted to in its native state.

Thrift is a good nectar plant, attracting many butterflies and bees to the garden during the early summer when, at peak flowering, the tufts carry many flowerheads.

# TORMENTIL
## *Potentilla erecta*

**Flowering season**
May to October.

**Suitable growing conditions**
Moist bare ground or rougher parts of the garden; acid soil of poor or reasonable fertility; a position in full sun.

**Growing guide**
Sow thinly in early spring or early autumn in carefully prepared permanent position; lightly cover seed; thin as required; spread can be up to 30cm (1ft). Preferably sow in a pot; prick out into a tray; move to final positions in autumn. Plants can be propagated by divisions of the roots in October or March, or from long basal cuttings in April.

The Potentillas, members of the Rose family, owe their generic name, which signifies small but powerful, to their use in medicine. The astringent roots of Tormentil were formerly used in the treatment of colic and it is from the Latin for this that its common name is derived.

This is a very widely distributed perennial in the northern hemisphere, being found as far east as Siberia. It is more common in northern Europe than in the Mediterranean area. In the British Isles, as elsewhere in its range, it shows a distinct preference for damp acid soils and is common in open woods and on heaths and fenland.

The specific name *erecta* leads one to expect a more upright plant than the rather sprawling specimen that Tormentil often is. However, this plant has a very wide distribution and there are forms showing rather different habits of growth. From a woody rhizomatous root-stock grows a rosette of three-lobed leaves, which tend to begin withering as the flowering stem develops. These carry five-lobed leaves and can reach a height of 50cm (20in). The bright yellow flowers are four-petalled and about 12mm (½in) across. The flowering season lasts throughout the summer. In the garden this is a pretty plant for a damp sunny bank, the edge of a pond or a moist pocket in a rockery.

The herbalists and apothecaries seem to have come to Tormentil rather late but once its astringent properties, particularly those of the root, were recognized it was used in a wide range of treatments. Culpeper thought highly of it, recommending it for internal and external use, including treatment of piles. The root was used as an astringent tooth powder.

The roots are sufficiently astringent for them to have been used in tanning as an alternative to oak bark. A local name, Blood Root, refers to the red juice that can be extracted from the roots to be used as a dye.

Silverweed *(P. anserina)* is another species that is widespread in Europe. The beautiful silky foliage adequately explains the common name. Many animals will eat the herb. Silverweed also favours damp ground and in the wild is most common on good loamy soil.

The creeping stems root as they go and throw up clusters of leaves that have a distinctive arrangement of a large leaflet alternating with a smaller one. The yellow flowers, which have five petals, start to appear in late spring.

# VIPER'S-BUGLOSS
## *Echium vulgare*

**Flowering season**
June to September.

**Suitable growing conditions**
Well-drained ground in borders and in wilder parts of the garden; neutral or alkaline soils of reasonable or low fertility; an open sunny position.

**Growing guide**
Sow thinly in May/June in carefully prepared permanent position; cover seed; keep well watered; thin out up to 45cm (18in) apart. Preferably sow in pots; prick out into pots as soon as possible; move to final positon in mid autumn, taking care not to disturb the tap-root.

This striking member of the Borage family owes its common name to a supposed resemblance of the seeds to a snake's head and an assumption that the plant was the *echion*, 'viper plant', mentioned by Dioscorides. Later writers perpetuated the belief that the plant was a specific against snake-bite, the stippling of the stems supposedly confirming the association between the plant and the serpent.

Viper's-bugloss is a widely distributed hardy biennial found wild in many parts of Europe and Asia and introduced to North America, where in some areas it has become a bad weed. In Britain it is most commonly found in the south east, either as a weed growing on the verges of arable land, or on chalky dry places or sea cliffs.

In its first year Viper's-bugloss forms a rosette of hairy pointed leaves from which, in the second season, develops the spotted hairy flower stem, sometimes reaching a height of 75cm (30in). The flower spike itself can sometimes be up to a foot long, each cluster of flowers accentuated by a leafy bract. The large flowers, with protruding anthers, are at first reddish purple but these soon turn to an intense blue, making this unusual plant one of the most conspicuous when in flower.

The brilliant blue of the flowers makes a really bold effect when clumps of Viper's-bugloss are planted in borders. However, it is only on light, free-draining soils that it is worth trying to naturalize it as a constituent of a grass and wild flower mixture because it will not stand up well to competition from vigorous grasses.

Viper's-bugloss is an outstanding nectar plant, attracting bees and numerous other insects, including hover-flies, butterflies and moths. In Germany before World War II it was one of a number of wild plants sown on roadsides and railway embankments to increase the sources of nectar available to bees. Its supposed virtue in the treatment of snake-bite has virtually eclipsed all other medicinal and herbal uses. However, a mild tonic infusion is said to have been effective as a treatment for the common cold and for headaches.

The Borage family includes several introduced plants with pretty blue flowers, including Borage itself *(Borago officinalis)*, Alkanet *(Anchusa officinalis)*, and the native Hound's-tongue *(Cynoglossum officinale)*, another plant of light soils.

# WATER AVENS
## *Geum rivale*

**Flowering season**
April to July.

**Suitable growing conditions**
Moist ground in borders or in rougher parts of the garden; acid or alkaline soil of reasonable fertility; a position in full sun or shade.

**Growing guide**
Sow thinly in early spring or early autumn in carefully prepared permanent position: lightly cover seed; thin out up to 30cm (1ft) apart. Preferably, sow in seed bed; transplant into growing bed and keep moist; move to final positions in autumn. Plants can be propagated by division of the roots in March or April.

Water Avens, a plant that had remained unnoticed in Britain until the early seventeenth century, takes its name from the more familiar Wood Avens *(G. urbanum)*. The name Avens is of obscure origin but the generic name *Geum* almost certainly refers to the aromatic root of the common species.

Water Avens is a European native more common in the north and east than in the south and west. In Britain it is found more frequently in Scotland and northern England than elsewhere. It is a moisture-loving plant, inhabiting damp woods, ditches and the water's edge, sometimes growing in the open but tolerating quite dense shade.

This is a downy plant which sends up a flower stem to a height of 60cm (2ft) from a rosette of lobed leaves, the terminal lobe being considerably larger than the others. The drooping flowers are of a dull purplish-orange and the calyces are also tinged with purple. The fruits on the seed-head look as though they might be hooked but they end in a feathery point.

Water Avens is a most attractive plant for any damp position in the garden and is particularly useful, provided the soil is moist, in shady borders.

It mixes well with other plants, so is also suitable for wilder parts of the garden.

Wood Avens is not such a suitable plant for borders, being rather straggly, but it is a good plant in woodland conditions of the kind that it favours in the wild.

The deep green hairy leaves of this species are three-lobed, those at the base rather round while those growing from the stems are narrower. The stems can be 60cm (2ft) high and carry throughout summer small yellow flowers with turned-back petals. Unlike those of the Water Avens, the fruits on the seed-heads of this species are hooked.

Wood Avens is sometimes known as Herb Bennet, a corruption of *herba benedicta*, meaning 'blessed herb', for this plant has had a formidable reputation for warding off the forces of evil. The clove scent of its root may be the primitive source of the belief in its virtue.

All the old authorities reckoned it a valuable medicinal herb, recommending it to be taken steeped in wine. Because of its smell the root was chewed to clean the breath and it was sometimes added as a flavouring to ale. It was believed that the roots, placed among linen, would preserve it from moths.

# WHITE DEAD-NETTLE
## *Lamium album*

**Flowering season**
March to December.

**Suitable growing conditions**
Free-draining rough or bare ground; moderately fertile soil that is not excessively acid or alkaline; a position in full sun.

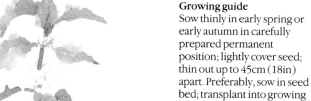

**Growing guide**
Sow thinly in early spring or early autumn in carefully prepared permanent position; lightly cover seed; thin out up to 45cm (18in) apart. Preferably, sow in seed bed; transplant into growing bed; move to final positions in autumn. Plants are easily propagated by division of the roots in October or March.

The superficial resemblance of the Dead-nettles to Stinging Nettle *(Urtica dioica)* has earned them their common name, 'dead' referring to the fact that they do not sting. When they are in flower it is clear that the Dead-nettles belong to a different family and they can be distinguished quite readily. Early in the year it is more difficult to pick out White Dead-nettle when it is growing in association with Stinging Nettle, which it frequently does. The Dead-nettle's square and hollow stems are, however, distinctive. Perhaps the common names Archangel and White Archangel refer to a belief that the plant gave protection from evil spirits.

This native European perennial, which is also found in other parts of the temperate world as an introduced species, is common as a wayside and hedgerow plant, particularly on fertile soils.

The plant has a spreading root system so that it is often found in large clumps. The stems, with paired nettle-like leaves, grow from 20 to 60cm (8 to 24in) tall. The greenish-white flowers are arranged in rings just above a pair of leaves. Usually a ring contains five to eight flowers but occasionally the whorl can be much more densely packed. A pretty local name from Somerset, Adam-and-Eve-in-the-Bower, refers to the black anthers that look like two little figures sheltering under the hooded upper lip. The arrangement of the flower favours pollination by large Bumble-bees. A barrier of hairs prevents shorter-tongued and smaller insects from reaching the generous supply of nectar, although some cheat the flower by piercing the tube at its base.

The White Dead-nettle can be an aggressive colonizer so that it is not something to combine with choice small plants. However, clumps of it in rougher parts of the garden are very attractive. At any one time throughout six months of a year you are likely to find at least one plant carrying flowers. In really fertile soil leafy growth can obscure the flowers. On poorer soil their rather neglected beauty is more obvious. In any case flowers picked for indoor decoration show up better if some of the leaves are cut away.

Purple Dead-nettle (*L. purpureum*), also known as Purple Archangel, is a very common annual that can be found almost everywhere in Britain. Its purplish flowers, which are carried in rings near the top of the plant, are conspicuous early in the year but their long season is often forgotten when other plants take over. Gerard says that the flowers can be 'baked with sugar as roses are'.

# WILD CARROT

## *Daucus carota*

**Flowering season**
June to August.

**Suitable growing conditions**
Well-drained mini-grassland; reasonably fertile neutral to alkaline soil; a position in full sun.

**Growing guide**
Sow thinly in autumn in carefully prepared permanent position; lightly cover seed; in spring, thin out to 45cm (18in) apart. Artificial stratification is necessary if sowing in spring (see page 106). Preferably sow in autumn in pots; over winter in sheltered spot outdoors; in spring, prick out into pots; move to final position in mid autumn, taking care not to disturb the tap-root.

It often requires a great leap of imagination to connect the cultivated vegetables that are such an important part of our diet with the plants from which they have been developed. As it happens, the parent of the cultivated Carrot is a sub-species of the Wild Carrot that is so common in the British Isles and other parts of Europe but it is still surprising that a fleshy root can have been developed from something that must be very similar to the woody root-stock of the wild plant which is familiar to us.

Wild Carrot is a biennial member of the Umbelliferae (often referred to as the Carrot family). In the British Isles it is frequently found on grassy wasteland or in fields, particularly near the sea or where the ground is chalky.

The branching stems, which are ridged and hairy, form an erect plant up to 60cm (2ft) in height. The leaves are a very attractive feature, being much divided, with the lower ones very much larger than those further up the stems. Flowering starts in early summer, the dense flat heads being as much as 75mm (3in) across. They are usually white but sometimes appear to be stained light purple. In white flowerheads the central flower is very often crimson. The local name Bird's Nest refers to the shape of the spiny seed-head, which is even more beautiful than the flowering umbel. Because of their long spines the fruits readily cling to the coats of animals, so aiding the spread of the plant.

Wild Carrot is an outstanding plant to include in a flowering meadow: it is beautiful in all its parts, it is attractive to a wide range of insects and after a long flowering season it has attractive seed-heads that are splendid for indoor decoration.

In times of famine people have turned to the roots of the Wild Carrot for food but it has never been much used for culinary purposes. The ancient Greeks considered it an aphrodisiac; however, it has generally been put to more sober medical uses.

Another umbellifer to be found on dry grassland, particularly on chalk, and one that is probably the parent of the cultivated plant bearing the same name is the Wild Parsnip *(Pastinaca sativa)*. The root of this sturdy species, which has lime-yellow flowers, is edible but in comparing it with the root of the cultivated plant Culpeper says that it 'is shorter, more woody and not so fit to be eaten and, therefore, more medicinal'.

# WILD DAFFODIL
*Narcissus pseudonarcissus*

**Flowering season**
February to April.

**Suitable growing conditions**
Reasonably moist ground in mini-meadows or borders; slightly acid or neutral soils of moderate fertility; positions in full sun or partial shade, including deciduous woodland.

**Growing guide**
Plants raised from seed take from three to six years to reach flowering size. Sow thinly in shallow drills in a growing bed in autumn; cover seed; in spring, thin out as required. After two or three years, move to final positions 10-20cm (4-8in) apart. Plant bulbs 5cm (2in) deep in clumps in early autumn.

The proliferation of Daffodil varieties is by no means a uniquely modern phenomenon. Writing in 1629 John Parkinson affirms that 'Of Daffodils there are almost an hundred sorts . . . every one to be distinguished from other, both in their times, formes, and colours'. The Wild Daffodil or Lent Lily has played an important part in the breeding that has resulted in the welter of varieties now available to the gardener, few of which ever grow with such convincing naturalness in damp meadows or woodland as the modest parent.

The name Lent Lily clearly refers to the flowering season but Daffodil and the more picturesque Daffydowndilly are corruptions of Asphodel, the flower of the classical underworld with which it was at one time erroneously associated.

Most authorities consider that the wild species is very variable with many distinct forms, having a wide distribution in western Europe, from Spain to Britain. Others view this complex of closely related plants as a number of separate species or as several species each with a series of subspecies.

The typical Lent Lily as found in Britain either wild or, more commonly, naturalized in old parks and woods, rarely grows more than 45cm (18in) high, the grey-green leaves often slightly shorter than the flower stem. The solitary flowers have creamy yellow petals with a trumpet, about 50cm (2in) long, of a deeper yellow.

There can hardly be a garden that does not have the space for a small clump at least of these most cheering flowers. They are seen to best advantage when allowed the space and time to build up large colonies in grass in company with other spring-flowering plants. After they have flowered they need to be left for a good six to eight weeks before the foliage is cut down. This means that mowing cannot begin until the middle or end of June but such a regime suits other spring flowers. If you are planting bulbs in lawns, it is best to keep clumps to edges and corners so that the central area of grass can be cut in spring and early summer. If you have your own bulbs the Daffodil is a very good plant for cutting, but remember never to take flowers from the wild.

The Daffodil is a happy case of a plant that the old authorities have valued more for its beauty than for any other virtues. The whole plant, but especially the bulb, is in some degree toxic. A number of cases have been reported of bulbs having been cooked and eaten, in the mistaken belief that they were onions, with unpleasant effects.

# WILD MARJORAM
## *Origanum vulgare*

**Flowering season**
July to September.

**Suitable growing conditions**
Well-drained ground in the border, herb garden or wild parts of the garden; neutral to alkaline soils of low fertility; an open sunny position.

**Growing guide**
Sow thinly in early spring or early autumn in carefully prepared permanent position; lightly cover seed; thin out up to 30cm (1ft) apart. Preferably, sow in seed bed; transplant into growing bed; move to final positions in autumn. Plants are easily propagated by division of the roots or from basal shoot cuttings in spring.

S weet Marjoram *(Origanum majorana)*, introduced to northern Europe from the Mediterranean region, has long been regarded as one of the subtlest culinary herbs. Pot Marjoram *(Origanum onites)*, a rather inferior culinary herb, was introduced to northern Europe in the eighteenth century. The native Marjoram or Oregano did not go entirely unnoticed: Culpeper remarks that various kinds of Marjoram 'grow commonly in gardens; some sorts there are that grow wild in the borders or corn fields, and pastures in sundry places of this land'. The botanical generic name, derived from Greek words for 'mountain' and 'joy', alludes to the loveliness of hillsides on which the plants bloom.

Throughout its range in Europe, including the British Isles, and western Asia, Marjoram is reasonably common, particularly on chalky soils. It is a plant of downland, hedgerows and verges.

Marjoram is a perennial that grows from a creeping root-stock, forming a rather hairy woody-stemmed aromatic bush up to 75cm (30in) tall. The leaves, which are about 25mm (1in) long, have a smooth or slightly toothed edge and are arranged in pairs. The small pink flowers, which form loose bunches at the top of the bush, have the characteristic form found in plants in the Mint family, to which Marjoram belongs.

It is worth reserving a place in the border or a corner of the herb garden for this well-flavoured native. Not only is it an attractive plant but it can also be used in cooking in much the same way as Sweet Marjoram, although it is a less refined culinary herb. Another way to use it is as part of a grass and flower mixture on rather poor alkaline soils. On a rich soil grasses will offer too much competition. Wherever it grows it will be an attractive nectar plant for bees and butterflies.

As well as being an excellent flavouring for meat dishes, the young leaves used discreetly make a piquant addition to salads. It is said that the leaves become sweeter when dried so it would be worth gathering and hanging up bunches in an airy room. Rub the leaves down and store in airtight jars as soon as they are brittle.

Various medicinal properties have been attributed to the plant. Culpeper, repeating antique wisdom, recommended it to treat the 'bitings of venomous beasts' and to help 'such as have poisoned themselves by eating hemlock, henbane or opium'. Marjoram tea helped less dramatic conditions, namely colds and fevers.

# WILD MIGNONETTE
## *Reseda lutea*

**Flowering season**
May to August.

**Suitable growing conditions**
Well-drained ground in
borders or rougher parts of
the garden; any soil that is
not excessively acid; a
position in full sun.

**Growing guide**
Sow thinly in early autumn
or early spring in carefully
prepared permanent
position; lightly cover seed;
thin out up to 30cm (1ft)
apart. Artificial stratification
is beneficial if sowing in
spring (see page 106).
Preferably, sow in a pot;
prick out into pots as soon as
possible; move to final
position in mid autumn,
taking care not to disturb the
short stout root.

The cultivated Mignonette *(R. odorata)*, an annual celebrated for its delicious sweet scent, is a native of North Africa. Wild Mignonette is a true European native and one that is common on chalk soils. In Britain it is a plant of the south and east rather than the north and west, but it is rarely seen growing in great numbers. It is most frequently found on disturbed ground at the side of roads and where earth has been ploughed.

Wild Mignonette is sometimes perennial but it commonly fades after flowering profusely in its second year. It makes a freely branched plant up to 60cm (2ft) tall with numerous divided leaves. The flower season begins in mid-spring and continues right through the summer; the spikes of greenish-yellow flowers are densely packed and surprisingly conspicuous although each flower is very small. Sadly this plant does not have the magical fragrance of its North African relative.

Wild Mignonette is a quiet unspectacular plant but one with a long flowering season, which is extended if the plant is grown in border conditions free of competition. Despite having almost no scent it is very attractive to insects and a useful source of nectar.

A closely related plant is Weld *(R. luteola)*. This is a native biennial that is common on chalky soils and, like Wild Mignonette, generally found where ground has been disturbed. It sends down a deep tap-root and in the first season forms a rosette of leaves. The flowering stem that develops in the second year can grow to a height of 150cm (5ft), the top portion forming a long flowering spike that makes an attractive, long-lasting cut flower. The flowers, which start to appear in early summer, are of a similar yellowish-green to those of the Wild Mignonette.

Another name for this plant is Dyer's Rocket, giving a clue to its great importance in medieval times as one of the main sources of yellow dye. It gives a very good colour that is fast in wool. As a result, Dyer's Rocket had much the same status as Woad and Madder, the sources respectively of blue and red dyes. So great was the demand for the dye that it could not be met from collections in the wild. Not only was the plant cultivated, but also quantities were imported from France. With the renewed interest in natural dyes in recent years, Weld is again being used to give a pure and reliable colour.

# WILD STRAWBERRY
## *Fragaria vesca*

**Flowering season**
April to July; fruit,
June to August.

**Suitable growing
conditions**
Well-drained ground
in wild parts of the
garden; alkaline or
slightly acid soils of
reasonable fertility; a
sunny or partly
shaded position.

**Growing guide**
Sow thinly in early
spring or early
autumn in permanent
position; lightly cover
seed; thin out up to
30cm (1ft) apart.
Preferably, sow in
seed bed; transplant
into growing bed;
move to final
positions in autumn.

The labour of collecting the delicious but tiny fruits of the Wild Strawberry has counted against it being grown for cropping ever since the introduction of the North American and Chilean species from which the modern garden strawberries have been developed. In some parts of Europe, however, the fruits are still much more commonly gathered than they are in Britain, being greatly valued as delicacies for their sweetness and flavour.

The Wild Strawberry is a common plant in Europe, including the British Isles, Asia and many other parts of the temperate world to which it has been introduced. It is found in woods and hedges on alkaline soils but also sometimes in great numbers on chalk. It seems that the seed can sometimes lie dormant for long periods before the right conditions favour germination. In *The Natural History of Selborne* Gilbert White writes of naked ground being covered by Strawberry plants within a year or two of old beech trees being cleared. He continues: 'One of the slidders or trenches down the middle of the Hanger, close covered over with lofty beeches near a century old, is still called Strawberry slidder, though no Strawberries have grown there in the memory of man.'

This creeping perennial grows from a sturdy root-stock, producing a rosette of toothed bright green leaves arranged in threes. On the underside these are paler with a silky down. The plant throws out numerous arching runners, which touch down to form independently rooted plants. The five-petalled white flowers with yellow centres are carried on stems up to 25cm (10in) high but the flowers, as the fruit, are often hidden in the leaves.

There is nothing new in bringing Wild Strawberries into the garden and in fact when the Wild Strawberry is grown in good conditions it bears more heavily. If we are to believe the Bishop of Ely in *King Henry the Fifth*, '... wholesome berries thrive and ripen best Neighbour'd by fruit of baser quality'.

Judged simply as a pretty plant, the Wild Strawberry is an attractive addition to the garden but it is too free-running to introduce incautiously into borders. It is best where its unchecked romping will cause no anxieties, particularly in semi-shade at the bottom of hedges or under trees.

The Wild Strawberry features in numerous medicinal and cosmetic preparations (the juice, for example, was used to clean teeth) but the rare flavour of its fruit has always been its chief virtue.

# WILD THYME
### *Thymus praecox* subsp. *arcticus*

**Flowering season**
July to August.

**Suitable growing conditions**
Well-drained ground among other plants or on its own; neutral to alkaline soil of low fertility; a position in full sun.

**Growing guide**
Sow thinly in early spring or early autumn in carefully prepared permanent position; barely cover seed; thin as required; spread can be up to 60cm (2ft). Preferably, sow in a pot; prick out into pots or trays; move to final positions in autumn. Plants can be propagated by division in September or March or by cuttings in May or June.

Garden Thyme *(Thymus vulgaris)*, so familiar as a culinary herb, is a native of the Mediterranean region, although it is easily grown in cooler areas. It is justly ranked above the other Thymes for its culinary value but all the many kinds of Thyme are shrubby aromatic herbs that share some of its qualities. The Wild Thyme found in Britain and other parts of Europe has, surprisingly, simply taken over the classical name, which is probably derived from a word meaning 'to fumigate' and refers to the plant's use as a sweet-smelling incense. Sometimes a qualifier anchors the name more firmly in a local tradition: Bank Thyme, Horse Thyme and Shepherd's Thyme are self-explanatory; Mother Thyme or Mother of Thyme probably alludes to the herb's use in the treatment of women in childbirth.

Wild Thyme is a reasonably common perennial of open places, particularly chalk downlands and upland areas, where it often forms cushion-like mats beneath a canopy of grass heads. It is said that sheep pastured on downland will crop it closely and some believe that this and other herbs give their meat a superior flavour.

The root-stock and stems of this sub-shrub are woody and the trailing branches with small paired leaves often rise no more than 10cm (4in) above the ground. In less exposed positions, however, the plant can grow in a more upright manner, reaching a height of 30cm (12in). The purplish flowerheads are conspicuous for the size of the plant and in the mass stain banks and slopes with their subtle colour.

Wild Thyme is much less aromatic than the garden variety, and can therefore never replace it as a garden herb. In its own right, though, it is a lowly creeping thing of great charm, a lovely plant to establish in grass on a sunny bank or to introduce into a rough lawn. It can even be used on its own to make a lawn that is beautifully springy and fragrant. Because it will make cushiony growth and will stand light wear, Wild Thyme is an excellent plant to lodge in paving, where it will work its way along cracks, thriving on a very meagre diet. In the rock garden it may sometimes need checking but can be successfully underplanted with vigorous small bulbs, which will come up through it in early spring.

Wild Thyme is an excellent nectar plant for a wide range of insects although it will never flavour honey as intensely as the Garden Thyme on the slopes of Mount Hymettus.

# WILD WALLFLOWER
## *Cheiranthus cheiri*

**Flowering season**
April to June.

**Suitable growing conditions**
Sharply drained ground in borders or in walls and rough banks; neutral to alkaline soil of poor or reasonable fertility; a positon in full sun.

**Growing guide**
Sow thinly in spring or autumn in carefully prepared permanent position; cover seed; thin out up to 20-30cm (8-12in) apart. Preferably sow in seed bed; transplant; move to final positions in autumn.

Precisely when the Wallflower was introduced as an ornamental to Britain and by whom is not known. Now it is probably the most widely planted biennial, its sweet warm scent and velvety blooms more firmly associated with mild spring days than the features of almost any other garden flower. For this we have to thank its popularity as a cottage garden plant. Whenever it was that this unassuming flower of southern Europe arrived in Britain – and it is certain that it was a favourite by the sixteenth century, when it often went by the name Wall Gilliflower – it took to its new environment to the extent that for several hundred years at least it has flourished as a near native, doing best where many plants could not find a toehold, let alone extract a living.

As a naturalized plant, Wallflowers are most commonly found growing on rocky outcrops, on cliffs, on crumbling and derelict buildings and on old walls. In these conditions it grows as a perennial; it appears that its chances of a long life are apparently improved by its having to scratch a meagre living.

As a wilding the Wallflower is a smaller plant than in its cultivated forms, rarely as tall as 60cm (2ft) and often making a rather spindly bush with woody stems bare at the base. The upper portion of the stem is rather crowded with pointed deep green leaves. The typical crucifer flowers, smaller than those of the cultivated forms, are bright yellow and wonderfully fragrant. The flowers are at their best in late spring and early summer but plants will sometimes continue to bloom over a long season.

This is an easy plant to grow in the garden, where a large patch of it can be used to attract butterflies and other insects. In borders it can be used in much the same way as the garden varieties. It is then probably best treated as they are, that is as a biennial that is sown in the late spring of one year for flowering in the spring and summer of the next. Plants will live on after flowering but if what you want is a bold and solid display of colour you may be disappointed by plants that then become rather straggly.

Good though it can be in a border, the Wild Wallflower looks best when it is encouraged to colonize the apparently inhospitable habitats where it has proved it can get a foothold and make a living. If you are lucky enough to have an old wall it is worth making some effort to get it started but once it is away it will self-seed freely.

# WILD WHITE CLOVER
## *Trifolium repens*

**Flowering season**
May to September.

**Suitable growing conditions**
Well-drained mini-grassland or bare ground; acid or alkaline soils ranging from poor to highly fertile; a position in full sun.

**Growing guide**
Sow thinly in early spring or early autumn in carefully prepared permanent position; lightly cover seed; thin as required; spread can be indefinite. Preferably, sow in seed bed; transplant into growing bed; move to final positions in autumn.

The Pea family includes many plants of out-standing economic importance. The Clovers are an example of plants that may be insignificant to the eye but that have an agricultural importance which it is difficult to exaggerate. The familiar expression 'to be in Clover' reminds us of how in a world more concerned with rural matters their rich feed represented the ultimate in luxurious living. The Clovers that dominate modern agriculture have moved a long way from the wild plants that were once constituents of pasture and weeds of wasteland. The White (or Dutch) Clover that is now sown in grazing land is the result of selective breeding that has produced a larger and more robust plant than that found in the wild in really old pasture. If you are looking for seeds of the wild plant a small number of merchants do supply it.

Before the seventeenth century the more common spelling of the old Anglo-Saxon name was Claver, which still survives in such place-names as Claverdon in Warwickshire. The name may be derived from the Latin word for a club, the arrangement of three leaves being likened to the three-headed club of Hercules.

White Clover is a creeping perennial, with prostrate stems that root very readily as they develop. The leaflets, arranged characteristically in threes, are carried on upright stalks up to 30cm (12in) high. The leaflets are generally marked with a whitish band at the base. The white flowers, which are sometimes tinged pink, are borne in dense globular heads on slightly longer stems than the leaves. Flowering starts in early summer and after pollination the dead flowers remain, brown and drooping, while the seeds develop.

For traditional gardeners White Clover is often a major headache, as a weed of lawns indicating a shortage of nitrogen. For the person establishing wild plants in the garden it is an attractive constituent of a flowering mini-meadow and to enjoy it at its peak grass should not be cut until July at the earliest. It can even be used in the way that Chamomile sometimes is to make a lawn on its own. Although the foliage is not aromatic, in such a dense planting you will be able to enjoy to the full the sweetness of its flowers. If checked, it can make a pretty low-growing clump in a border.

All the Clovers are important nectar plants and White Clover is probably the source of more honey than any other single flower. This sweet harvest is in itself a very good reason for growing Clovers, which are also food plants for the caterpillars of several butterflies and moths, including those of the Common Blue and Mother Shipton.

# WOOD ANEMONE
*Anemone nemorosa*

**Flowering season**
March to May.

**Suitable growing conditions**
Well-drained ground in wilder parts of the garden; slightly acid to markedly alkaline soils of reasonable or high fertility; a position that is open in early spring although it can be densely shaded in summer.

**Growing guide**
Plants raised from seed often take two to four years to produce flowers. Sow thinly in early autumn or spring in a pot; lightly cover seed; prick out into a tray; move to growing bed in autumn and grow for one or two years before planting out in final positions up to 15cm (6in) apart.

According to Pliny, the Anemone, the flower of windy places and sometimes simply called Windflower in English, owes its name to the fact that it opens its flower not of its own accord but only when the wind blows. He almost certainly was thinking of the more brightly coloured *Anemone coronaria* but the name Windflower does seem appropriate for the Wood Anemone when sheets of flowers are set trembling by the blasting winds of March. Local names include Crowfoot and Smell fox, the former referring to the shape of the leaves, the latter to the faint but disquieting smell.

The Wood Anemone, a perennial, is a widely distributed plant in Europe and western Asia, in Britain being a common species of deciduous woodland. Although it is not hard to please, it prefers moist soils and when conditions suit it the creeping underground rhizomes spread freely, quickly building up large flowering colonies.

The single flowers are borne on slender stems up to 25cm (10in) high, which also carry three deeply divided leaves. These protect the developing bud but the flower opens well above them. The flowers are up to 40mm (1½in) across and consist of six or seven white petal-like segments, slightly flushed on the reverse, with a little yellow boss in the centre. Even in wild populations specimens can be found with flowers that are tinted blue or pink. At night and in bad weather the flowers close and droop. The fruits form a downy globular cluster. By early summer the plant has disappeared, depending on its fleshy root-stock to see it through to the following spring.

The Wood Anemone has long been admired by gardeners, who have brought selected forms into cultivation. These generally have larger flowers than the wild plant, markedly blue or pink in tone and occasionally double. However, in the wild garden such as in woodland, underplanting small clumps or trees, at the foot of hedges and even in more open positions, it is the broad effect of ground strewn prettily with starry flowers that the Wood Anemone creates so effectively in early spring. For this effect the simple wild plant is as appropriate as any of the selected forms.

Preparations of the plant were once widely employed in various remedies. Culpeper advised chewing the root. However, the Wood Anemone is a member of the Buttercup family and like other members is poisonous to animals and to humans. On the skins of those who are allergic the juices can cause blistering.

# YARROW
## *Achillea millefolium*

**Flowering season**
June to November.

**Suitable growing conditions**
Well-drained ground in the border or wild parts of the garden; slightly acid to alkaline soils of reasonable fertility; a position in full sun.

**Growing guide**
Sow thinly in early spring or early autumn in carefully prepared permanent position; barely cover seed; thin out up to 30cm (1ft). Preferably, sow in seed bed; transplant into growing bed; move to final positions in autumn. Plants are easily propagated by division of the root clumps which is best done in early spring.

As one might expect of a plant that is so common on roadsides, dry grassland and wasteland, Yarrow has many common and local names.

Yarrow descends directly from its Anglo-Saxon name but Nosebleed and Carpenter's Weed refer to the belief that the leaves could staunch bleeding. The same belief underlies the botanical generic name for, it is said, this is the herb that the Greek hero Achilles used to heal the wounds of his men. Milfoil, another name by which it is known, is simply an anglicized form of the specific name, which refers to the fine divisions of its foliage.

Yarrow is common throughout Europe and western Asia and has inadvertently been spread to many parts of the world. In *The Herball* of 1597 John Gerard gives a sharp portrait of a plant many loathe as a pestilential lawn weed. He says that it 'hath a thicke rough roote, with strings fastened thereto; from which immediately rise up divers stalkes, very greene and crested, whereupon do growe long leaves composed of many small jagges, cut even to the middle rib; the flowers stand at the top of the stalkes in spokie umbles or tufts, of a yellowish colour, and pleasant smell'. Wild plants, which grow to a height of 60cm (2ft), show some variation in flower colour, ranging from dingy white to yellow, pink and red forms.

Many gardeners have laboured prodigiously to exclude Yarrow from their territory, cursing it for its invasive roots and its capacity to self-seed very freely. Others have recognized in it a plant of considerable ornamental value. For those who do not require a tightly controlled and manicured garden Yarrow is a splendid plant for a flowering meadow, combining well with other summer-flowering plants. More than most wild flowers it is tolerant of mowing, something that those who are scrupulous about their lawns find rather tiresome. This tolerance means, however, that it can be sown in meadows with widely varying mowing regimes.

Wherever it is grown, as a constituent of a hayfield or as a clump in the border, Yarrow is a useful summer nectar plant for butterflies and other insects. Some maintain that it has a favourable influence on other plants, merely by its presence giving them vigour. It makes an excellent flower for cutting and for drying.

All the old authorities rank Yarrow as a valuable medicinal plant. Yarrow tea, for most an infusion needing sweetening, has been widely used as a remedy for colds.

# YELLOW RATTLE
*Rhinanthus minor*

**Flowering season**
May to August.

**Suitable growing conditions**
Reasonably dry mini-grassland; acid to mildly alkaline soil of low to average fertility; a position in full sun.

**Growing guide**
For a border clump, sow thinly with two parts low-maintenance grass seed mixture, in early spring or early autumn, in carefully prepared permanent position; cover seed; do not remove the grass seedlings; thin out as required. Preferably, sow as part of a wild flower or grass and wild flower mixture in early spring or autumn.

Yellow Rattle is a pretty annual of grassland and roadsides but its sweet demeanour hides a scrounging nature. It is semi-parasitic, contriving to tap the root system of the grasses among which it grows, taking up nutrients and water that they extract from the ground. It can reduce the quality of grassland in which it grows and in the past it is said to have been a troublesome weed in rye, greatly reducing the harvest if not checked in time.

It has many local names, most of which refer to the way the seeds rattle in the capsule when they are ripe. The generic name *Rhinanthus*, from Greek words meaning 'nose' and 'flower', refer to the hooked shape of the petal tube.

Yellow Rattle develops quickly into an erect mature plant. The rigid stem, which can be up to 60cm (2ft) but is generally rather less, is smooth and irregularly spotted purplish-black. The narrow oblong leaves are rough, toothed and conspicuously veined. The yellow flowers, which begin to open in late spring, have large lime-green calyces. These are swollen at the base but contract at the mouth where the tube emerges so that it looks rather pinched by the four calyx teeth. The large upper lip curves over two violet teeth; the lower lip is divided into three small segments, of which the middle one is the largest.

Although the farmer may not see this plant as benign, it is a characteristic feature of meadowland, where its particular quality of yellowness is quite distinctive. When recreating a mini-meadow, either by the gradual transformation of a lawn or by a more radical approach involving the resowing of a whole area, Yellow Rattle ought to be included in the sowing mixture. If anything, the goodness it takes from grasses will benefit other wild flowers growing with it, for most do best when grasses do not compete too aggressively.

Yellow Rattle was believed to be an effective treatment of eye conditions, either taken internally or applied to the eyes.

Two other plants that are semi-parasitic on grasses are Eyebright *(Euphrasia officinalis)* and Lousewort *(Pedicularis sylvatica)*, sometimes known as Dwarf Red Rattle. Of these the former shared with Yellow Rattle a reputation as a cure for eye complaints.

Lousewort is a plant of damper pasture. It earned its name in the mistaken belief that sheep became diseased and lousy because of eating it, when the condition of the animals was the direct consequence of their poor pasture.

# WILD FLOWERS IN THE GARDEN

One approach to gardening with wild plants that at first sight might appear very attractive is simply to abandon any attempt at cultivation and management. What a seductive proposition this can seem when we are pinned to a wall trying to prune an obstreperous rose or achingly double-digging the vegetable garden.

I must make clear at the outset that the kind of gardening with wild flowers that I recommend is not an excuse for total neglect. Quite a lot of work may be needed in the initial stages, for instance if you are going to create a successful flowering meadow, and, although in the long term gardening with wild flowers will be less arduous than conventional gardening, it does call for a certain level of sustained basic management. Otherwise you may find yourself a suburban Sleeping Beauty trapped in a miniature tangled forest.

However, there is no need to make unnecessary labour out of gardening with wild flowers. By answering two elementary questions before embarking on any major schemes you can save yourself a great deal of work and also a lot of disappointment. How do you want to use your garden? What growing conditions does it offer?

A garden containing wild flowers, just like any other garden, has to satisfy many requirements, ranging from the severely practical to the aesthetic and romantic. You need somewhere to hang out the washing and to tuck away the rubbish bins. You prefer the view from close neighbours to be screened so that there is the sense at least of privacy. You want a clear area in a sunny part of the garden for sitting out and relaxing. There must be a spot within sight of the living-room where there is space for a children's sandpit. Notwithstanding, you would like to create the feeling of a small woodland glade in the remnants of an orchard, a summer border of cornfield annuals at the bottom of the lawn or a stretch of mini-meadow that will be thick with bulbs and other spring flowers. There is no simple solution to the competing claims that we make on our increasingly small gardens but you can make a start by drawing up a ranked list of priorities.

It helps, too, if you draw up a reasonably accurate plan of your garden, indicating the position of the house, any other buildings and main features, including trees, all points of access and paths. Mark the compass point North to make it easier to read those parts of the garden that will be in full sun and those that will be in part or full shade.

Your assessment must also establish what kind of soil you have in your garden, how well drained it is and to what extent areas of the garden are shaded through the day.

If you have been living in the same place for any length of time you will probably know whether your soil is acid or alkaline. At first this seems a curious subject for gardeners to concern themselves with. While a number of plants will tolerate both acid and alkaline conditions there are others, however, that are quite particular. Those who have had conventional gardens on chalky soil will know that several important categories of ornamentals, including Rhododendrons and Camellias, will not thrive on these alkaline soils. Some European wild flowers, Heather being the best-known example, are also lime-haters. On the other hand, a number of very attractive wild flowers show a marked preference for the thin alkaline soils of chalky downland, among them being Horseshoe Vetch, Rockrose and Wild Thyme.

Talking to your neighbours and observing what is in their gardens will give you a good idea of how acid or alkaline the soil in your area is.

By using a simple soil-testing kit, of the kind readily available in hardware stores and garden centres, you will be able to get a more accurate reading of the acidity or alkalinity of your soil. This is measured on a pH scale that runs from 0 to 14, a neutral soil giving a reading of 7, acid soils give readings below 7, alkaline soils above.

Few soils are the well-drained but moisture retentive fertile loams so beloved of gardening correspondents. The best way to find out about the structure and quality of the soil in your garden is by working it with a spade or fork. You will soon be able to tell if it is a heavy clay, light and sandy, moist and rich in humus, or thin and crumbly. Not all parts of the garden are likely to be drained to the same degree even though some soils are in general much freer draining than others. Find out where there are damp pockets and where you have got a dry sunny slope and add this information to the plan of your garden.

Plants vary enormously in their tolerance of shade so before you begin any planting you should work out the areas of the garden that enjoy full sun and the degrees of shade that are cast in other parts of the garden. The shade on the north side of buildings and walls and in the vicinity of evergreen trees can be heavy and unrelieved but under deciduous trees the ground can be fully exposed to sunlight in spring, when many interesting woodland plants flower. Even later in the year many deciduous trees will probably cast only a light dappled shade.

This process of assembling information may seem unnecessarily laborious, although I have discovered that most people interested in establishing wild flowers find it a comfortable lead-in to the quiet pleasures of making a wild garden. With wild flowers we stand a much better chance than ever we do with cultivated varieties of matching a plant to the conditions in which it grows best without having to make radical adjustments to soil and drainage. Knowing the ecological niches that our garden has to offer is the beginning of success in the growing of wild flowers.

Another part of the pattern that should not be neglected is the natural vegetation of the area in which you live. For those who live in towns and cities it is very hard to get any sense of the sort of plants that might once have grown on areas now covered by miles of road and acres of buildings. Those who live in small towns and villages, however, should be able to get a much better feel of the plants that belong to the locality. When you are out walking, note the wild flowers that you see growing in hedgerows, meadows and woodland because it is plants such as these that you will probably find you are able to grow most successfully in your own garden.

### Mixing wild flowers and cultivated plants

To combine wild flowers with ordinary garden plants might seem like an admission of defeat before you have even begun. Many busy gardeners will, however, welcome a chance to test their cultivation techniques on a limited range of wild flowers before embarking on a grander scheme. Starting with a few wild flowers growing among other ornamentals may also be the best way of converting other members of your family to the merits of some of the showiest wild species. The reluctance of some to take up gardening with wild plants is often based on a belief that all species are going to be ragged untidy things with no merit recommending them other than their nativeness.

There is no doubt that gardening with wild flowers creates a looser, softer effect than you get with the formal arrangement of cultivated ornamentals. But it is precisely the sort of effect that many discriminating gardeners go to great trouble to achieve with the use of exotic plants.

The border is the obvious place to begin mixing wild and cultivated plants. Make your selection on the basis of the growing conditions available and also try to place wild flowers in company that shows them to good advantage. Among obvious favourites to start with are Cowslips and Primroses but if these are mixed with cultivated varieties of Polyanthus it will be to the detriment of the wild plants, which may seem altogether too subdued – and to the detriment of the garden plants, which will look too florid and coarse.

Good summer-flowering perennials that can hold their own with a wide range of cultivated plants include Musk Mallow, Jacob's-ladder, Meadow Crane's-bill and Purple-loosestrife. Their effect is almost always enhanced when grown in clumps rather than dotted about. A biennial of magnificent proportions that assorts well with many ornamentals is the Great Mullein, which can give any cottage garden an air of distinction.

Some of the low-growing wild flowers are excellent as a skirting to larger perennials and shrubs. Wild Pansy is one of the best for this purpose, making a good underplanting in rose beds and particularly useful with some of the older roses that have only one flush of flower.

A few wild flowers are also excellent for incorporating in hedges or as climbers working their way through other plants. One species of outstanding quality for this purpose is the Narrow-leaved Everlasting-pea, its purplish-red flowers making a good splash of colour in summer.

The purists may be disappointed by what they might see as a half-hearted attempt to garden with wild flowers but for many people growing them in combination with cultivated plants will be an excellent starting point and even in the long term the most convenient way to grow them. My only serious reservation about this use of wild flowers is that so often only a very limited range of species is tried. Once you have got started, branch out and try new species each year.

## A SHOW BORDER

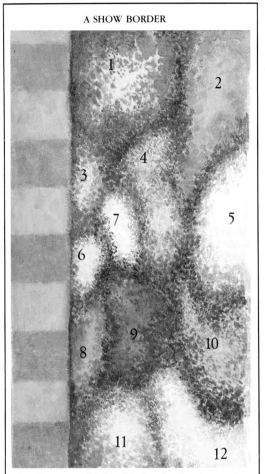

*The plants assembled in this show border give convincing proof that wild flowers can give a really colourful display. These plants respond well to good cultivation, growing more vigorously and flowering over a longer period than they do in the wild.*

1  Field Poppy, *Papaver rhoeas*
2  Soapwort, *Saponaria officinalis*
3  Wild Marjoram, *Origanum vulgare*
4  Betony, *Stachys officinalis*
5  Musk Mallow, *Malva moschata*
6  Columbine, *Aquilegia vulgaris*
7  Cowslip, *Primula veris*
8  Red Campion, *Silene dioica*
9  Common Toadflax, *Linaria vulgaris*
10  Sneezewort, *Achillea ptarmica*
11  Meadow Crane's-bill, *Geranium pratense*
12  Small Scabious, *Scabiosa columbaria*
13  Jacob's Ladder, *Polemonium caeruleum*

## Wild flowers in sunny borders

Even within the framework of a conventional garden you could decide to select wild species only as your plants. It could be argued that in this kind of gardening wild flowers are being expected to perform something like a circus act, masquerading as something that they are not. The simple fact is that our own wild flowers, like the wild flowers of many exotic countries, include some really beautiful plants that need no explanation or apology wherever they are grown. When skilfully planted in borders, combinations of these plants create effects that are worthy of the best conventional gardening but can also be ecologically sound.

Wild perennials can be used in much the same way as the constituents of the traditional herbaceous border. Just as with the conventional cultivated plants, height is an important factor to take into account when grouping the various kinds.

The most widely grown of the really tall plants are Foxglove, Great Mullein and Teasel, all of which are suitable as backing for shorter perennials. To these three could be added Common Evening-primrose and Purple-loosestrife, the former growing to 90cm (3ft), the latter reaching 1.2m (4ft).

There are many plants to choose from for the middle ground of a bed, including Red Campion, White Campion and Ragged-Robin (all three lovely members of the Pink family), Meadow Crane's-bill (a plant that understandably has been commandeered by the nursery trade), Field Scabious, the Knapweeds and Meadow buttercup. Greater Stitchwort, Lady's Bedstraw and Selfheal might make an interesting alternative as low-growing plants to the more familiar Cowslip, Speedwells and Wild Pansy.

To get the best effect from any of these plants they really do need to be grown in clumps. Indeed it is better to have reasonable sized clumps of a few different kinds than odd plants of many different species. However, you could add to the plants of middle height single specimens of Feverfew, a prodigious seeder, and Viper's-bugloss, a plant with flowers of a very striking colour that makes a strong impact even when grown singly.

One of the easiest and loveliest borders to create in a free-draining sunny part of the garden

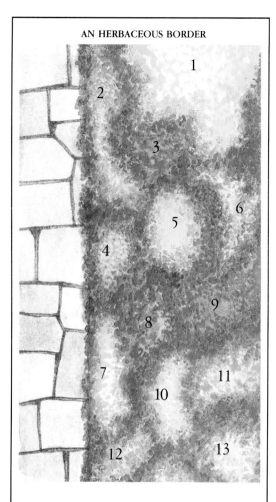

**AN HERBACEOUS BORDER**

*The traditional herbaceous border depends for its effects on a happy combination of clumps of flowers arranged so that the taller plants do not obscure those of shorter growth. A well-chosen selection of wild flowers will give a long summer display.*

1  Meadow Crane's-bill, *Geranium pratense*
2  Teasel, *Dipsacus fullonum*
3  Heart's-ease, *Viola tricolor*
4  Field Scabious, *Knautia arvensis*
5  Primrose, *Primula vulgaris*
6  Cowslip, *Primula veris*
7  Wild Strawberry, *Fragaria vesca*
8  Ragged-Robin, *Lychnis flos-cuculi*
9  Red Campion, *Silene dioica*
10  Purple-loosestrife, *Lythrum salicaria*
11  Greater Knapweed, *Centaurea scabiosa*
12  Great Mullein, *Verbascum thapsus*

brings together some of the bright and attractive annuals that were once a conspicuous feature of cultivated land. The Corncockle, because its seed was formerly a poisonous contaminant of flour, is now hardly ever seen in the wild, its spread checked by efficient seed cleaning methods and the use of herbicides. Cornflower, too, is now rarely seen and even the Field Poppy no longer reddens the corn with the same lavish splendour it used to thirty or forty years ago. Deciding how we balance the demands of efficient agriculture and the survival of wild plants is too large a subject to embark on in this book but we can at least spare a nostalgic look back to the colourful weeds of the field that were once so familiar. If there is no longer a place for them in the field that is a reason in itself to bring them into the garden.

These annuals are best grown in drifts, tall ones, such as the three already mentioned, at the back of the border. With them you could grow Charlock, one of the quickest annuals to bring from seed to flowering, Corn Marigold, Field Forget-me-not and White Campion. Corn Chamomile and Scentless Mayweed can also be added, these two somewhat similar plants grown in combination between them giving an extended flowering season.

For a fringe of shorter plants you could grow Scarlet Pimpernel, the Speedwells or Wild Pansy.

### Wild flowers in shade

It is a common complaint that there is a shortage of interesting plants for the shady parts of the garden. There are plenty of shade-loving species and varieties among our native wild plants.

Some of the loveliest are woodlanders that come into flower early in the year while the trees are still bare and which have almost vanished by the time the canopy is in full leaf. Lesser Celandine, Wood Anemone and Wood-sorrel, three cheering flowers of spring, flourish in conditions that are shady in full summer. A spring collection for a shady corner or border could include as well as these some of the most popular wild flowers, such as Daffodils, Primroses, Bluebells and Sweet Violets. It is certainly worth trying to include some of the very early plants. Winter Aconite, for instance, shows its yellow globular flowers surrounded by bright green ruffs as early as February.

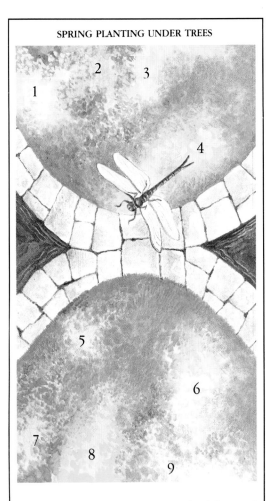

**SPRING PLANTING UNDER TREES**

*Even a single tree can be underplanted with flowers of woodland origin. A number of early-flowering plants are particularly suitable for growing under deciduous trees, making a striking springtime feature well before the trees have broken into leaf.*

1 Primrose, *Primula vulgaris*
2 Sweet Violet, *Viola odorata*
3 Lesser Celandine, *Ranunculus ficaria*
4 Archangel, *Lamiastrum galeobdolon*
5 Ground Ivy, *Glechoma hederacea*
6 Lords and Ladies, *Arum maculatum*
7 Wood Anemone, *Anemone nemorosa*
8 Wild Daffodil, *Narcissus pseudonarcissus*

This species is probably a naturalized plant in Britain, not a true native but it is likely that the Snowdrop, another delightful early flowerer, is a genuine but rare native. It would be interesting to know what proportion of the naturalized stock derives from plants sent back from the Crimea.

Lords and Ladies or Cuckoo Pint might not flower until mid-spring but it is a great asset in a shady corner of the garden for its leaves appear in the dead of winter, defying the coldest weather. The startling red of the fruit late in summer catches the eye even when the plant is growing in the darkest shade.

Stinking Hellebore is another unusual plant for early in the year. The dark, handsome foliage is worth having at any time, as many traditional gardeners recognize. But to this asset is added in late winter and early spring green flowers subtly finished with a deep maroon rim.

It might not be too frivolously macabre to set out with the intention of assembling a collection of poisonous plants, though nurturing a toxic medley might not go well with the successful rearing of a family. It is obviously sensible not to put temptation in the form of brightly coloured and poisonous fruit, such as those of Lords and Ladies, in the way of young children, but adults should be able to cope with the presence of poisonous wild plants just as they do the numerous poisonous cultivated varieties that are common in gardens.

Of the shade tolerant plants mentioned so far Lesser Celandine, Lords and Ladies, Stinking Hellebore, Winter Aconite and Wood Anemone are all poisonous to some degree. Among other plants of sinister fascination that could be added to these are both the Black and White Bryony, Dog's Mercury, Foxglove, Honeysuckle and various members of the Nightshade family.

### Wild flowers for damp places

Very few gardens contain a natural pond but the availability of flexible liners makes the creation of a small piece of water something that can be managed almost anywhere. Although the preformed rigid shapes that are also available sometimes attempt to imitate the outlines of a natural pool, in the garden they almost invariably look awkward and contrived.

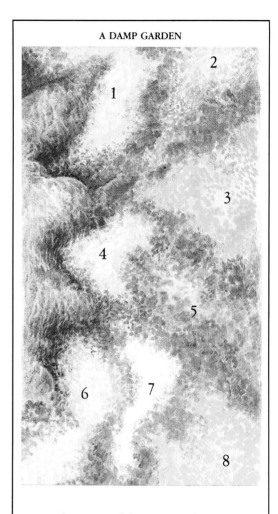

**A DAMP GARDEN**

*A natural or contrived damp area in the garden gives scope for growing some of the loveliest wild flowers, plants that grow lushly and produce an abundance of flower. The pond margin can accommodate plants that like their feet in water and those that prefer slightly drier conditions.*

1 Yellow Iris, *Iris pseudacorus*
2 Water Mint, *Mentha aquatica*
3 Meadowsweet, *Filipendula ulmaria*
4 Marsh-marigold, *Caltha palustris*
5 Brooklime, *Veronica beccabunga*
6 Water Avens, *Geum rivale*
7 Woundwort, *Stachys palustris*
8 Betony, *Stachus officinalis*
9 Monkeyflower, *Mimulus guttatus*
10 Purple-loosestrife, *Lythrum salicaria*

Of the liners, those made of synthetic rubber are the most expensive but also the most durable, provided they are well laid and there is no risk of them being punctured. Of the cheaper materials, nylon-reinforced PVC lasts longer than plastic.

Whatever kind of liner you use, it needs to be laid over a surface that is free of sharp stones, preferably a hole excavated so that there are deep and shallow areas. A layer of sand provides a sound base on which the liner can be laid. The shallow areas are particularly important for some of the emergent and marginal plants that like to have their feet in water. Many other plants of the water's edge do not want their roots submerged but nonetheless do best in quite boggy soil. One way of creating the damp conditions that suit them best is to extend the pond liner back from the water's edge by a metre or two (3-6ft), using it to line a soil-filled trough about 50-80cm (20-30in) deep. The liner of this trough can have a few holes pierced in it to allow excess moisture to drain away but the aim should be to imitate the boggy con-ditons that are often found at the edges of ponds and lakes and even slow-moving streams.

A natural stretch of water has distinct communi-ties of plants that belong to different water levels and to different degrees of dampness at the edge. The submerged oxygenators, such as Water Milfoil and Curled Pondweed, are an important group to include in your own pond for as well as perform-ing their oxygenating role they provide food and cover for various kinds of aquatic life that might be introduced or become established. Some of the floating aquatics, such as the White Water-lily, can be difficult to accommodate in a very small piece of water but if you have a large enough pond they are well worth including. The emergent plants and marginals also include some very vigorous spe-cies. The Bulrushes, for example, can quickly spread and take over a small piece of water. There are, however, other plants suitable for the margins of even quite small ponds. Two of the most attrac-tive are the Flowering-rush and the Yellow Flag. The choice of plants for boggy conditions is very wide and includes some of our most striking native plants. A magnificent plant to add to perennials such as Globeflower, Marsh-marigold, Water Forget-me-not, Meadowsweet and Purple-loose-

*Some gardeners will be lucky enough to have a real wood-land area that can be planted with Bluebells, Foxgloves, Wood Avens, Yellow Archangel and other flowers that like shade and dappled light.*

strife is the Royal Fern, a handsome green in sum-mer that turns to rich brown in autumn. The broader the range of plants that you can use to surround your pond, the wider the range of wild-life you are likely to attract into your garden.

### Woodland planting

Some gardeners are lucky enough to have the scope to garden with wild flowers on a grand scale, or at least on a grander scale than is possible in a small town garden. Fortunately, you do not need a wood to bring together in an unforced natural planting the wild flowers of woodland. Bluebells may look at their best growing in broad masses under an extended deciduous canopy. But many woodland plants, including Bluebells, can be brought together in a truly authentic combination under a single tree. If you have the remnants of an old orchard, one of the best ways to give it a new lease of life is to use the old trees as the framework of a wild, lightly shaded woodland garden.

In this kind of planting the aim is to create as nearly as you can a self-sustaining woodland community so that you have to intervene less and less as manager. The repertoire of plants suitable for such a setting includes those mentioned in the section on wild flowers in shade and a more extensive selection is listed on page 132. With most species the best results are achieved by planting out young plants that have been reared in a nursery bed.

Although you will probably want flowering plants to dominate your small woodland community their effect can be much enhanced by establishing among them some of the common native ferns. Two of the most versatile are the Hart's Tongue Fern and the Male Fern, the latter astonishingly resilient even in dry shady conditions. Ferns are particularly useful for areas of dense shade, where many will flourish and serve as an attractive background to the wild flowers that prefer lighter dappled shade.

### Flowering meadows

It is not only the loss of woodland and hedgerows that have contributed to the transformation of familiar landscapes. The species-rich pastures and meadows have been dramatically altered by changes in agriculture so that the spring and summer flowering of grasslands risks becoming no more than a memory. The ploughing of old pasture, the draining of meadows to allow cultivation, the addition of fertilizers and seeding with new and vigorous varieties of grass, have all contributed to changes of habitats where once numerous wild flowers flourished and created one of the loveliest features of a typically British landscape.

We have been slow to recognize the enormous impact that changes in agriculture have had on old grassland and the wild flowers that are to be found in them so that only a vestige of these habitats now survives untouched. However, conservation-minded authorities, landowners and landscapers with responsibility for putting down and maintaining areas of amenity grassland have become increasingly aware of the possibility of using mixtures of native grasses and wild flowers rather than simply sowing with vigorous grass seed mixtures. It is not possible overnight to recreate all the features of a meadow habitat that has been built up over a period of hundreds of years but attractive flowering grassland can be successfully created in a few years.

The one feature of the garden that on the face of it seems ideally suited for transformation into a small-scale flowering meadow is the lawn, provided we can escape the fixed idea that plants such as Bird's-foot-trefoil, Daisy and the Speedwells are not weeds that must be removed. From the outset you should recognize that a flowering meadow is an alternative to a lawn, not something that you can easily transform a lawn into. Only when lawn grass is in very poor condition growing on a soil of low fertility is it likely that you can find or create adequate gaps in the sward to allow introduced plants to become established. Generally the competition is much too fierce, the rather slow-growing perennial broad-leaved herbs becoming swamped by vigorous, closely-sown grasses before they have made sturdy growth. Attempting to sow directly into an established sward is not likely to give any worthwhile results for the same reason.

The most successful method for establishing a flowering meadow is given in more detail in the following chapter. It involves preparing an area so that it is free of weeds and grasses, sowing a mixture of suitable, commercially available grasses and native wild flower seed thinly and then managing the planted area for the first year so that the wild flowers have a chance to become established. Suitable wild flowers are listed on page 136 but for most gardeners commercially available mixtures are the most convenient way of getting a well-balanced mixture of grass and wild flowers.

The subsequent cutting regime you adopt should take into account the flowering time of the seeds you have sown. This may seem a formidable exercise but it is very similar to what is necessary to sow a new lawn successfully and once the flowering meadow is established it will require very much less attention than is needed to keep a traditional lawn in good condition.

Many gardening writers do not recommend lawns for very small gardens, because of the problems of wear and maintenance. Enthusiasts have undoubtedly made successful miniature flowering meadows but my advice for those who have small

*The town gardener with no more than a small paved area can still grow many wild flowers successfully in containers, such as old sinks, barrels and half barrels. These must be watered regularly in dry weather.*

gardens is to grow wild flowers in other ways. To get the maximum effect from an almost random mixture of grasses and wild flowers they need to be growing on the scale of a medium-sized lawn at least. The more space they are given the more attractive and natural they look.

### Pocket-sized wild gardens

While the generous effects of a flowering meadow or a woodland planting cannot be simulated on a small scale there are plenty of ways of growing wild flowers even in a tiny urban garden, where a touch of the wilderness can be a welcome and original surprise.

Because their space is so limited many town gardeners wanting to grow wild flowers will choose to combine a small selection of them with cultivated plants. Another option to consider is to grow a medley of the showiest wild flowers, modifying and adapting the sort of scheme represented on page 97.

Another approach is to make a collection of small plants suitable for growing in a rockery or raised bed. Among plants to consider are Water

and Mountain Avens, Rock-rose, Sea Campion, the Stonecrops, Thrift and Tormentil. These small species could even be accommodated in a container, for example a half barrel or an old glazed sink, perhaps one that has been improved with a rough peat and cement exterior so that once it starts to weather it will take on the appearance of a stone trough.

Many other wild flowers are suitable for growing in a wide range of containers, as the illustration on this page shows. In most cases plants will look best when grouped with species coming from a similar habitat. Sometimes the addition of a little grass seed, as with the annuals in the old sink illustrated on this page, will give additonal weight and substance to the planting.

For those who have no gardens but enjoy window box gardening, there are many attractive, low-growing wild flowers which combine well with cultivated plants to give a good display. Cowslips, Wild Pansies, Primroses, Ivy-leaved Toadflax and Bird's-foot-trefoil are amongst those which have proved to be very successful.

### Conclusion

In pointing out the many ways in which wild flowers can be grown in the garden I have failed perhaps to lay sufficient stress on one very attractive feature of almost all our native plants. Once you have fitted them in to an appropriate corner of the garden, you will find that they are remarkably untroubled by pests and diseases, showing much greater resistance to attack than most cultivated exotic plants.

You may find this a useful argument if other members of your family are reluctant to give the garden over to what they see as weeds. The last thing you want to do is to alienate their interest in a subject that extends beyond the private garden to the landscapes about us and the wildlife that belongs to them. To begin with it may be diplomatic to think of your garden as being divided into an area near the house which is gardened in a fairly conventional way and an area beyond that is gradually transformed into a wildlife habitat and one in which wild flowers are a conspicuous feature. A hedge, even a low one, can provide a natural break from the well-groomed to the wilder garden.

# GROWING WILD FLOWERS

It is all very well wanting to have a garden brimming with wild flowers but how do you start? Can you simply find the plants you want in the wild, uproot them and bring them home for planting in the garden?

Unfortunately that is precisely what, in the past, many people have done. This often well-intentioned but reckless plundering of natural habitats has contributed to the destruction of many plant communities and has helped make some plants rare or very rare. Sadly, of the many plants taken from the wild state few will have survived and flourished in their garden settings. This is often because people uplift them, on impulse, when they are in flower and at the wrong time of year for successful transplanting.

The recognition that plants and other wild life are everywhere under threat has led, in most countries, to the passing of protective legislation. In Britain the Wildlife and Countryside Act, 1981, gives full protection to a list of 62 scheduled plants (see page 138), but also makes it illegal to uproot any wild plant unless you are an authorised person (generally the owner or occupier of the land, or someone with the permission of the owner or occupier). If you were to decide to take from the wild to fill your garden you would in any case almost certainly have a low success rate and you might just find yourself in court.

There is now no need to go to the wild to obtain seeds or plants for the garden. Most garden centres sell wild flower seeds, though the range may be limited to the most popular kinds. You may also find young plants of popular species. Many major mail-order seedsmen also offer a small selection of wild flowers. However, there are a few specialist seedsmen offering large comprehensive seed lists of wild flower species and mixtures mainly by mail order, but also through garden centres and shops. They are also making available on a more limited scale a range of nursery-grown plants. A comprehensive list of suppliers is given on page 140.

The wild flower seeds and plants being offered for sale by most specialist seedsmen for garden use are probably all of British origin. Because the production of one or two species such as Bird's-foot-trefoil and Kidney Vetch is still rather limited, large scale users may be offered seed of foreign commercial production. If this is being done, the customer should be informed of the situation by the seedsman's sales literature. British seed is produced from plants which have been raised under nursery or field conditions from seed taken from wild populations.

## Growing plants from seed

By far the best and cheapest method of establishing wild flowers in the garden is to grow from seed. In addition to other advantages there is with this method the enormous satisfaction experienced by most gardeners in participating in the whole life cycle of a plant.

It is a mistake to think that wild flowers are in some mysterious way fundamentally different from plants well established in cultivation. After all, many favourite garden subjects are the wild plants of other countries. However, selection and breeding over hundreds if not thousands of years has generally resulted in cultivated plants having much more rapid and regular germination patterns than their wild counterparts. Most wild forms tend to produce fewer seedlings at any one time over a much longer period.

As with cultivated plants, annuals and biennials are far the most straightforward. Most are quick to germinate and rapidly come to maturity so that the plant's life cycle can be completed in favourable weather conditions.

Seed of many perennials, such as Cowslip, Oxlip, Primrose, Bluebell and Ramsons, require exposure to a cold period in the soil during winter before they will germinate satisfactorily. The simplest way of dealing with such seeds is to sow outdoors in carefully prepared ground in autumn. With valuable seed that is difficult to obtain it is worth sowing in pots or seed trays which should be carefully labelled, and left in the open or placed in a cold frame. Germination should occur in the spring as soon as the temperature of soil becomes warm enough to promote growth. You sometimes need to be very patient; if seedlings do not appear in the year following sowing they may require yet another alternation of warm and cold phases. Keep pots for at least a further year to give the seeds the chance of late germination.

The vernalization process, in which a cold period precedes the expected germination phase, can sometimes be imitated successfully by subjecting the seed to a relatively low temperature in the main compartment of a domestic refrigerator (not in the freezer). In the Wild Flower Guide (pages 13-93) I have called this technique 'artificial stratification'. The normal practice is to mix the seed with wet compost or sand in a polythene bag and to keep it in the refrigerator with the thermostat on a low setting for a period of six to eight weeks before sowing. Sometimes this technique produces very good results but not consistently enough for it to be considered a simple alternative to sowing outdoors in autumn.

Hard-coated seeds of some members of the Crane's-bill family and most members of the Pea family will only germinate after a period of being exposed to conditions in the soil, during which time the seed coat is broken down by these conditions, finally allowing water to penetrate it and reach the seed inside. This natural process can take many weeks, but it can be greatly accelerated by 'scarifying' the seed before it is sown. 'Scarification' involves rubbing seed between two sheets of glass paper or sandpaper, to wear down the seed coat enough to promote water absorption by the seed. Rub until the seed coat looks well scraped but take care not to expose the seed inside. Bloody Crane's-bill, Meadow Crane's-bill, Bird's-foot-trefoil, Clovers, Kidney Vetch and Sainfoin are well known examples of seeds which can be successfully treated in this way.

Hard-coated species being sown in the autumn outdoors should not need to be scarified before sowing because over-wintering in the soil will break down the seed coat. Equally, seed which is artificially stratified should not require scarification either before or after treatment.

## Routine sowing techniques

Although the seed of some very desirable plants require a cold phase before they will germinate and others, such as Harebell, Columbine, Soapwort, Crane's-bill and most legumes, germinate much more freely after one, most wild flowers can be grown from seed without catering for this need.

In the most straightforward routine, one that gives good results with a large number of species, the seed is sown directly in the permanent position. Annuals particularly respond well to this sort of treatment. A mistaken belief persists, and is a cause of some disappointment, that it is enough to sprinkle seed in spare parts of the garden in supposed imitation of nature's own methods. Success depends on good preparation of the ground in advance and control of weeds that would compete for space nutrients and water.

Choose a position appropriate to the plant you want to sow, taking account of light, moisture and soil requirements, and dig or fork it over, removing all perennial and annual weeds. Getting rid of the perennial weeds is particularly important, for once the seed is sown it will be difficult to deal with them. Many wild flowers respond well to fertile conditions but fertility is best built up by the addition of well-rotted organic matter such as garden compost, rather than applications of chemical fertilizers.

Prepare a good firm bed and work the surface to a reasonable tilth before sowing thinly. Very fine seed, such as that of Foxglove, is simply sown on the surface and firmed in or lightly covered with a little sharp sand. Larger seed, such as that of Wild Pansy, should be covered with its own depth of soil. Bulky seed, such as that of Corncockle, should be put in at twice its own depth.

After sowing and firming, water gently with a very fine rose. Early autumn and early spring sowings can both give good results, but annuals sown in autumn are likely to be sturdier than those sown in spring. Annuals are well worth sowing in succession – in autumn, early spring and mid-spring – to give a long period of display from late spring through to the second half of summer.

Once the seed has been sown the most important job is to keep any weed competition under control. As the seedlings develop they will almost certainly need to be thinned, the ultimate spacing depending on the species. Many of the smaller plants such as Daisies can be as close as 15 to 20cm (6 to 8in); really large plants such as Teasel need about 75cm (30in) between plants. Try to thin the plants to create natural groups, for most wild flowers look uncomfortable when they are organized in the rigid patterns that are sometimes used for cultivated plants.

Other than watering in periods of prolonged drought, there is very little other work involved in looking after your plants.

In the case of some biennials and perennials, which are not going to flower in their first year, you may find it is more convenient to sow them first in a seed bed from which they are transplanted to a growing bed at seedling stage, to be moved eventually to the permanent position in the autumn of their first year. Choose a sheltered but not overshadowed part of the garden for the seed bed and dig thoroughly well in advance of sowing. The incorporation of well-rotted compost (or peat) and sand will help to provide open, well-drained soil conditions that will enable young roots to develop quickly. Winter weathering will help break down the surface to give a fine tilth for spring sowing. In a seed bed it is most convenient to sow in drills. Remember to label all sowings and keep a record of the dates either on the label or in a notebook.

Have the growing bed prepared well in advance of germination. It, too, should be in a sheltered position and must offer your young plants the best chance of developing sturdy and vigorous growth. When digging it over incorporate plenty of well-rotted compost. Seedlings should be transferred to the growing bed once the true leaves have started to develop and the plants are large enough to handle. Plant out in rows and space almost as generously as you would in the final position, because by the autumn your plants will be nearly the size of mature specimens. To give the young plants the full advantage of the growing bed it must be kept weed free and watered in periods of prolonged dry weather.

The final position needs to be well prepared before planting out in autumn. Remove weeds and dig over ground, incorporating compost in the soil. Plants sown in autumn are easily forgotten the following spring. Check all planted areas at the beginning of the growing season to ensure that there is no competition from weeds.

The seed of some species of wild flowers is difficult to produce and for that reason tends to be expensive. A packet of Bugle, Celandine or Primrose contains a relatively small quantity. In such cases I recommend sowing in pots. The seed of Foxgloves is so fine and the seedlings so small that I prefer to sow them in this way too.

Use an ordinary seed compost (John Innes rather than the peat-based loamless composts). Distribute the seed evenly and thinly over the surface of the pot. Very small seed is best thoroughly mixed with dry sharp sand in order to make sowing easier. Firm down the surface of the compost to make sure that the seed is in contact with the soil. Very small seeds can be left uncovered. Larger seed should be covered with its own depth of sharp sand or soil. Bulky seed should be put at twice its own depth.

After sowing, water gently with a fine rose. In order to prevent evaporation, cover the pot with a sheet of newspaper and a piece of glass so that watering can be kept to a minimum. Remove the paper and glass as soon as seedlings appear.

When the seedlings show their first pair of true leaves they can be pricked out. They are probably best moved on to a tray containing a slightly richer potting compost, but they could also be moved to a bed to be grown on before planting out in autumn.

### Establishing a flowering mini-meadow

It is tempting to think that an attractive flowering grass area can be created without very much effort, simply by overseeding an area that is already grassed with a suitable wild flower mixture. It is, regrettably, an approach to wild flower gardening that offers almost no chance of success! Few of the broad-leaved herbaceous plants that are the most desirable constituents of a flowering meadow are vigorous enough to establish themselves when competing against well-established, closely sown grasses that are commonly found in lawns, playing fields and pastures. Successfully creating a mini-meadow from seed is only possible if the site to be sown is thoroughly cultivated, prepared and carefully maintained, especially during the first year while both wild flower and grass plants are becoming established.

You stand the best chance of success if the site you choose is an open and sunny one where the soil is naturally of low fertility. It should also be well drained and not infested with weeds, which would compete with and threaten the survival of the species being sown. The more fertile the soil the more vigorous the competition from grasses and unwanted plants. Wild flower seedlings, most of which are relatively slow growing, are more likely to be squeezed out before they reach maturity. This is one kind of gardening where a poor thin soil is ideal – even if it is poorly drained there are a number of attractive plants that will do well on it.

Obviously an area that has been well cultivated and fertilised, such as a vegetable garden or herbaceous border, is less suitable for conversion. If it is very fertile then it should be cropped for a few years in an attempt to reduce fertility.

If the area to be sown is already grassed, the grass should be eradicated by digging or rotovating it in. On larger areas it may be necessary to use a non-selective contact or translocated herbicide. In a relatively small area the best method may be to slice off the turf with a spade (you may be able to use part or all of the turf in another part of the garden or you might prefer to use it as the basis of a compost for a part of the garden that needs good soil). Removing the turf in this way also disposes of a good layer of top soil which might otherwise provide too rich a bed for your meadow.

The eradication of large, vigorous, perennial weeds such as Docks, Nettles and Thistles is absolutely essential. Many wild flower gardeners who would prefer to pull, fork or dig them out will be uncomfortable about using herbicides. However, a non-selective translocated herbicide (containing non-residual glyphosate) does offer one of the best ways of getting a piece of land clear so that the meadow herbs have a chance of getting established. Some weeds will be very difficult to get rid of in any other way; on a larger site hand weeding is not a practical proposition.

A seed bed should be prepared by forking or digging, firming and raking in the usual way. Lar-

*A flowering meadow cannot be established satisfactorily simply by oversowing an area that is already grassed. As a first step it is essential to remove competition.*

ger areas could be rotovated. The importance of a firm seed bed cannot be over-emphasised. For an early autumn sowing this needs to be done by mid-summer so that any weeds that germinate after the ground is worked can be cleared.

Some excellent results have been achieved where infertile subsoils have been spread over a site before sowing. This seems an extreme measure and is probably not warranted when you are creating a mini-meadow on a small scale, but it is an option to consider if you have subsoil to dispose of. Sand can also be used.

Getting the seed mixture right is essential if the meadow is to be a success. Several seedsmen market a range suitable for different soil conditions, situations and purposes. The mixtures should contain a selection of slender-leaved aggressive grasses and a fairly wide range of broad-leaved plants, usually as many as twenty different species. Most of the grasses used are relatively inexpensive, commercially available varieties of commonly used amenity and sportsfield grasses often used in lawn seed mixtures. Typical grasses include Browntop (Common) Bent, Chewing's Fescue, Slender and Strong Creeping Red Fescue, Smooth and Rough-stalked Meadow-grass plus Meadow Foxtail, Sweet Vernal-grass and Yellow Oat-grass. To these are added a small number of relatively expensive nursery-grown and hand-collected grasses which have extremely attractive flower heads such as Common Quaking-grass, Crested Hair-grass and Meadow Barley. In order to allow and encourage the establishment of any wild flowers sown with them, mixtures containing these grasses must be sown very thinly. Large, vigorous, leaf-producing agricultural grasses such as Rye-grass, Cock's Foot, Timothy (Cat's-tail), Couch-grass and Yorkshire Fog must be avoided. These will soon take over and any other plants – grasses or wild flowers – will stand very little chance of survival.

The wild flower species should be typical grassland plants commonly found in different types of grassland throughout Britain, and not be localised or rare. The majority should be colourful, long-lived perennials, preferably capable of freely reproducing themselves by seed and vegetative means. As many as possible should be of value to insects. A few suitable annuals and biennials can

also be used. Nearly all the seed used will be nursery or field grown and 'hand-collected' and therefore relatively expensive.

Mixtures of different types are formulated using percentages of suitable constituents mainly based upon the number of seeds and germinable seeds per gram and the height and spread of the mature plant. Approximately half the wild flower species used in mixtures formulated for major soil types are common to each mixture. The species most likely to succeed on clay, lime or loam soils include Bird's-foot-trefoil, Black Medick, Cowslip, Hoary and Ribwort Plantain, Kidney Vetch, Lady's Bedstraw, Oxeye Daisy, Selfheal and Yarrow. To these bases other suitable species most likely to be found on the soil in question could be added. Similar principles are applied when formulating mixtures suitable for acid and sandy soils, for pond-edge, hedgerow and woodland situations, or for early and late flowering grassland purposes. Mixtures can also be made up to contain plants especially attractive to butterflies, bees, and other insects and birds.

Most standard grass and wild flower seed mixtures consist of 80 per cent grasses and 20 per cent wild flowers. It is generally recognised that satisfactory results can be obtained from a 20 per cent wild flower content sown under average conditions. If the time of sowing and soil preparation were ideal a reduced 15 per cent content would probably be just as effective. Alternatively, an increased flower content could be expected to improve if not accelerate results, but it would dramatically increase the price. In a standard mixture, the 20 per cent wild flower content would account for 90 to 95 per cent of its value.

If you have special requirements you should discuss these with a seed merchant. It may be possible to have a mixture prepared for your own requirements and conditions.

### Sowing the meadow

For those who have had experience of sowing lawn seed it comes as a surprise to discover how thinly a meadow mixture should be sown. With a lawn the aim is to get a dense, vigorous cover as quickly as possible but when you are establishing a mini-meadow it is essential that there is room for development. Lack of growing space will not encourage the establishment of slower growing species and will probably be responsible for their suppression by more vigorous species. Instead of sowing at something like 45 to 60gm per square metre (1½ to 2oz per square yard), as you would when sowing a lawn, you need to sow at a rate of 25gm per square metre (¾oz per square yard).

To get a thin even distribution of a relatively small amount of seeds with widely varying sizes and weights is not easily done by straightforward broadcast sowing. For the best possible results the seed must first be very well mixed and combined with a thoroughly dry carrier. This gives the mixture bulk and makes it visible when distributed, so that you can see where it has been sown. The most commonly used materials are barley meal, sand or fine sawdust from untreated timber mixed in proportions of nine parts carrier to one part seed.

Mixing with a carrier is not in itself enough to ensure that seed is spread evenly. It will help, however, if you mark out your site with tape or twine in square metre (square yard) sections and if you then divide the seed mixture up into equal portions. You will find it much easier to spread the seed and carrier mixture evenly over small areas than over the whole surface of your site. Dividing the mixture to be sown into two lots, and sowing in opposite directions, will allow even distribution.

On a really large area sowing by hand may not be feasible. An applicator for spreading lawn fertilizer is reasonably efficient but you must ensure either that a carrier is used or that the seed is kept well mixed throughout the whole operation.

Early autumn (late August to mid-September) has many advantages as a sowing season, including the fact that seed requiring a period of cold temperature to break dormancy will germinate the following spring whereas the same seed sown in spring will not germinate until the following year. The earlier seed is sown the longer seedlings have to get established before growth slows up and stops as winter develops. Well developed plants are less susceptible to damage from frost and cold. Seed sown in late autumn is not likely to germinate until the following spring, when temperatures start to rise, and where the site is sloping there is the likelihood of surface water washing away a high proportion of the seed. After early autumn the next best time for sowing is early spring from March to the end of April. Seed can also be sown during May. It is advisable to sow as early as possible to ensure that seedlings are well established before the likelihood of dry hot weather in June or July which will adversely affect growth. It is best to avoid sowing in windy conditions and after prolonged periods of wet or dry weather. In some areas the use of a bird repellent is a wise precaution.

*Grass and wild flower seed mixtures are sown much more thinly than lawn mixtures. To ensure even seed distribution mark out the area in regular divisions, mix the seed with a carrier such as sand or sawdust and then scatter evenly across the area.*

After sowing go over the site using a tined rake or a brush to work the surface lightly so that the seed gets covered by a thin layer of soil (when a large area is being sown the normal procedure is to go over the ground with a chain harrow). Then firm the surface by rolling it lightly, using, for example, the heavy roller of a lawn mower. An alternative is to tread the seed in, working evenly and systematically across the site. Seeds well firmed in will be in contact with moisture in the soil and likely to germinate more rapidly and evenly. The sowing operation is completed by watering the whole site using a very fine rose so that seed is not washed away.

### Meadow maintenance

In the first year after sowing a meadow has to be looked after more carefully than will be necessary in subsequent years. Neglect at this stage will almost certainly lead to failure. The first plants to germinate will probably be annual weeds such as Chickweed and Groundsel. These may even give some protection to the developing seedlings and will not persist once the mowing regime begins. Perennial weeds are another matter. They should be handweeded as soon as they develop but take care when pulling them out that seedlings of sown species are not dislodged or damaged. The use of a systemic contact herbicide in gel form will deal with persistent perennial weeds.

When the young sward has grown to about 10cm (4in) tall, it is ready to be cut for the first time. There is a danger of small plants being uprooted by the mower when their root systems are still just developing. For this reason it is worth rolling the surface lightly, for the pressure will help firm the plants in the soil. Cut to a height of 5cm (2in) and remove the cuttings. Whenever the growth reaches a height of 10cm (4in) cut back to 5cm (2in); you may find that your meadow needs cutting three or even four times in its first year, especially on fertile soils. It is essential that cuttings are not allowed to remain, because their gradual decomposition will significantly increase soil fertility. Repeated cutting during the first year will encourage the establishment of wild flowers and prevent the grasses gaining ascendency over them. By the end of the first year, the young sward should consist of a well balanced, open mixture of relatively prostrate grasses interspersed with wild flowers in various stages of development. Vigorous, fast-growing species such as Black Medick, Common Sorrel, Kidney Vetch, Oxeye Daisy, Ribwort Plantain, Selfheal and Yarrow will be noticeable as well developed plants. Slower growing plants like Common and Greater knapweed, Field Scabious, Hoary Plantain, Lady's Bedstraw, Rough Hawkbit, Meadow Buttercup, Salad Burnet, Small Scabious and Wild Carrot will probably be less robust. Although not easily recognisable, plantlets or seedlings of slow growing subjects such as Harebell, Cowslip and Meadow Crane's-bill may also be present, depending upon when they were sown. Spring-sown seeds may only germinate after they have spent one winter in soil.

In the second year, the wild flowers are allowed

*Perennial weeds such as Docks and Thistles need to be controlled. They can be dug out or treated with a wipe-on herbicide. It is essential for them to be checked long before they set seed.*

to grow, mature, flower and set seed. Ideally they are not cut until the seed produced has been shed into the sward. Cutting the sward two or three times a year will be required on most soils. The first cut would be made in early or late April. The second would take place after most seeding had finished and plant growth was looking untidy and unattractive. The third and final cut would be necessary if the sward needed to be tidied up in readiness for the following year's growth. In subsequent years you will notice variations in the relative proportions of species from year to year, as the meadow matures the balance gradually shifting in favour of those plants that are best suited to the conditions of your site.

There are three principal aspects of minimeadow management if you are aiming to maintain a species-rich sward. The main activity consists of mowing about two or three times a year according to a regime that fits in with the flowering period of the majority of plants in your sward. For example, some meadows contain a high proportion of plants that flower in spring or early summer and include a range of bulbs. If the foliage of bulbous plants is cut down shortly after flowering the bulbs will be weakened and the quality of the flowering display will steadily deteriorate (the leaves are one source of the food supply that is stored during the dormant period in the bulb). Early cutting will also prevent the setting and maturing of the seeds of many species. A mowing regime that suits an early-flowering meadow begins not sooner than mid-summer with a repeat cut at least once before the end of autumn.

Swards which are rich in summer-flowering species, many of which are especially attractive to butterflies, should be treated differently. To avoid cutting these before they set seed the most appropriate mowing regime consists of one or two mowings in spring and another in late autumn after all seed has been shed.

The mowing regimes outlined here are by no means rigid and there is plenty of room for variation. A meadow should never be close-mown in the way a lawn is; 8cm (3in) is quite close enough,

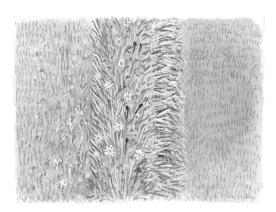

*A spring-flowering meadow should be left uncut until mid-June and then cut to a height of 5cm (2in). It can then be mown regularly or left and cut only once or twice before mid-autumn.*

except where you want a path cut through the sward. What is important as the second principal aspect of management, as we have seen, is that the cut grass is removed. The job of collecting grass is less laborious if the mowings are allowed to stand for a day or two to dry out before being collected and taken off the site.

The control of troublesome perennial weeds such as Ragwort, Cow Parsley, Thistles and Dock is the third aspect of management that must not be neglected. Handweeding may be effective in some cases but the use of a herbicide such as glyphosate in gel form will be the most practical solution. The indiscriminate use of chemicals to kill weeds of course runs counter to the whole spirit of ecological gardening.

### Adding wild flowers to a grassy area

As I have previously mentioned, I do not recommend using a wild flower mixture to overseed an existing grass area as a method of increasing its number and range of flowering species. However, there are a number of other ways in which wild flowers can be successfully introduced into established grassland. The success of these methods is very dependent upon the vigour, density and type of grasses present in the sward. A self-sown grassy area would be more suitable than a well-fertilised lawn or amenity area left uncut. The grass species found in lawns, with the exception of rye grass, would be quite acceptable but their unnaturally closely-sown density would not be appropriate.

Mixtures to be used should consist of wild flowers only and be formulated exclusively from species which are most likely to succeed against competition from tall growing vigorous grasses. They would contain more taller species than mixtures intended to be sown with the non-aggressive grasses used to create a mini-meadow. 100 per cent wild flower mixtures can be successfully used to sow patches or strips in existing grass. Cut the surrounding grass short in early autumn or early spring and prepare, cultivate and sow the areas as carefully as previously described for sowing grass and wild flower mixtures. On a larger scale, the same type of wild flower mixtures are sown directly into established grassland by a specially adapted drilling machine which sows seed in rows.

For a small grassy area, established plants from growing beds or pot grown plants can be introduced into the sward. For the best possible results, cut the sward closely before implanting in early autumn or early spring. The area round the spots to be planted should be cleared in order to reduce competition from surrounding plants. A bulb planter can be successfully used for planting, by removing a core of soil and leaving a hole into which a pot plant is firmly placed. Use plants grown in

*After a meadow is cut, the hay should be removed by raking, otherwise as a result of the processes of decay nutrients will be returned to the soil and encourage vigorous plants that compete with wild flowers.*

ordinary soil potting compost to avoid the risk of shrinkage in dry weather. Thoroughly water the plants in after planting, and keep well watered, especially during dry weather, until they are established.

Alternatively, seed boxes or potato trays sown with a 100 per cent wild flower mixture can be used to produce species-rich turves which can be planted out directly into a tight-fitting rectangular 'hole' dug to receive it.

Taller-growing annuals, such as Corn Chamomile, Corn Marigold, Corn Poppy, Corncockle and Cornflower, can be used to add unique first-year colour to an area sown with a standard grass and wild flower mixture. Their addition will not be to the detriment of the formation of the mini-meadow. Usual first-year management of such an area would require the young sward to be cut at regular intervals and any annuals present would be eradicated before they could flower. Therefore, the first cut has got to be delayed until after the majority of annuals have finished flowering. This will probably be in late July or early August. Cut the young sward back to the usual height of 5cm (2in), removing the cuttings, and continue to cut as required until the end of the year. The annuals will not reappear in the following year as they will not have had a chance to set seed.

An area entirely devoted to wild annual flowers can be maintained for a number of years. Sow the mixture either in early autumn or early spring and allow the plants to grow without being cut. After flowering has finished, allow the plants to set seed which should be encouraged to spread over the area sown. At the beginning of September, ensure that all seed has been shed before removing dead and dying plants. Remove all unwanted plants, especially grass, and rake the area vigorously in order to prepare a seed bed. Germination of the majority of species present should occur rapidly and they should be established before winter starts. Some rigorous thinning will be necessary in the autumn and probably in the spring.

**Planting bulbs**

Bulbs are undoubtedly some of the most attractive plants and create more powerfully than almost all other flowers the feeling that winter is over. Most bulbs are best planted in autumn. In the case of Daffodils the sooner they can be got into the ground the better, for they start making root growth very promptly.

When planting in grass place the bulbs so that they are covered by a depth of soil equal to three times the height of the bulb. If you have only a small number of bulbs to plant it may not be too tedious to use a trowel to make holes, before dropping in the bulbs and covering them over. If you are planting a really large area a bulb planter will make the job much less tedious. You use it to lift out a plug of earth before dropping in the bulbs and then covering with the plug. It is important to make sure that each bulb is well bedded in its hole, in particular that there is no air gap between it and the soil underneath.

Remember that the leaves of bulbs must not be cut prematurely; they must be left for at least six weeks after flowering. Bear this in mind when you decide where they are best planted; you may well find that they are best kept to corners or the borders of your site, even under areas lightly shaded by deciduous trees. Eventually bulbs will build up their own colonies, forming irregular clusters of plants. At the initial stage it is worth going to some trouble to get a natural look. The traditional advice given to gardeners is to cast handfuls of bulbs loosely on the ground and to plant individual bulbs where they have fallen. In practice you may find it easier to arrange irregular clumps, allowing for the subsequent expansion, but with some quite close together and a few more scattered.

Native bulbs will need very little further attention but if flowering starts to deteriorate it may be worth lifting and dividing clumps after the flowering season.

### Harvesting seed

With few exceptions most wild flowers set seed quite readily and the seed produces plants identical with the parents. The only time when this is not likely to happen is when there are cultivated plants very closely related to the wild species you are growing in the near vicinity.

Taking seed from plants in the wild should be discouraged, but gathering seed from your own plants is well worth doing if you want to extend your own plantings or if you want to encourage a friend to sow wild plants. It is not always easy to tell when seed is on the point of ripening. In the case of many plants there is an obvious change of colour just as the seed ripens but you will find that collecting seed at just the right moment is a matter of frequent inspection.

In the case of many plants collection is quite straightforward. It is best to hand collect in dry weather just before the seed is ripe. Because most seeds are produced in succession, either select only mature capsules, fruit or seed or wait until the whole flower head is ripe (and risk losing the earliest ripened seed). For many plants the easiest collection method is to hold a plastic seed tray, bowl or bucket underneath the majority of the plant and vigorously shake the seed out. Without causing any damage, the whole plant can be carefully bent over the rim of a bucket and shaken. Shaking seed out from plants ensures that only mature seed is collected, leaving immature seed to be gathered at a later date. With plants such as Common and Greater Knapweed, Oxeye Daisy and Field Scabious either the ripening seed-head can be picked or ripe seed can be removed from it. Seed of low-growing plants can often be easily collected by cutting off stems bearing ripening seed-heads and putting them in a suitable place to mature fully. Lady's Bedstraw, Cowslip, Selfheal and Common Restharrow are typical examples.

*Many perennial wild flowers, including Cowslips and Primroses, are easily propagated by division. In most cases the best time to do this is in autumn. Discard any damaged or decaying material.*

Provided the capsules are taken with a small piece of stem attached they will continue to ripen after being picked.

Some plants, such as Bird's-foot-trefoil, Tufted Vetch and Meadow Crane's-bill, have pods, capsules or fruits which burst open explosively, firing the seed away from the plant. Remove them before they are fully ripe and put in a covered container to prevent the seed being lost as it is shed.

With species such as Dandelion, Goat's-beard and Rough Hawkbit which have seeds with a parachute pappus the easiest collection method is to pick nearly ripened seed-heads from the plant. Remove the pappus from the head and put it in a suitable place where the seeds can fully ripen.

After collecting the seed, remove debris and coarse plant material as quickly as possible. Cleaning can most easily be done by hand-picking or sieving. Fanning or winnowing by gently and slowly tossing a handful of seed up and down in a shallow receptacle or tea tray is also an excellent way of separating the seed from the chaff. Dust and light dirt are blown away by the passage of air underneath the seed. Immature seed and plant material lighter than the seed being cleaned move to the front of the receptacle and can be removed. When clean, spread the seed out thinly on paper in seed trays in a dry, preferably sunny, well-ventilated place so that it can dry out and fully ripen naturally. Capsules, fruits, pods, seed-heads and flowering stems should also be spread out in order to complete the drying and ripening processes before the seed is removed, cleaned and dried. Natural drying can be aided by blowing unheated air from a fan heater over the seed. On no account should seed be either dried by hot air or put in an oven to dry.

Seed to be stored must be clean and dry otherwise moulds will develop during storage. Pack in paper or linen bags but not in polythene bags. Put the seed in a plastic container or air-tight tin to be kept in a place with as even a temperature as possible. A cool dark room, preferably without windows, where there is not a great fluctuation from day-time to night-time temperatures is ideal.

Seed collecting from groups of garden plants can often produce surprisingly large quantities of precious seed – especially in a good year. All seed collected should be for use in gardens only. It should never be scattered in the countryside. Reintroducing species in this way is usually unsuccessful because of the considerable difficulties encountered when trying to establish plants by this method. However, it is also biologically undesirable because if plants do establish themselves, this could lead to the crossing of strains from different areas and changes in plant populations. Cultivated flower seed should never be scattered in the wild either. This can lead to hybridisation and provide unnecessary competition to wild plants.

### Encouraging self-seeding

Many wild plants will build up more or less permanent communities by self-seeding. You can give them encouragement by giving old plants a chance to set seed before taking them out, and by giving the old plants a good shake before removing them. The aim is to dislodge as much ripe seed as possible and to give it the best chance of germinating and establishing sturdy plants.

The same principles apply as in other gardening with wild flowers, in particular that plants stand the best chance of giving good results if they are allowed to grow in reasonably fertile soil free of competition.

### Other means of propagation

The adventurous wild flower gardener will soon discover that a wide range of gardening techniques normally applied to cultivated plants are just as applicable to wild flowers. This is particularly true of the various techniques of propagation, almost all of which can be applied without significant modification to wild flowers.

Numerous plants are easily increased from cuttings of different kinds. A number of leafy perennials are easily propagated from tip cuttings, which are normally taken at the beginning of autumn. The cuttings need to be kept in a fairly close environment for several weeks until they begin to root, when they can be potted up individually and overwintered in a cold frame before being planted out the following spring.

A large number of perennials are very easily increased from basal cuttings, which are taken in spring. Young shoots about 10cm (4in) long are taken from the base of established plants in early spring and inserted in pots of compost. Cuttings that take should be grown on and planted out in the flowering position in autumn.

Plants with fleshy roots can also be propagated from root cuttings, which are generally taken in autumn. Mulleins, for instance, can be increased in this way. Sections of root are laid in trays or pots of compost and when the cuttings have rooted in the following spring the plants are potted up and grown on before being planted out in the following autumn.

By far the most useful way of increasing perennials is division. The time for this to be carried out is the dormant period between late autumn and early spring. Lift plants or clumps of plants and discard all dead and damaged growth. Gently separate the clump into two or more parts, each with a good supply of roots and a crown. Many plants can be separated by hand but tough or woody clusters may need to be cut or separated with two forks.

# THE WILDLIFE GARDEN

Suddenly, or so it seems, we have discovered that we are on a shrinking planet. A dramatic plunge in the fortunes of a few high-profile species – to take two examples, the otter and the tiger – has brought an awareness (though not much more than a dull one) that human exploitation of the world's resources has up till now rarely taken into account the fate of all the other forms of life with which humanity shares the earth. The age-old conflict between human needs and what is required to sustain all the astonishing variety of other forms of natural life has moved into a quite new phase. Changes in land use and agriculture are taking place at such a speed and on such a devastating scale that they may yet prove as perilous for humanity as they have for many other species.

While we in Europe wonder whether the great rain forests of the tropics will survive in any recognizable form into the twenty-first century, our own grasslands, hedgerows, wetlands and woodlands melt away. Monitoring the changes in the British landscape since World War II has been like writing an obituary of the traditional landscape; we cling to the idea of that landscape in our imagination but it is increasingly difficult to find in reality. The decisions to bring about changes, it must be admitted, are often very well intentioned; there is no im-

penetrable plot to pick off species one by one. But the destruction or transformation of habitats has meant the loss not just of wild flowers but of whole communities of species – animals, birds, insects, plants and a myriad micro-organisms.

At national and international levels conservation bodies can and do put the case for the preservation of habitats and of endangered species. Giving these bodies our full support, although enormously important for increasing public awareness of conservation issues, sometimes seems to fall short of the involvement many people would like to have in the care and management of our landscape and wildlife. Our gardens may offer us the best opportunity for making a small but practical contribution to maintaining wild plant and animal life.

Although our gardens are individually often very small, when all the little fragments are added up they represent a significant element, hundreds of thousands of acres, in the national landscape. Despite its fragmentation, with individual holders managing their own plots according to their own interests, there may be here a greater resource for conservation than has as yet been recognized.

We look back now on the vanishing hedgerows of Britain as an integral part of the landscape but

## A BUTTERFLY BORDER

*Wild flowers, so beautiful on their own account, are valuable sources of nectar for butterflies and moths. A border such as that shown here will entice an interesting range of these most colourful insects into the garden throughout the summer months.*

1  Greater Knapweed, *Centaurea scabiosa*
2  White Campion, *Silene alba*
3  Wild Marjoram, *Origanum vulgare*
4  Oxeye Daisy, *Leucanthemum vulgare*
5  Field Scabious, *Knautia arvensis*
6  Vetch, *Vicia hirsuta*
7  Thrift, *Armeria maritima*
8  Hawkweed, *Hieracium vulgatum*
9  Wild White Clover, *Trifolium repens*

the planting of many hedges took place as recently as 150 or 200 years ago, when much common land was enclosed. The animals, plants and insects of the woodland edge seized their opportunity and slipped into what seemed like an extension of the habitat they already knew. Hedgerows have assumed their own distinctive character, they are not simply a linear version of the woodland edge, but their importance as a wildlife refuge increased partly because of the shrinkage of broadleaved woodland. Gardens friendly to wildlife may, unfortunately, be widely separated, quite different in this respect to the criss-crossing patterns of hedges that were so important as thoroughfares as well as residential areas for many forms of wildlife. Pocket refuges are, however, very much better than no refuges at all and if more and more gardeners adopt a welcoming attitude to wildlife there may be a much brighter future ahead.

### Luring butterflies into the garden

Butterflies, the most decorative and conspicuous of the insects, are among the best equipped forms of wildlife to take advantage of scattered but well-placed supplies of food. Flower nectar, a watery solution of several different kinds of sugar, is the main energy source for most species, although some butterflies are not at all squeamish about feeding on carrion. Many of our wild flowers are particulary attractive to native species of butterfly, which are lured to them both by scent and by colour pattern.

Many cultivated plants are so highly developed that the mechanisms for attracting insects or allowing them to feed, and in the process pollinate the flowers, have been distorted. Monster heads that may now be particularly appealing to the human eye no longer indicate the availability of a meal to butterflies and other insects. There are, however, several cultivated plants that are particularly good sources of nectar and should be included when planning a garden if you are keen to make it a regular haunt of butterflies. Three of the best to consider are Buddleia, Michaelmas Daisy and Iceplant.

One approach to attracting butterflies is to plant a border with a good collection of nectar-rich plants, wild flowers mixed with suitable cultivated plants or wild flowers only, as in the scheme illustrated here. Other species worth trying in a border are included in the list on page 131. An advantage of concentrating nectar plants in a relatively small area is that it makes the pleasurable activity of observing butterflies so much easier. It might be worth including a seat in your plan for you will have a very good excuse for taking things easy and watching the various species that find their way even into town gardens. They may be relatively common but Brimstones, Peacocks, Red Admirals and Small Tortoiseshells are nonetheless very welcome visitors.

A less managed arrangement of plants will suit some gardeners better and there it will be easier to make room for some of the weedier wild flowers, not least among them the Dandelion. Early-flowering species, such as this and the Lesser Celandine, are particularly useful for overwintering butterflies that are coaxed out of hiding by unseasonably warm weather very early in spring.

Getting a flowering meadow established may need quite a lot of work but once it has reached maturity it will require very little management from one year's end to the next. A well-balanced mixture containing a good representation of nectar-rich species – Field Scabious, Hawkbits, Hawkweed, Knapweeds, Wild Thyme, Wild White Clover and Yarrow, to name but a few – will come close to recreating the natural habitat of characteristic meadowland butterflies, such as the Common Blue, Meadow Brown, Orange-tip, Skippers and Small Copper. A meadow in full bloom aflutter with these butterflies of the countryside is a real achievement for the wildlife gardener.

It is not always easy to persuade the drifting population of nectar drinkers to settle to the business of breeding and laying eggs just where we want them. Even when the food plants of the caterpillars are plentiful (generally not the same plant as the source of nectar favoured by the mature insect) there may be many other factors that it is difficult to get right in a recreated habitat. Despite their reputation for weediness, I must make a plea for the inclusion of a patch of Nettles in the garden but you are very unlikely to find the caterpillars of Peacocks, Small Tortoiseshells and Red Admirals on your plants unless they are growing in full sun.

There are limits to the number of species that can be catered for in the garden but by maintaining a species-rich meadow and growing a species-rich hedge you stand the best chance of providing nursery areas for a good range of the sixty or so butterfly species native to Britain.

In the interests of butterflies a hedge is an especially valuable asset, breaking the force of the wind and creating sheltered areas in the garden which will be favoured by butterflies on the wing. In winter, a hedge may provide the sheltered retreat needed by hibernating specimens.

### Other insects in the garden

There is no denying the beauty and fascination of butterflies but it would be a shame if in singling out this one group of insects we were to forget all others. There is no harm in our fastening on the obvious and showy, especially if we use their occurrence as an indicator of the health of the habitats about us.

Some of the moths are almost as splendid as the highly coloured butterflies but because most are night-flying they are relatively little known. One that is better known than most is the Garden Tiger but more for its caterpillar, the 'woolly bear', which feeds on such common weeds as Chickweed, Dandelion, Dock and Groundsel, than for the adult insect, even though this is very handsomely marked.

The inclusion of good nectar plants in your garden will encourage moths to visit and feed. Some, such as the Humming-bird Hawk-moth, a common migrant that flies by day, you may see visiting flowers but the moth population often has to be gauged from the numbers swarming about outside lights or fluttering at lighted windows.

Bees are a much easier group of insects to observe taking nectar and gathering pollen to feed their young. The importance of their role as pollinators can be seen in the sometimes elaborate floral mechanisms specifically adapted to them. In the case of the White Dead-nettle, for example, the rich supply of honey is so positioned that only the large Bumble-bees with long tongues can reach it, a barrier of hairs preventing small insects from plundering it. When a Bumble-bee alights on the lower lip any pollen on its back is rubbed against the projecting stigma, so that the flower is fertilized. As the bumble-bee thrusts down it fits snugly into the shape of the corolla, getting dusted with pollen from the stamens, which is picked up by the stigma of the next flower that is visited. All being well, only an insect with the right configuration for fertilizing the flower with pollen from another flower can get at the store of nectar. Sometimes, however, rogue insects that might not otherwise be able to reach the nectar manage to get at it by puncturing the tube at its base.

There are many other arrangements far more complicated and ingenious than that securing the fertilization of the White Dead-nettle, and in the Orchids the mechanisms can be bizarrely sophisticated. The point of this example is to underline the degree to which many flowers are precisely engineered to a narrow range of pollinators, which are attracted by scent and guided in to the nectar source by vivid markings, the so-called honey guides that are not always visible to the human eye in normal light. Native wild flowers will attract far more species than you will be able to identify readily; in Britain there are about 250 species of bees, some solitary and some social.

Another group of nectar feeders that you might easily mistake for wasps or bees are the Hover-flies, insects which in themselves are quite harmless but which in shape and markings mimic stinging insects. They are insects to encourage not only because they are major flower pollinators but also because the larvae feed on aphids, pests that can be troublesome in the garden because they sap the strength of plants and spread virus diseases. Hover-flies are especially attracted to the members of the Carrot family because, even with the short tongues most of them are equipped with, they can get at the exposed nectar and pollen of these flowers.

The categories of insects I have mentioned may have a special interest for those who grow wild flowers but they represent only a small proportion of a hugely varied and fascinating sector of the animal world. The more similar to a natural habitat you are able to make your garden, the richer in insect species and other interesting creatures, ranging from large spiders to micro-organisms, it will become.

## Birds in the garden

Even the most common birds are welcome in the garden, transforming the dull and humdrum by their lively movement and song. One way to ensure that birds are attracted is to maintain a plentiful supply of food and water. If you have no pond, keep a shallow trough or pan of water in a clear part of the garden. Feeding with fruit, nuts, seeds and vegetables can make a tremendous difference in winter, particularly at the end of the season, but at other times of the year it is much better if birds can find a plentiful supply of natural food. A garden well stocked with insects and other small creatures is a great enticement for certain birds while what others need is a plentiful supply of seed. Some of the weedier wild flowers – among them Chickweed, Colt's-foot, Fat-hen, Groundsel and Shepherd's Purse – are an especially valuable source of food, characteristically seeding heavily and over an extended season. Some of these will probably be in your garden whether you like it or not. Knowing that they are important to birds, particularly when other food is scarce, may encourage you to adopt a lenient attitude towards them. Of less weedy species the most striking is the Teasel, a plant whose stiff gaunt winter outline comes alive when a flock of Goldfinches alights to feed on its seeds. A list of seed-producing plants attractive to birds is given on page 000. When you are planting any of these it is worth giving some thought to positioning so that you can observe birds feeding without disturbing them.

Birds will also be encouraged to visit your garden – and may even take up residence – if you have trees and shrubs offering shelter, song posts and nesting sites. In a small garden there is not much scope for tree planting but even in a moderately sized garden there is room for one or two trees. The ideal is to combine a few specimens of such species as Silver Birch and Rowan with bushy shrubs such as Blackthorn, Guelder Rose and Hawthorn. To these you can add Dog Rose, Honeysuckle and Traveller's Joy and the many plants that are perfectly at home along the hedge bottom.

## Small animal sanctuary

Some gardeners do not welcome the small mammals such as Bank Voles and Wood Mice that sometimes do damage to bulbs, seeds and young plants. Those with an interest in conservation probably feel that it is worth having them whether they are well behaved or not. About one species, the Hedgehog, there is general agreement. It may go off duty for four or five months of the year, hibernating in a thick pile of leaves, but for the rest of the year it is a busy feeder on beetles, slugs and snails, just the sort of pests the gardener wants to control without resorting to chemical warfare.

A thick hedge not too scrupulously tidied at the bottom is the ideal habitat for almost all our small mammals, from the Hedgehog to the Pigmy Shrew, and the less obviously managed the garden is the better pleased they will be.

*A pond is one of the most rewarding small-scale habitats to create, providing a setting for many attractive plants and encouraging insects and amphibians to visit and, perhaps, take up residence in the garden.*

### Wildlife and the pond

The pond and its marshy edge are, as I have already stressed on page 101, an ideal habitat for many lovely moisture-loving plants. Its interest, however, goes far beyond the plants that can be grown in and around it.

One way to get the pond off to a really good start is to introduce a pint or two of muddy water taken from the bottom of an already well-established pond. The water will be rich in the minute organisms that feed on decaying vegetation, even one another; they are essential for sustaining a healthy pond because these are the food of creatures higher up the chain.

If you want fish in your pond that is something you will have to introduce but you may find frogs, toads and newts making their own way there. If you want the amphibians, and it is a very good idea for gardeners to make room for them, given that the larger stretches of water where they were once common are more and more frequently drained or polluted, fish are not such a good idea. They will eat spawn and tadpoles so if you want to have them and the vulnerable amphibians you will need to keep them separated.

### Ecological gardening

I am often asked for my views on which are the most desirable and achievable kinds of wildlife habitat that the keen gardener can create. There is no doubt that for me the flowering meadow is a very special achievement, that wonderful medley of bloom and seedheads above which flutter a bright assortment of butterflies, evocative of parts of our landscape which are now relatively rare but which until recently we took completely for granted. I acknowledge that there is quite a bit of work involved in getting a flowering meadow started and that it does need space.

A species-rich hedge (not necessarily an alternative to a flowering meadow for the two together make a superb combination) is something that can be built up even on quite a modest scale in a garden of moderate size and it caters for a very wide range of animal and plant life.

The pond does give those who garden on a small scale the chance to create in miniature something like a coherent habitat and one of unlimited fascination.

If you have the time and space, my advice is to try them all and any other natural associations that your garden lends itself to. Avoiding the use of insecticides, herbicides and fertilizers or using them only very sparingly will allow the broadest range of species a chance to find a home at your back door.

# TRADITIONAL USES FOR WILD FLOWERS

In the eighteenth and nineteenth centuries a flood of previously unknown exotics entered European gardens. These were the discoveries of a remarkable group of plant hunters who probed every accessible corner of the world for new species to meet the demands of wealthy connoisseurs with an insatiable appetite for botanical novelties. Not all the plants lavishly cultivated in the grand gardens designed for them are still widely grown – many varieties and species have been lost for ever – but these relatively recent introductions and the horticultural developments of them are the major plants of the modern garden. This period of very active introduction has left its mark for we have inherited a dismissive attitude to native plants, favouring instead the outsider.

Two other developments in the nineteenth century helped to change attitudes to wild flowers. Progress in medical science, particularly in pharmacology, led to the modern rational of therapeutic medicine. After centuries of relying on plants or plant parts as the form in which medication was administered, mainstream medicine, wanting to refine its understanding of exact cause and effect, concentrated on isolating chemical substances and then on manufacturing them. Eventually even the tradition of folk medicine was undermined.

The second main development concerned changes in patterns of diet. The population drift to towns from the country gathered momentum and perhaps because of better conditions in the country itself there was less and less reliance on wild plants for food. Although in other European countries the peasant habit of enjoying the wild harvest has managed to survive, in Britain it has almost disappeared.

The growing awareness of the threat to wild flowers and their habitats has coincided with and, possibly, revived an interest in the uses of native plants, especially medicinal and culinary but also for cosmetics, as dyes and as a source of decoration for the home. This interest is certainly a healthy one that in the long term can only lead to a fuller appreciation of the qualities of our wild flowers. There is a danger, however, that many people may turn to plants in the wild, gather unscrupulously and so do further damage to habitats and reduce the populations of individual species. The case for growing wild flowers if you want to gather their blooms, fruits or foliage is a very strong one.

Of course, there are some species – Blackberry, Dandelion and Elder among them – that continue to be common and are not likely to be damaged by collection in the wild. Bear in mind, however, the following general points whenever you are thinking of collecting plants for food or for any other purpose. Under the Conservation of Wild Creatures and Wild Plants Act 1975 it is illegal to uproot a plant without reasonable excuse when it is on someone else's property without the owner's permisson; and some protected species cannot be picked at all without a licence. When you are taking leaves, fruit or flowers from plants in the wild gather only small quantities from each plant and do so in a way that will not damage its health or appearance. Bear in mind, when you are gathering plants for food, that land nearby may have been recently sprayed with insecticides and weedkillers. It is also best to avoid taking plants from the edges of busy roads as these may be contaminated by exhaust fumes.

One final warning may seem unnecessary, particularly as we have very few plants that are highly poisonous. You should never, however, eat any wild plant, whether it is gathered in the hedgerow or in the garden, that you cannot identify with absolute certainty.

### Wild flowers for cutting

One of the simplest ways of enjoying wild flowers when they are growing in quantity is to bring a few indoors, but not all wild flowers are suitable for cutting. Comfrey, for example, collapses when it is cut and no blandishments will revive it. There are, nonetheless, a large number of native species that are sadly undervalued as flowers for cutting, giving a distinctive character to large and small arrangements. Flowers that are particularly long-lasting include many of the Daisy family, such as Corn Chamomile, Corn Marigold, Cornflower, Yarrow and Oxeye Daisy; also Daffodils, Campions and the Mallows.

Care at picking time will give the best chance of a long display. Gather flowers early in the day and aim to get them in a deep container up to their necks in tepid water as quickly as possible. Except in the case of plants with hollow stems, splitting the stems will encourage them to take up water and become firm. After an hour or so standing in deep water, the flowers can be arranged. With wild flowers simple arrangements are generally more effective than elaborate ones.

*Once you have your own wild flowers, but not before, you can think about using them for picking and indoor decoration, either fresh or as dried material, as has been used on this mirror frame.*

As with cultivated flowers, the addition of a commercially available cut flower life lengthener to the water will be very effective. It will keep the water fresh and, by feeding the flowers, really will extend their lives.

Some flowers, including Violets, can be freshened by a light spray but keep water off the petals of Cowslips, Hearts-ease and Primroses for it will mark them.

Keep the water in the vase topped up and if it starts getting dirty change it. Daffodils and Bluebells produce a slimy sap and their water will need frequent changing.

### Wild flowers and medicine

The interest that the medical world is again taking in herbs that for centuries enjoyed enormous prestige among herbalists and practitioners of folk medicine, only to be discarded when the modern drug industry was confident of conquering all human ills, is sober and measured. It is not based on a blind acceptance of ancient authorities, nor is there a fixed dogma to which the evidence must conform. Medical science now wants to know what the true values might be of the constituents of many herbs, European and exotic, that have enjoyed high reputations without their efficacy or mode of operation being accurately assessed or understood.

The sixteenth- and seventeenth-century writers who are often quoted in the Wild Flower Guide – especially Nicholas Culpeper, John Gerard and John Parkinson – passed on to us an amazing body of information combining observed fact, vivid fantasy and an uncritical acceptance of anything handed down from the ancient world as the ultimate authority on matters botanical and medical. The two subjects went hand in hand; it was not until the works of Carl Linnaeus were published in the second quarter of the eighteenth century that botany became a subject fit for enquiry independent of medicine. The link was part of the ancient inheritance, the most influential works, such as *De Materia Medica*, the massive compilation of Dioscorides, a physician of the first century AD who was attached to the Roman army, recording botanical information for its medical value.

Another source of distortion in the old herbals was the general doctrine used to justify the use of specific herbs for particular complaints. The ideas were current long before the sixteenth century but it was in the first half of that century that they were articulated by Paracelsus, a Swiss physician. According to the dogma, which came to be known as the Doctrine of Signatures, there was a God-given clue in the form and character of a plant clearly indicating the affliction that it could remedy. The plant resembled either the part of the body to be treated (for instance the markings on the Clover leaf resembled the heart) or the disease (the spotted leaves of Lungwort brought to mind ulcerated lungs).

In rejecting this rationalization of herbal medicine we have risked throwing out the baby with the bath water. It is not my purpose in this book to provide a manual of medical self-help based on traditional and newly verified treatments. This is, after all, a subject that the amateur must approach with very great caution, but it may help in under-

standing more specialist literature to explain the three main methods used in the preparation of herbal remedies.

Decoctions are prepared by hot-water treatment of plant parts that are fibrous or woody, such as roots, stems, bark and seed. The proportions used are generally 30 g of material to 500 ml (1 oz to 20 fl oz). The material is steeped in the water for about 10 minutes, then covered and brought to the boil, simmered for about 15 minutes, and left in the water for a further ten minutes before straining and cooling.

Infusions extract the water-soluble constituents from leaves and other non-woody parts of plants. The normal procedure is to pour 500 ml of boiling water over 30 g (20 fl oz over 1 oz) of the material in a vessel with a tight-fitting lid. It is left with the lid on for about 15 minutes and then the liquid is strained and cooled.

Poultices are made either from fresh plant material that is pulped and mixed with a small quantity of hot water or from dried material that is made into a paste with a substance such as bran or flour that is mixed with hot water. The most convenient way to apply poultices is with the mixture sandwiched between two pieces of thin cloth.

While the curative and tonic effects of many herbal remedies are indisputable, you should seek specialist advice for any condition that requires prolonged treatment.

### The culinary uses of wild flowers

We would not have rich pickings if we were left to scrape a living exclusively from our native wild plants; searching and preparation might need more energy than we would get from the food we would eventually be able to consume. Nevertheless over 150 of our native plants can provide a useful and interesting supplement to our ordinary diet, a supplement that until quite recently country people were very glad to take advantage of in difficult times.

One of the best ways of using wild plants is as an addition to salads. Always select young and tender leaves for as the season develops the leaves become coarse and very strong or bitter flavoured. Even the most succulent leaves can be much more strongly flavoured than cultivated vegetables.

Two particularly good and tasty wild plants which can be used as an addition to salads are Salad Burnet, which has a fresh, cucumber-like flavour, and Sorrel, with its superb sharp and lemony taste. Another useful plant, Dandelion, is widely-used as a salad vegetable in Europe. In France selected forms are cultivated and sold at times of the year when relatively few green vegetables are available. Plants can stand repeated picking if only a few leaves are taken at a time. The natural bitterness of the plant can be moderated by blanching whilst growing.

The flowers of some wild plants are in themselves edible and make an attractive addition to a salad. Keep the amount used in proportion for their principal interest is as decoration. The most suitable are Cowslips, Daisies, Primroses, Roses, Violets and Wild Pansies.

A number of weedy plants can also be served as cooked greens. Among the best are Fat Hen, Chickweed, Ground Elder, Bistort, Common Sorrel, Stinging Nettle and Common Comfrey. The best method of using Comfrey is probably in fritters as it is a very mucilaginous plant. With the others prepare them as you would Spinach, washing them thoroughly, placing them in a pan with no water other than that clinging to the leaves after washing, throw in a large knob of butter and cook gently until the leaves are tender. A good method of cooking Sorrel is to combine it with equal parts of Spinach, which will help to moderate its strong flavour. It can also be made into a delicious sauce to be served with fish.

One of the best ways of using Nettles is as a soup. You need to gather a good half litre (pint) of fresh young tops, which are prepared with a litre of milk or stock to which has been added a knob of butter and about 50 g (2 oz) of rolled oats. Simmer the soup for about 45 minutes and just before serving stir in a generous sprinkling of chopped parsley.

Sea-kale is a wild plant that used to be sold as a vegetable, the young stems being forced and blanched. Do not gather it in the wild as it is no longer a common plant but it is worth growing for its distinctive flavour. The blanched stems are prepared in the same way as asparagus, tied in bundles, cooked in a deep pan of water and served with a hollandaise sauce or with melted butter and lemon juice.

Some wild plants are best used simply as flavourings. This is true of Wild Marjoram and Wild Thyme. They can be used fresh or dried, the flavour of the fresh herb, however, being superior to the dried form. Both of these herbs are most effective added to meat dishes; Wild Thyme needs to be used lavishly as it is not as strongly flavoured as the cultivated varieties.

Another common plant that makes a magnificently pungent flavouring is an old introduction that has escaped and become a common weed of roadsides and waste places. The roots of Horseradish, cleaned, peeled and finely grated, added with castor sugar, vinegar and salt to lightly whisked cream, or just grated and added to plain yogurt, makes one of the best accompaniments to beef and smoked fish.

Tansy is one herb formerly grown widely, not only for its supposed medical value but also as a flavouring that most who have tried it consider too bitter for the modern palate. It was traditionally used in omelettes and puddings at Easter; perhaps the explanation of this potent flavour is a matter of religion not of cuisine.

Much easier for us to accept is the use of wild plants in the preparation of sweetmeats, conserves and jams. Blackberry jam is as popular as ever but why not try a Blackberry fool made from half a litre of blackberries to 600 ml of cream (one pound to one pint)?

There are numerous early recipes for the making of syrups, conserves and pastes of Violets. Commercially prepared candied Violets are a curious survival of the old banqueting conceits. Primroses lend themselves just as well to candying. Gather them when dry and detach the flower from the green calyx. Prepare a syrup by boiling icing sugar in water. You can test when it is ready by dropping a little into cold water; when ready it should set firm. Put the Primroses in for a minute, then take them out and leave to dry in a well-aired place. When dry sprinkle with icing sugar.

Numerous wines and beers have also been prepared from wild plants and their flowers. Cowslip wine is probably the best known and is said to be the finest flavoured but collecting enough flowers could devastate the colony in your garden. Dandelion wine makes an interesting alternative and the plant is not one in short supply. For every 4.5 litres (gallon) of water you need the same measure of Dandelion flowers, two large oranges, one large lemon, 60 g (2 oz) raisins, two tablespoons of yeast and 1.5 kg (3¼ lb) sugar. Rinse the flowers and make sure that they are free of insects. Place in a large pan with the water and bring to the boil. Add the sugar and the rinds of the oranges and lemons. Bring to the boil again and simmer for one hour. Strain and let cool. When tepid add the raisins and

*Leaves and flowers of many of our wild plants are easily pressed and can be used to make attractive decorations arranged on cards or mounted under glass. Pressing takes about six weeks.*

the juices of the oranges and lemon. Leave it a week then strain and put into clean bottles. When fermentation has finished, about a month after bottling, cork firmly and let stand for about six months before using.

The recipes given here far from exhaust the possibilities wild plants offer you. It is a particularly interesting subject to pursue through old herbals and recipe books for it gives us a refreshingly direct insight into the way people in the past looked on the plants around them.

## Pressing and preserving flowers

Pressing flowers, an activity passionately pursued by Victorian ladies, was an extension of polite society's interest in botany and wild flowers. Fortunately we can escape the prim and cloying overtones of the Victorian parlour and avoid their sometimes thoughtless plundering of wild plants in their native habitats. By growing your own plants you will have excellent material on your doorstep that can be gathered when it is in peak condition and when you know that you have the time to give it your full attention.

The best time to pick is when there is no moisture on the petals but before the heat of the day takes the freshness off the flowers. Use scissors to detach the flowers, as this way you will cause least damage to the plant, and place the collected material in a basket or box.

Cheap and efficient presses are once again readily available and are easier to manage than telephone directories or other makeshift arrangements. The flowers need to be arranged so that they do not touch, placed between sheets of absorbent paper before even pressure is applied. Flowers and foliage need to be left for a good six weeks in a well-ventilated room before the press is opened. Once the material is adequately dried it can be arranged on cards and to form pictures that are put under glass.

Many wild flowers and seedheads are suitable for drying on the stem for winter decoration and use in flower arrangements. These include Corncockle, Common Toadflax, Foxglove, Lady's Bedstraw, Poppy and most members of the Cow Parsley and Dock families (even the most notorious wild plants have their uses). The infinite variety and decorative uses of most grasses, both cultivated and wild, gives the fresh or dried flower arranger the opportunity to make use of their interest and charm. Many common grasses, such as Bents, Bromes, Cock's-foot, Meadow Foxtail, Quaking Grasses, Timothy or Cat's-tail, Rushes and Sedges are freely obtained from any uncut grassy area. A wide range of wild flowers can be preserved by using the silica-gel technique. The flowers and their stems are completely covered for five or six days by the gel, which absorbs the moisture in the plant material.

# ANNUAL WILD FLOWERS FOR BORDERS

| Plant name | Flowering | Colour | Height guide |
|---|---|---|---|
| Charlock<br>*Sinapsis arvensis* | April-June | yellow | tall |
| Common Field-Speedwell<br>*Veronica persica* | Feb-Oct | blue | small |
| Common Fumitory<br>*Fumaria officinalis* | May-Oct | purple | medium |
| Corn Buttercup<br>*Ranunculus arvensis* | June-July | yellow | medium |
| Corn Chamomile<br>*Anthemis arvensis* | June-July | white | small |
| Corncockle<br>*Agrostemma githago* | June-Aug | purple | tall |
| Cornflower<br>*Centaurea cyanus* | June-Aug | blue | tall |
| Corn Marigold<br>*Chrysanthemum segetum* | June-Aug | yellow | medium |
| Field Forget-me-not<br>*Myosotis arvensis* | April-Sept | blue | medium |
| Field Pansy<br>*Viola arvensis* | April-Sept | cream | small |
| Field Poppy<br>*Papaver rhoeas* | May-Aug | red | medium |
| Ivy-leaved Speedwell<br>*Veronica hederifolia* | April-July | blue | small |
| Long-headed Poppy<br>*Papaver dubium* | June-July | red | medium |
| Pale Flax<br>*Linum bienne* | May-Sept | blue | medium |
| Pheasant's-eye<br>*Adonis annua* | May-July | red | medium |
| Scarlet Pimpernel<br>*Anagallis arvensis* | May-Aug | scarlet | small |
| Scented Mayweed<br>*Matricaria recutita* | May-Aug | white | medium |
| Scentless Mayweed<br>*Tripleurospermum inodorum* | July-Sept | white | medium |
| White Campion<br>*Silene alba* | May-Aug | white | tall |
| Wild Pansy<br>*Viola tricolor* | April-Sept | violet & yellow | small |

*Height guide:* small = average height less than 30cm (12in); medium = average height between 30 and 60cm (12 and 24in); tall = average height in excess of 60cm (24in)

# WILD FLOWERS FOR SUNNY BORDERS

| Plant name | Flowering | Colour | Height guide | Type |
|---|---|---|---|---|
| Agrimony<br>*Agrimonia eupatoria* | June-Aug | yellow | medium | compact |
| Alkanet<br>*Anchusa officinalis* | June-Sept | blue | medium | bushy |
| Betony<br>*Stachys officinalis* | June-Sept | purple | medium | bushy |
| Bloody Crane's-bill<br>*Geranium sanguineum* | May-Aug | purple | medium | compact |
| Cheddar Pink<br>*Dianthus gratianopolitanus* | June-July | pink | medium | clump-forming |
| Clustered Bellflower<br>*Campanula glomerata* | May-Sept | blue | small | leafy |
| Columbine<br>*Aquilegia vulgaris* | May-June | blue | tall | open |
| Common Dog-violet<br>*Viola riviniana* | April-July | violet | small | spreading |
| Common Evening-primrose<br>*Oenothera biennis* | June-Sept | yellow | tall | coarse-leaved |
| Common Knapweed<br>*Centaurea nigra* | June-Sept | purple | medium | loosely bushy |
| Common Restharrow<br>*Ononis repens* | June-Sept | pink | medium | spreading |
| Cowslip<br>*Primula veris* | April-May | yellow | small | rosette-forming |
| Devils'-bit Scabious<br>*Succisa pratensis* | June-Oct | mauve | tall | open, erect |
| Dusky Crane's-bill<br>*Geranium phaeum* | May-June | maroon | medium | large-leaved, compact |
| Elecampane<br>*Inula helenium* | July-Aug | yellow | tall | large, erect |
| Feverfew<br>*Tanacetum parthenium* | July-Aug | white | medium | loosely bushy |
| Field Scabious<br>*Knautia arvensis* | June-Sept | mauve | tall | open, bushy |
| Foxglove<br>*Digitalis purpurea* | June-Sept | purple | tall | erect |
| Globeflower<br>*Trollius europaeus* | June-Aug | yellow | medium | open, bushy |
| Goldenrod<br>*Solidago virgaurea* | July-Sept | yellow | medium | erect |
| Greater Celandine<br>*Chelidonium majus* | May-July | yellow | tall | large-leaved |
| Greater Knapweed<br>*Centaurea scabiosa* | July-Sept | purple | tall | open, bushy |

*Wild Flowers for Sunny Borders contd*

| | | | | |
|---|---|---|---|---|
| Greater Stitchwort<br>*Stelleria holostea* | April-June | white | medium | compact |
| Great Mullein<br>*Verbascum thapsus* | June-August | yellow | tall | erect |
| Harebell<br>*Campanula rotundifolia* | July-Sept | blue | small | open, bushy |
| Hemp-agrimony<br>*Eupatorium cannabinum* | July-Sept | pink | tall | compact, erect |
| Hoary Mullein<br>*Verbascum pulverulentum* | June-July | yellow | tall | erect |
| Hoary Plantain<br>*Plantago media* | May-Aug | pink | small | rosette-forming |
| Jacob's-ladder<br>*Polemonium caeruleum* | May-July | blue | tall | erect |
| Lady's Bedstraw<br>*Galium verum* | June-Aug | yellow | medium | clump-forming |
| Meadow Clary<br>*Salvia pratensis* | June-July | blue | tall | erect |
| Meadow Crane's-bill<br>*Geranium pratense* | May-Sept | blue | tall | open, large-leaved |
| Meadowsweet<br>*Filipendula ulmaria* | June-Aug | white | tall | open, bushy |
| Musk Mallow<br>*Malva moschata* | June-Aug | pink | tall | loosely bushy |
| Narrow-leaved Everlasting-pea<br>*Lathyrus sylvestris* | June-Aug | red | tall | climbing |
| Nettle-leaved Bellflower<br>*Campanula trachelium* | July-Sept | blue | tall | erect |
| Oxeye Daisy<br>*Leucanthemum vulgare* | May-Aug | white | tall | free-flowering, bushy |
| Perforate St John's-wort<br>*Hypericum perforatum* | June-Sept | yellow | medium | erect |
| Purple-loosestrife<br>*Lythrum salicaria* | June-Aug | purple | tall | erect |
| Ragged-Robin<br>*Lychnis flos-cuculi* | May-June | red | tall | slender, erect |
| Red Campion<br>*Silene dioica* | May-Nov | red | tall | erect |
| Russian Comfrey<br>*Symphytum × uplandicum* | May-Aug | mauve | tall | large-leaved, bushy |
| Sainfoin<br>*Onobrychis viciifolia* | May-Aug | pink | medium | open, bushy |
| Small Scabious<br>*Scabiosa columbaria* | June-Aug | mauve | medium | open, bushy |
| Sneezewort<br>*Achillea ptarmica* | July-Aug | white | tall | erect |
| Soapwort<br>*Saponaria officinalis* | July-Sept | pink | tall | open, erect |

*Wild Flowers for Sunny Borders contd*

| | | | | |
|---|---|---|---|---|
| Sweet Violet<br>*Viola odorata* | Feb–April | violet | small | spreading |
| Teasel<br>*Dipsacus fullonum* subsp. *sylvestris* | July–Aug | mauve | tall | gauntly upright |
| Viper's-bugloss<br>*Echium vulgare* | June–Sept | blue | tall | open, bushy |
| Water Forget-me-not<br>*Myosotis scorpioides* | May–Sept | blue | medium | compact |
| Wild Strawberry<br>*Fragaria vesca* | April–July | white | small | spreading |

*Height guide:* small = average height less than 30cm (12in); medium = average height between 30 and 60cm (12 and 24in); tall = average height in excess of 60cm (24in)

# NECTAR PLANTS FOR BUTTERFLIES

**Short-growing plants**
*on average*
*less than 30cm (12in)*

Bird's-foot-trefoil
  *Lotus corniculatus*
Bulbous Buttercup
  *Ranunculus bulbosus*
Carline Thistle
  *Carlina vulgaris*
Cowslip
  *Primula veris*
Daisy
  *Bellis perennis*
Dandelion
  *Taraxacum officinale*
Lesser Celandine
  *Ranunculus ficaria*
Mouse-ear Hawkweed
  *Hieracium pilosella*
Orange Hawkweed
  *Hieracium aurantiacum*
Primrose
  *Primula vulgaris*
Sea Campion
  *Silene maritima*
Sweet Violet
  *Viola odorata*
Thrift
  *Armeria maritima* subsp. *maritima*
Tormentil
  *Potentilla erecta*
Wild Pansy
  *Viola tricolor*
Wild Thyme
  *Thymus praecox* subsp. *arcticus*
Wild White Clover
  *Trifolium repens*

**Plants of middle height**
*on average between*
*30 and 60cm (12 and 24in)*

Autumn Hawkbit
  *Leontodon autumnalis*
Bluebell
  *Hyacinthoides non-scriptus*
Cat's-ear
  *Hypochoeris radicata*
Common Hawkweed
  *Hieracium vulgatum*
Common Knapweed
  *Centaurea nigra*
Corn Marigold
  *Chrysanthemum segetum*
Cuckooflower
  *Cardamine pratensis*
Feverfew
  *Tanacetum parthenium*
Heather
  *Calluna vulgaris*
Kidney Vetch
  *Anthyllis vulneraria*
Oxeye Daisy
  *Leucanthemum vulgare*
Ragged-Robin
  *Lychnis flos-cuculi*
Rough Hawkbit
  *Leontodon hispidus*
Sheep's-bit
  *Jasione montana*
Small Scabious
  *Scabiosa columbaria*
Wild Marjoram
  *Origanum vulgare*
Yarrow
  *Achillea millefolium*

**Tall-growing plants**
*on average*
*more than 60cm (24in)*

Bladder Campion
  *Silene vulgaris*
Cornflower
  *Centaurea cyanus*
Dame's-violet
  *Hesperis matronalis*
Devils'-bit Scabious
  *Succisa pratensis*
Field Scabious
  *Knautia arvensis*
Fuller's Teasel
  *Dipsacus fullonum* subsp. *fullonum*
Greater Knapweed
  *Centaurea scabiosa*
Hemp-agrimony
  *Eupatorium cannabinum*
Meadow Buttercup
  *Ranunculus acris*
Michaelmas-daisy
  *Aster novi-belgii*
Musk Mallow
  *Malva moschata*
Purple-loosestrife
  *Lythrum salicaria*
Red Valerian
  *Centranthus ruber*
Water Mint
  *Mentha aquatica*
White Campion
  *Silene alba*
Woundwort
  *Stachys* sp.

# Contents

Some words are shown in bold, **like this**. You can find them in the glossary on page 23.

# WILD FLOWERS FOR LIGHT SHADE

| Plant name | Flowering | Colour | Height guide | Type |
| --- | --- | --- | --- | --- |
| Betony<br>*Stachys officinalis* | June-Sept | purple | medium | Perennial |
| Bluebell<br>*Hyacinthoides non-scriptus* | April-June | blue | medium | Bulb |
| Bugle<br>*Ajuga reptans* | May-July | blue | small | Perennial |
| Common Dog-violet<br>*Viola riviniana* | April-July | violet | small | Perennial |
| Cowslip<br>*Primula veris* | April-May | yellow | small | Perennial |
| Dark Mullein<br>*Verbascum nigrum* | June-Oct | yellow | tall | Biennial |
| Devils'-bit Scabious<br>*Succisa pratensis* | June-Oct | mauve | tall | Perennial |
| Dog-rose<br>*Rosa canina* | June-July | pink | tall | Shrub |
| Enchanter's-nightshade<br>*Circaea lutetiana* | June-Aug | white | medium | Perennial |
| Field Forget-me-not<br>*Myosotis arvensis* | April-Sept | blue | medium | Annual |
| Foxglove<br>*Digitalis purpurea* | June-Sept | purple | tall | Biennial |
| Garlic Mustard<br>*Alliaria petiolata* | April-June | white | tall | Biennial |
| Germander Speedwell<br>*Veronica chamaedrys* | March-July | blue | medium | Perennial |
| Greater Stitchwort<br>*Stellaria holostea* | April-June | white | medium | Perennial |
| Great Mullein<br>*Verbascum thapsus* | June-Aug | yellow | tall | Biennial |
| Ground-ivy<br>*Glechoma hederacea* | March-May | blue | small | Perennial |
| Hairy St John's-wort<br>*Hypericum hirsutum* | July-Aug | yellow | tall | Perennial |
| Hedge Woundwort<br>*Stachys sylvatica* | May-Aug | purple | tall | Perennial |
| Herb-Robert<br>*Geranium robertianum* | April-Oct | pink | medium | Annual |
| Honeysuckle<br>*Lonicera periclymenum* | June-Sept | yellow-orange | tall | Shrub |
| Lesser Celandine<br>*Ranunculus ficaria* | March-May | yellow | small | Perennial |
| Lesser Periwinkle<br>*Vinca minor* | March-May | blue | small | Perennial |
| Lords-and-ladies<br>*Arum maculatum* | April-May | green | medium | Perennial |

*Wild Flowers for Light Shade contd*

| | | | | |
|---|---|---|---|---|
| Oxlip<br>*Primula elatior* | April-May | yellow | small | Perennial |
| Primrose<br>*Primula vulgaris* | March-May | yellow | small | Perennial |
| Ragged-Robin<br>*Lychnis flos-cuculi* | May-June | red | tall | Perennial |
| Ramsons<br>*Allium ursinum* | April-June | white | medium | Bulb |
| Red Campion<br>*Silene dioica* | May-Nov | red | tall | Perennial |
| Sanicle<br>*Sanicula europaea* | May-Aug | pink | medium | Perennial |
| Stinking Hellebore<br>*Helleborus foetidus* | March-April | green | medium | Perennial |
| Sweet Violet<br>*Viola odorata* | Feb-April | violet | small | Perennial |
| Teasel<br>*Dipsacus fullonum* subsp. *sylvestris* | July-Aug | mauve | tall | Biennial |
| Tufted Vetch<br>*Vicia cracca* | June-Aug | blue | tall | Perennial |
| Upright Hedge-parsley<br>*Torilis japonica* | July-Aug | white | tall | Annual |
| White Bryony<br>*Bryonia dioica* | May-Sept | white | tall | Perennial |
| Wild Strawberry<br>*Fragaria vesca* | April-July | white | small | Perennial |
| Winter Aconite<br>*Eranthis hyemalis* | Jan-March | yellow | small | Perennial |
| Wood Anemone<br>*Anemone nemorosa* | March-May | white | small | Perennial |
| Wood Avens<br>*Geum urbanum* | May-Aug | yellow | medium | Perennial |
| Wood Forget-me-not<br>*Myosotis sylvatica* | May-July | blue | medium | Perennial |
| Wood Sage<br>*Teucrium scorodonia* | July-Sept | yellow | medium | Perennial |
| Wood-sorrel<br>*Oxalis acetosella* | April-June | white | small | Perennial |
| Wood Spurge<br>*Euphorbia amygdaloides* | March-May | green | tall | Perennial |
| Yellow Archangel<br>*Lamiastrum galeobdolon* | May-Aug | yellow | medium | Perennial |

*Height guide:* small = average height less than 30cm (12in); medium = average height between 30 and 60cm (12 and 24in); tall = average height in excess of 60cm (24in)

# WILD FLOWERS FOR DAMP CONDITIONS

| Plant name | Flowering | Colour | Height guide | Type |
|---|---|---|---|---|
| Brooklime *Veronica beccabunga* | May-Aug | blue | medium | Perennial |
| Common Fleabane *Pulicaria dysenterica* | July-Sept | yellow | medium | Perennial |
| Cuckooflower *Cardamine pratensis* | April-July | pink | medium | Perennial |
| Gipsywort *Lycopus europaeus* | June-Sept | pink | tall | Perennial |
| Greater Bird's-foot-trefoil *Lotus uliginosus* | June-Aug | yellow | medium | Perennial |
| Hemp-agrimony *Eupatorium cannabinum* | July-Sept | pink | tall | Perennial |
| Lesser Bulrush *Typha angustifolia* | June-July | brown | tall | Perennial |
| Lesser Spearwort *Ranunculus flammula* | May-Sept | yellow | tall | Perennial |
| Marsh-marigold *Caltha palustris* | March-July | yellow | medium | Perennial |
| Marsh Woundwort *Stachys palustris* | July-Sept | purple | tall | Perennial |
| Meadow Buttercup *Ranunculus acris* | April-May | yellow | tall | Perennial |
| Meadowsweet *Filipendula ulmaria* | June-Aug | white | tall | Perennial |
| Musk *Mimulus moschatus* | July-Sept | yellow | medium | Perennial |
| Purple-loosestrife *Lythrum salicaria* | June-Aug | purple | tall | Perennial |
| Ragged-Robin *Lychnis flos-cuculi* | May-June | red | tall | Perennial |
| Water Avens *Geum rivale* | April-July | brown-yellow | medium | Perennial |
| Water Figwort *Scrophularia auriculata* | June-Sept | red | tall | Perennial |
| Water Forget-me-not *Myosotis scorpioides* | May-Sept | blue | medium | Perennial |
| Water Mint *Mentha aquatica* | July-Oct | lilac | tall | Perennial |
| Yellow Iris *Iris pseudacorus* | May-July | yellow | tall | Perennial |
| Yellow Loosestrife *Lysimachia vulgaris* | July-Aug | yellow | tall | Perennial |

*Height guide:* small = average height less than 30cm (12in); medium = average height between 30 and 60cm (12 and 24in); tall = average height in excess of 60cm (24in)

# SEED-PRODUCING WILD FLOWERS TO ATTRACT BIRDS

| Plant name | Height guide | Type |
|---|---|---|
| Betony<br>*Stachys officinalis* | medium | Perennial |
| Common Bird's-foot-trefoil<br>*Lotus corniculatus* | small | Perennial |
| Common Dandelion<br>*Taraxacum officinale* | medium | Perennial |
| Common Evening-primrose<br>*Oenothera biennis* | tall | Biennial |
| Common Knapweed<br>*Centaurea nigra* | medium | Perennial |
| Cow Parsley<br>*Anthriscus sylvestris* | tall | Biennial |
| Field Forget-me-not<br>*Myosotis arvensis* | medium | Annual |
| Greater Burdock<br>*Arctium lappa* | tall | Biennial |
| Greater Knapweed<br>*Centaurea scabiosa* | tall | Perennial |
| Hoary Plantain<br>*Plantago media* | small | Perennial |
| Hogweed<br>*Heracleum sphondylium* | tall | Biennial |
| Large-flowered Evening-primrose<br>*Oenothera erythrosepela* | tall | Biennial |
| Lesser Burdock<br>*Arctium minus* | tall | Biennial |
| Meadowsweet<br>*Filipendula ulmaria* | tall | Perennial |
| Michaelmas-daisy<br>*Aster novi-belgii* | tall | Perennial |
| Milk Thistle<br>*Silybum marianum* | tall | Annual |
| Musk Thistle<br>*Carduus nutans* | tall | Biennial |
| Pale Flax<br>*Linum bienne* | medium | Annual |
| Scotch Thistle<br>*Onopordum acanthium* | tall | Biennial |
| Teasel<br>*Dipsacus fullonum* subsp. *sylvestris* | tall | Biennial |
| Woolly Thistle<br>*Cirsium eriophorum* | tall | Biennial |

*Height guide:* small = average height less than 30cm (12in); medium = average height between 30 and 60cm (12 and 24in); tall = average height in excess of 60cm (24in)

# WILD FLOWERS FOR MEADOWS

| Plant name | Flowering | Colour | Height guide | Type |
|---|---|---|---|---|
| Black Medick<br>*Medicago lupulina* | April-Aug | yellow | medium | Annual |
| Cat's-ear<br>*Hypochoeris radicata* | May-Sept | yellow | medium | Perennial |
| Clustered Bellflower<br>*Campanula glomerata* | May-Sept | blue | small | Perennial |
| Common Bird's-foot-trefoil<br>*Lotus corniculatus* | May-Sept | yellow | small | Perennial |
| Common Knapweed<br>*Centaurea nigra* | June-Sept | purple | medium | Perennial |
| Common Restharrow<br>*Ononis repens* | June-Sept | pink | medium | Perennial |
| Common Sorrel<br>*Rumex acetosa* | May-June | pink | tall | Perennial |
| Common Vetch<br>*Vicia sativa* | April-Sept | purple | tall | Annual |
| Cowslip<br>*Primula veris* | April-May | yellow | small | Perennial |
| Cuckooflower<br>*Cardamine pratensis* | April-July | pink | medium | Perennial |
| Dropwort<br>*Filipendula vulgaris* | June-Aug | white | tall | Perennial |
| Field Scabious<br>*Knautia arvensis* | June-Sept | mauve | tall | Perennial |
| Germander Speedwell<br>*Veronica chamaedrys* | March-July | blue | small | Perennial |
| Goat's-beard<br>*Tragopogon pratensis* | June-July | yellow | medium | Annual |
| Great Burnet<br>*Sanguisorba officinalis* | June-Sept | red | tall | Perennial |
| Greater Knapweed<br>*Centaurea scabiosa* | July-Sept | purple | tall | Perennial |
| Harebell<br>*Campanula rotundifolia* | July-Sept | blue | small | Perennial |
| Hoary Plantain<br>*Plantago media* | May-Aug | pink | small | Perennial |
| Horseshoe Vetch<br>*Hippocrepis comosa* | May-July | yellow | small | Perennial |
| Kidney Vetch<br>*Anthyllis vulneraria* | May-Sept | yellow | medium | Perennial |
| Lady's Bedstraw<br>*Galium verum* | June-Aug | yellow | medium | Perennial |
| Marsh-marigold<br>*Caltha palustris* | March-July | yellow | medium | Perennial |
| Meadow Buttercup<br>*Ranunculus acris* | April-May | yellow | tall | Perennial |

*Wild Flowers for Meadows contd*

| | | | | |
|---|---|---|---|---|
| Meadow Crane's-bill<br>*Geranium pratense* | May-Sept | blue | tall | Perennial |
| Meadow Saxifrage<br>*Saxifraga granulata* | April-June | white | medium | Perennial |
| Meadowsweet<br>*Filipendula ulmaria* | June-Aug | white | tall | Perennial |
| Oxeye Daisy<br>*Leucanthemum vulgare* | May-Aug | white | tall | Perennial |
| Pepper-saxifrage<br>*Silaum silaus* | June-Aug | yellow | medium | Perennial |
| Perforate St John's-wort<br>*Hypericum perforatum* | June-Sept | yellow | medium | Perennial |
| Pignut<br>*Conopodium majus* | May-July | white | medium | Perennial |
| Ragged-Robin<br>*Lychnis flos-cuculi* | May-June | red | tall | Perennial |
| Ribwort Plantain<br>*Plantago lanceolata* | April-Aug | brown | medium | Perennial |
| Rough Hawkbit<br>*Leontodon hispidus* | May-Sept | yellow | medium | Perennial |
| Sainfoin<br>*Onobrychis viciifolia* | May-Aug | pink | medium | Perennial |
| Salad Burnet<br>*Sanguisorba minor* subsp. *minor* | May-Aug | green | medium | Perennial |
| Selfheal<br>*Prunella vulgaris* | June-Sept | purple | medium | Perennial |
| Small Scabious<br>*Scabiosa columbaria* | June-Aug | mauve | medium | Perennial |
| Tufted Vetch<br>*Vicia cracca* | June-Aug | blue | tall | Perennial |
| Weld<br>*Reseda luteola* | June-Aug | yellow | tall | Biennial |
| White Campion<br>*Silene alba* | May-Aug | white | tall | Perennial |
| Wild Basil<br>*Clinopodium vulgare* | July-Sept | purple | medium | Perennial |
| Wild Carrot<br>*Daucus carota* subsp. *carota* | June-Aug | white | tall | Biennial |
| Wild Mignonette<br>*Reseda lutea* | May-Aug | yellow | medium | Biennial |
| Yarrow<br>*Achillea millefolium* | June-Nov | white | medium | Perennial |
| Yellow-rattle<br>*Rhinanthus minor* | May-Aug | yellow | medium | Annual |

*Height guide:* small = average height less than 30cm (12in); medium = average height between 30 and 60cm (12 and 24in); tall = average height in excess of 60cm (24in)

# PROTECTED PLANTS

The Wildlife and Countryside Act 1981 has given special protection to the 62 wild plants listed below. Removal of any part of these plants is an offence. The Nature Conservancy Council has recently recommended to the government that a further 31 species should be added to the list. Details of 317 threatened species are given in *British Red Data Book I: Vascular Plants* (Royal Society for Nature Conservation, 2nd edition, 1983).

Adder's-tongue Spearwort
*Ranunculus ophioglossifolius*
Alpine Catchfly
*Lychnis alpina*
Alpine Gentian
*Gentiana nivalis*
Alpine Blue-sow-thistle
*Cicerbita alpina*
Alpine Woodsia
*Woodsia alpina*
Bedstraw Broomrape
*Orobanche caryophyllacea*
Blue Heath
*Phyllodoce caerulea*
Brown Galingale
*Cyperus fuscus*
Cheddar Pink
*Dianthus gratianopolitanus*
Childing Pink
*Petrorhagia nanteuilli*
Diapensia
*Diapensia lapponica*
Dickie's Bladder-fern
*Cystopteris dickieana*
Downy Woundwort
*Stachys germanica*
Drooping Saxifrage
*Saxifraga cermia*
Early Spider-orchid
*Ophrys sphegodes*
Fen Orchid
*Liparis loeselii*
Fen Violet
*Viola persicifolia*
Field Cow-wheat
*Melampyrum arvense*
Field Eryngo
*Eryngium campestre*
Field Wormwood
*Artemisia campestris*
Ghost Orchid
*Epipogium aphyllum*
Greater Yellow-rattle
*Rhinanthus serotinus*

Jersey Cudweed
*Gnaphalium luteo-album*
Killarney Fern
*Trichomanes speciosum*
Lady's-slipper
*Cypripedium calceolus*
Late Spider-orchid
*Ophrys fuciflora*
Least Lettuce
*Lactuca saligna*
Limestone Woundwort
*Stachys alpina*
Lizard Orchid
*Himantoglossum hircinum*
Military Orchid
*Orchis militaris*
Monkey Orchid
*Orchis simia*
Norwegian Sandwort
*Arenaria norvegica*
Oblong Woodsia
*Woodsia ilvensis*
Oxtongue Broomrape
*Orobanche loricata*
Perennial Knawel
*Scleranthus perennis*
Plymouth Pear
*Pyrus cordata*
Purple Spurge
*Euphorbia peplis*
Red Helleborine
*Cephalanthera rubra*
Ribbon-leaved Water-plantain
*Alisma gramineum*
Rock Cinquefoil
*Potentilla rupestris*
Rock Sea-lavender
*Limonium paradoxum*
Rock Sea-lavender
*L. recurvum*
Rough Marsh-mallow
*Althaea hirsuta*
Round-headed Leek
*Allium sphaerocephalon*

Sea Knotgrass
*Polygomon maritimum*
Sickle-leaved Hare's-ear
*Bupleurum falcatum*
Small Alison
*Alyssum alyssoides*
Small Hare's-ear
*Bupleurum baldense*
Snowdon Lily
*Lloydia serotina*
Spiked Speedwell
*Veronica spicata*
Spring Gentian
*Gentiana verna*
Starfruit
*Damasonium alisma*
Starved Wood-sedge
*Carex depauperata*
Teesdale Sandwort
*Minuartia stricta*
Thistle Broomrape
*Orobanche reticulata*
Triangular Club-rush
*Scirpus triqueter*
Tufted Saxifrage
*Saxifraga cespitosa*
Water Germander
*Teucrium scordium*
Whorled Solomon's-seal
*Polygonatum verticillatum*
Wild Cotoneaster
*Cotoneaster integerrimus*
Wild Gladiolus
*Gladiolus illyricus*
Wood Calamint
*Calamintha sylvatica*

# FURTHER READING

Jonathan Andrews, *The Country Diary Book of Creating a Wild Flower Garden* (Webb & Bower, 1986)

Chris Baines, *How to Make a Wildlife Garden* (Elm Tree Books, 1985)

Chris Baines, *Wild Life Garden Notebook* (Oxford Illustrated Press, 1984)

Michael Chinnery, *The Living Garden* (Dorling Kindersley, 1986)

Stephen Dealler, *Wild Flowers for the Garden* (Batsford, 1977)

John Dony, Stephen Jury, Franklyn Perring, *English Names of Wild Flowers* (The Botanical Society of the British Isles, 1974, 2nd edition 1986)

Alastair Fitter, *An Atlas of the Wild Flowers of Britain and Northern Europe* (Collins, 1978)

Richard Fitter, Alastair Fitter and Marjorie Blamey, *The Wild Flowers of Britain and Northern Europe* (Collins, 1974)

Richard Gorer, *Growing Plants from Seed* (Faber & Faber, 1978)

Mrs M. Grieve, *A Modern Herbal* (Jonathan Cape, 1931; Peregrine Books, 1976)

Geoffrey Grigson, *The Englishman's Flora* (Phoenix House Ltd, 1958; Paladin, 1975)

International Bee Research Association, *Garden Plants Valuable to Bees* (International Bee Research Association, 1981)

Gertrude Jekyll, *Wall, Water and Woodland Gardens* (reprinted Antique Collector's Club, 1982)

Michael Jordan, *A Guide to Wild Plants: The Edible and Poisonous Species of the Northern Hemisphere* (Millington, 1976)

W. Keble Martin, *The New Concise British Flora in Colour* (Michael Joseph/Ebury Press, 1982)

John Killingbeck, *Creating and Maintaining a Garden to Attract Butterflies* (National Association for Environmental Education, 1985)

Richard Mabey, *Food For Free: A Guide to the Edible Wild Plants of Britain* (Collins, 1972; Fontana, 1975)

Helen McEwan, *Seed Growers' Guide to Herbs and Wild Flowers* (Suffolk Herbs, 1982)

B. E. Nicholson, S. Ary and M. Gregory, *The Oxford Book of Wild Flowers* (Oxford University Press, 1960)

F. H. Perring and L. Farrell, *British Red Data Book I: Vascular Plants* (2nd edn, Royal Society for Nature Conservation, 1983)

Roger Phillips, *Wild Flowers of Britain* (Pan Books, 1977)

Reader's Digest, *Field Guide to the Wild Flowers of Britain* (Reader's Digest, 1981)

William Robinson, *The Wild Garden* (1870, reprinted Century Hutchinson, 1983)

Miriam Rothschild and Clive Farrell, *The Butterfly Gardener* (Michael Joseph/Rainbird, 1983)

John Stevens, *The National Trust Book of Wild Flower Gardening* (Dorling Kindersley, 1987)

Violet Stevenson, *The Wild Garden* (Windward, 1985)

Urban Wildlife Group, *Gardening for Wildlife* (Urban Wildlife Group, 1986)

Terry Wells, Shirley Bell and Alan Frost, *Creating Attractive Grasslands Using Native Plant Species* (Nature Conservancy Council, 1981)

Terry Wells, Alan Frost and Shirley Bell, *Wild Flower Grasslands from Crop Sown Seed* (Nature Conservancy Council, 1986)

# USEFUL ADDRESSES

Listed below are various organisations who are concerned with the preservation and/or cultivation of wild plants and the protection of wildlife.

The British Butterfly Conservation Society
Tudor House, Quorn, Loughborough, Leicestershire.

Council for the Protection of Rural England – C.P.R.E.
4 Hobart Place, London SW1.

Farming and Wildlife Group
The Lodge, Sandy, Bedfordshire, SG19 2DL.

Fauna and Flora Preservation Society
Zoological Gardens, Regent's Park, London NW1.

Good Gardeners' Association
Arkley Manor Farm, Arkley, Nr Barnet, Hertfordshire.

Hardy Plant Society
10 St Barnabas Road, Emmer Green, Reading, Berkshire.

Herb Society
34 Boscobel Place, London SW1.

National Council for the Conservation of Plants and Gardens
C/O RHS, Wisley, Woking, Surrey.

Nature Conservancy Council
Northminster House, Peterborough, Northants.

Royal Society for Nature Conservation
The Green, Nettleham, Lincolnshire

The Royal Society for the Protection of Birds
The Lodge, Sandy, Bedfordshire, SG19 2DL.

Wild Flower Society
69 Outwoods Road, Loughborough, Leics.

World Wildlife Fund
Panda House, 11-13 Ockford Road, Godalming, Surrey, GU7 1QU.

# SUPPLIERS

Key to abbreviations
S = Separately packed
    species
M = Mixtures
G = Grass and wild flower
    mixtures
P = Plants
B = Bulbs
C = Catalogue supplied free
    but SAE appreciated

The following wild flower seed packet specialists will supply by mail order:

John Chambers
15 Westleigh Road
Barton Seagrave
Kettering
Northants NN15 5AJ
Tel: 0933 681632
(S, M, G, P, B, C)

Emorsgate Seeds
Terrington Court
Terrington St Clement
King's Lynn
Norfolk PE34 4NT
Tel: 0553 829028
(S, M, G, P, C)

Naturescape
Little Orchard
Main Street
Whatton in the Vale
Nottinghamshire NG13 9EP
Tel: 0949 51045
(S, M, G, P, C)

Suffolk Herbs
Sawyers Farm
Little Cornard
Sudbury
Suffolk CO10 0NY
Tel: 0787 227247
(S, M, G, C)

The following mail order seed packet merchants include wild flowers in their range:

Chiltern Seeds
Bortree Stile
Ulverston
Cumbria LA12 7PB
(No telephone. Write, enclosing 48p in stamps.)
(S, C)

Samuel Dobie & Son Ltd
PO Box 90

Paignton
Devon TQ3 1XY
Tel: 0803 616281
(S, M, C)

Mr Fothergill's Seeds Ltd
(see above)
(S, M)

Mr Fothergill's Seeds Ltd
Kentford
Newmarket
Suffolk CB8 7BR
Tel: 0638 751161
(S, M, G, P, C)

Sutton's Seeds Ltd
Hele Road
Torquay
Devon TQ2 7QJ
Tel: 0803 62011
(S, M, C)

Thompson & Morgan
London Road
Ipswich
Suffolk IP2 0BA
Tel: 0473 688588
(S, M, C)

Unwins Seeds Ltd
Histon
Cambridge CB4 4LE
Tel: 022 023 2270
(S, C)

The following seed packet merchants include wild flowers in their flower range. These are available from shops and garden centres:

Carters Ltd
Hele Road
Torquay
Devon TQ2 7QJ
Tel: 0803 62011
(S, M)

Cuthberts Ltd
Hele Road
Torquay
Devon TQ2 7QJ
Tel: 0803 62011
(S)

Fisons PLC
Horticulture Division
Paper Mill Lane
Bramford
Ipswich
Suffolk IP8 4BZ
Tel: 0473 830492
(S, M)

Mr Fothergill's Seeds Ltd
(see above)
(S, M)

Hurst
Unit 7
Cromwell Centre
Stepfield
Witham
Essex CM8 3TA
Tel: 0376 515811
(S, M, G)

W. W. Johnson Ltd
London Road
Boston
Lincolnshire PE21 8AD
Tel: 0205 65051
(S)

Sutton's Seeds Ltd
(see above)
(S, M)

Unwins Seeds Ltd
(see above)
(S)

The following suppliers specialise in larger amounts of wild flower seeds but are prepared to deal with the general public:

Ashton Wold Seeds Project
Ashton Wold
Ashton
Peterborough PE8 5LE
Tel: 0832 73575
(S, M, G, P, C)

John Chambers
(see above)
(S, M, G, P, B, C)

Emorsgate Seeds
(see above)
(S, M, G, P, C)

Naturescape
(see above)
(S, M, G, P, C)

Suffolk Herbs
(see above)
(S, M, G, C)

The following wholesale seed merchants are prepared to offer larger amounts of wild flower seed to the general public:

British Seed Houses Ltd
Bewsey Industrial Estate
Pitt Street
Warrington
Cheshire WA5 5LE
Tel: 0925 54411
(M, G, C)

Hurst
(see above)
(G, C)

W. W. Johnson Ltd
(see above)
(S, M, G, C)

Mommersteeg International
Station Road
Finedon
Wellingborough
Northants NN9 5NT
Tel: 0933 680891
(S, M, G, C)

The following wild flower plant suppliers offer a mail order service:

G. & J. E. Peacock
Kingsfield Tree Nursery
Broadenham Lane
Winsham
Chard
Somerset TA20 4JF
Tel: 046030 697
(Wide range of wild flower plants, ferns, grasses and water plants. Also native trees, shrubs and climbers from predominantly native seed. C)

Stapeley Water Gardens Ltd
London Road
Stapeley
Nantwich
Cheshire CW5 7JL
Tel: 0270 623868
(Specialise in native wetland and water plants. C)

Ruth Thompson
Oak Cottage Herb Farm
Nesscliffe
Shropshire DY4 1DB
Tel: 074381 262
(Wide range of wild flower plants. C)

# INDEX

# ACKNOWLEDGEMENTS

Artists:
Lalage Daily (c/o Perrins Art Gallery):
3, 9, 13-93, 95, 105, 117, 123
Philip Hood: 97-100, 118
Dorothy Tucker: 2, 8, 94, 101, 103, 104,
108, 110-11, 112-13, 114, 116, 121,
122, 124, 127